READER PRAISE FOR THE FIRE INSIDE

"This book will have you smiling and crying about the everyday life of firefighting and their ties with families and their coworkers. It was wonderful to catch up with all of the other firefighters and their families from previous stories."

"Wonderful account of the world of firefighters. It was so interesting to read what recruits go through in their training. I have read each Hidden Cove story and they have all touched my heart. Thank you, Kathryn. Fantastic book and greatest series ever!!"

"What a surprise getting to know and adore Jack Harrison. Sweet and complex. Steady and uber sexy. He meets a woman who challenges him to be a better man. A win-win for all. Loved it."

"I have read all of the Hidden Cove Fire Department stories. This one is just as wonderful as the rest. Cant wait for the next HCFD story."

ALSO BY KATHRYN SHAY

The
FIRE INSIDE

KATHRYN
SHAY

NEW YORK TIMES BESTSELLING AUTHOR

ISBN: 1939501288
ISBN-13: 978-1939501288

CHAPTER 1

"**G**et the lead out, old man." The insulting remark came from the lips of Captain Tess Righetti, an instructor at the Rockland Fire Academy in upstate New York.

Jack Harrison, aka John Mason on this little venture, had gotten the censure from her because he'd stopped to adjust his face mask—he hadn't worn the damn thing in years and now had trouble making it fit. Attempting to conceal his annoyance, he said to the very crabby woman, "Yes, ma'am." Hell, she'd had a bug up her ass since he'd gotten here.

She arched a brow. Her short brown hair was thick and all uneven, its color matching her dark eyes. "And try not to croak on me."

"I'll give it my best shot."

Turning, he hurried into the simulated-burning building for the first maneuver. The structure was filled with mist, which mimicked smoke. Every time Jack went into a fire, even a pretend one, he was struck once again by the pitch blackness. Firefighters operated blind most of the time and he knew fear of the darkness was one of the hardest to overcome.

He followed five recruits carrying hose up three flights of stairs, feeling the strain of the sixty pounds of gear he wore. He'd stayed in shape in the Academy gym back home, thank God, but he *was* forty-five.

The drill involved splitting into teams of two and rescuing a tied-down dummy in a fake fire. The recruits were to extricate one of the "bodies."

"All right," the recruit-in-charge, Rob Hanley, said to the others. His breathing was fast from climbing the steps. "Pair up. Go low and feel your way for victims. We don't know how many or where they are."

Jack guessed there would be more than one. Three probably, since six recruits were participating in the first rotation. Following his partner, Jack entered a room and headed right. Hanley took the left.

As he felt around for the dummy, he heard in his ear, "This is taking a freakin' long time, guys and gals. Has *anybody* got something?"

Right as she spoke, Jack's hand came upon heavy padding. The dummy. "Me and Mason just found one."

"Well, hallelujah." Because all the recruits could hear, he heard her say, "You let Grandpa beat you out, weaklings."

Groans from several mics. Hell, he was still trying to figure out why the woman harped on his age. It had never happened to him in all his years of voluntary training.

"Hand me the wire cutters," Hanley said.

Jack did. The recruit needed the experience of freeing the victim, which wasn't as easy as it seemed when he couldn't *see* anything, so Jack backed off and let the kid do the work.

Ten minutes later, he allowed Hanley to walk backward down the staircase—the hardest position—as they carried the heavy dummy out.

Righetti met them at the door and got in Hanley's face. "Why isn't Grandpa doing the hard part? You coddling him?"

Jack's temper spiked. She should be praising the young man's performance of a difficult task.

Blank faced, Hanley answered, "I wanted the hard part, ma'am."

The kid was definitely an overachiever. Jack knew that particular malady. It had afflicted him all his life. And his drive to be the best reached its peak in his role as a staff psychologist for three hundred firefighters in Hidden Cove.

o0o

Tess stayed on Mason's ass because something was off about him. For one thing, he'd entered the class halfway through for the practical part, skipping the book learning. Fire Chief Lincoln had given a paltry explanation—how Mason had transferred from one academy to another for personal reasons. She'd never heard of that happening before. He was also middle-aged, which wasn't that much older than her, but was double the age of the other recruits so the moniker fit. But he wasn't getting any special treatment from her because of his age. Nobody under her watch would. Maybe if Joey…

Pushing thoughts of her brother aside, she glanced at the clock, then back to the recruits. "Take twenty laps around the gym, and you're done for the day."

Not one single person grumbled. Not even Mason. Actually, he seemed in pretty good shape. About six feet, linebacker shoulders, and now, after discarding the turnout gear, wearing shorts and T-shirt, she could see corded muscles in his legs and arms. He passed her as he ran—still not winded—and saluted. She hid a grin, though sass from recruits was unacceptable.

When the day ended, Tess headed for the shower in her office. Before she reached the door, Mason caught up to her. "Captain Righetti, a word?"

She stopped. His voice held authority. And something else she couldn't name. She pivoted. He was taller than her, but she stiffened her spine and stepped back so she didn't have to look up at him. "What is it, recruit?"

"Stop looking for me to make mistakes and concentrate on the others who need your support."

"Excuse me? You dare question an officer? I could have you booted out of this class for that behavior."

He leaned in closer. His dark hair was damp, and his gray eyes burned with intensity. His scent was sweat and man. "In my other life, I was the boss. I know how to treat people who work for me or those I'm training. Taunting *me* shouldn't be your focus; these young kids need all your attention."

"Now, wait just a minute. Do *not* tell me how to do my job. I don't care who you are and where you came from."

Easing back, he held up his hands arrest-style. "Okay, okay, I won't again. Just think about what I said."

Tess watched him jog to the men's locker room. She'd overreacted to his suggestion, but he was way out of line to talk to her like that. And he was wrong. She knew it was vital to be hard on recruits. Otherwise, bad things could happen to them. She dismissed Mason and went into her office.

oOo

The maze was always a problem for recruits. In order to pass the practicals, they had to crawl blindfolded through a miniature house-like structure equipped with several barriers. As Tess Righetti tied the cloth around Hanley, who Jack sensed would make a great firefighter, she said, "This isn't going to be a piece of cake, Hanley. Let's see what trips up the big man on campus."

Hell. Jack had warned her two days ago that she needed to be more supportive. Most of the line firefighters at any fire academy were tough—should be tough—but this woman was downright mean. And it didn't set well with him.

Ms. By-the-Book held a stopwatch. "Go."

Minutes ticked by. The kid should be out by now.

Righetti shook her head. "Looks like he isn't such a hotshot after all." Catching Jack's eye, she arched a brow. "Go find him, Grandpa."

Angry at her apparent joy in the kid's failure, Jack stalked to the door of the maze, yanked it open and went inside. He'd done this blind, right before Hanley, but it was a lot easier when you could see. He circled the wall put up to stop the recruits, hit a bench placed in the only pathway and climbed up a few steps. He found the boy sitting on a ledge. It was the only way down and then out of the maze, but blindfolded you didn't know how steep the fall was.

"Hey, Hanley. It's me, Mason. Take the blindfold off."

"Gotta finish." Jack could hear the boy's labored breathing.

"It's too late this time around. Righetti already called you out." What the hell? What did he have to lose? Jack sat next to him. "Remove the blindfold, son."

After Hanley pulled the cloth off, he looked down. "Shit. It's only a couple of feet."

"But could have been more. You know, there are techniques you can master for working in blindness."

The kid removed his helmet and mask. His hair was plastered against his head, and his skin beaded with sweat. "Yeah?" He frowned. "You did it, right?"

"Uh-huh. But I had to learn how." An idea struck him. "You know what, if you want, I can help you with your training."

"What the hell is going on in here?" Righetti had come into the maze.

"Just conversing with Hanley."

"It's not your job to *converse*. Get out of here, Hanley. With your tail between your legs, so to speak." Then her gaze lasered in on Jack. "Meet me in my office at the end of the day."

"Yes, ma'am."

When she started out, he whispered to Hanley, "Tonight, at the Radcliff Hotel where I'm staying. We'll go over some stuff." He glanced at Righetti's retreating back. "No matter what she thinks, you're going to be a top-notch firefighter."

oOo

Tess had showered and changed into jeans and a hooded RFD sweatshirt before John Mason showed up. So had he, she saw when he arrived. He looked different out of the firefighter uniform. Wearing a soft-looking gray sweater that accented the smoky color of his eyes and made his shoulders seem broader, he didn't appear contrite at all.

Standing with his legs apart, he dug his hands in the pockets of his jeans. "So, what did you want to see me about?"

She didn't invite him to sit. "You damn well know what this is about. You're interfering in Hanley's training."

"No, *I'm* helping the kid. Instead, you set up more roadblocks than the maze itself."

Her eyes flamed. "That's it. I'm calling the chief. You're out of this class, Mason. I don't care what strings you pulled to get into the Academy halfway through. I'm going to have you tossed."

"Go ahead and call." He took a seat of his own.

She clicked into her phone, searched for a number and punched it in. "Hi, Mary. It's Tess Righetti. How are you? The grandkids?"

It was his turn to look surprised.

"Super. My youngest went to kindergarten."

"What's his name again?"

"Mark. Thanks for asking." They chatted a bit more. "Can I help you with something, Tess?"

"Yeah, I need to talk to the chief." She waited, drumming her fingers on the desktop while the call was transferred. Then, "Hey, Chief Lincoln."

"Tess. What can I do for you? Is the recruit class going well?"

"The class is fine except for one recruit, John Mason. He's disrupting my supervision."

"Ah, Mason. Good guy. He's from downstate. Came here to train when he unexpectedly had to move to Rockland."

"Be that as it may, he's out of line in his treatment of other recruits."

"In what way?"

She filled him in on Mason's interference.

"Sounds to me like he's trying to help."

Seriously? She could feel her face heat. She liked Chief Lincoln, and usually he supported the Academy staff. "What's going on here, Chief?"

"He knows a lot about firefighting from his past...job."

"I don't care what he knows."

A pause. Then, "Just work with him, Righetti."

The use of her last name told Tess the conversation was over. "Yes, sir."

When she disconnected, she glanced at Mason. He sat with his arms crossed, but his expression was neutral. Not gloating as it should have been. "Lincoln says you're staying."

"Good for me. And I'll apologize for having challenged you in front of the kids."

"And promise not to do it again?"

Shaking his head, he stood and moved closer to her.

"I won't do it in front of them, but please think about letting up a bit."

"Not going to happen. Coddling recruits is the wrong thing to do."

"And you know that how?"

"Life experience."

His brows knitted. "Would you like to talk about that? Maybe there's a root cause for your rigidity."

"I'm not frigid."

He blinked. "I said rigid." Now, he chuckled. "But the other's good to know."

"You can leave. I don't want to analyze my personality or views on firefighting with you."

Reaching out, he grasped her arm. His touch was firm but gentle, a feat almost impossible to pull off. "I'm sorry for whatever happened to you. The offer stands, anytime you want to take it."

With that, he let go of her, turned and walked out.

What the hell? A recruit offering to talk things out with her? Invading her personal space? Something was *definitely* different about him. She glanced at her computer. Hmm. Circling the desk, she sat down and called up a browser. Typed in John Mason, New York State. The chief had said, *He's had experience with firefighting.* She added firefighting to the search. So many names came up she couldn't possibly find him that way. Damn, she was going to have to keep a close eye on the guy. When the thought made her uncomfortable, she switched off the computer and stood.

What she needed was a glass of chardonnay and a bath. That would erase all thoughts of the maddening man who'd just left her office.

o0o

Later that night, Jack pulled open the door to his hotel room and found five recruits lined up like soldiers going to their deaths. "Hey there, Hanley. You brought your friends?"

"Yeah. I hope it's okay. They get…well…you know."

He smiled warmly at them. Poor kids. "Yeah, I know. Come on in."

When he'd moved up to Rockland, Jack had booked a suite with a sizable bedroom and a large sitting area filled with cushiony chairs and a couch. He said, "Not sure there's enough furniture, though."

"We can sit on the floor." A young blonde girl stood close to an equally blond guy; they dropped down on the rug, while the others found seats.

They'd left him a chair, so he took it. "You all look nervous. Don't be. Start with telling me your names."

Jill and Jordan were the two on the floor. Twins, like his children. The others were Mae, Mick and, of course, Rob Hanley.

Hanley spoke first. "Can I ask something before we start?"

"Sure."

"You're not a recruit, are you?"

"I'm in your class," Jack hedged.

"Yeah, but you know a lot and you don't act like us, plus you're old."

"Thanks for reminding me. But I assure you, I'm here to get as much information from the recruit training as I can."

Jordan on the floor asked, "Are you a plant?"

"Excuse me?"

"Like, undercover for the officers."

He laughed out loud. "No. And I give you my word, nothing said tonight will go any further."

They exchanged glances. One nodded, then the others followed suit. Again, Hanley began. "You said you had some techniques for operating blind. For, um"—his Adam's apple bobbed—"for fear."

"I do. Let's start with the fact that seasoned, line firefighters get scared sometimes. It'll happen when you're in a burning building or afterward, and could crop up at any point in your career." He was reminded of Tony Ramirez and Sydney Sands, who'd had the experience. "I know of one case where the man had been fighting fires for almost twenty years and got trapped. He told me later he was scared to death."

Jack had to smile at the hope that came over their faces, one by one. Damn, he was good at this. He could have an effect on kids just starting out.

And he knew, in his heart, he'd made the right decision to conduct biweekly support groups for recruits at the Anderson County Fire Academy come spring. That was the reason he was attending this particular class.

"Let's start with visualization."

oOo

The hot water soothed every bone in Tess's body, especially the one in her ankle that she'd broken a year ago. The one that still wasn't strong enough to allow her back on the line. Instead of dwelling on her disappointment, Tess luxuriated in the sweet jasmine-scented bubbles in the tub—the water pulsing out from six jets—and the candles that glowed all around the bathroom. Picking up her chardonnay, she relished the tart taste of the wine and how it went down smooth, how it settled her nerves. Nerves that one very annoying man had activated.

Who the hell *was* he? She went back over what he'd told her, what the chief had implied, and she guessed she could live with his secretiveness, but she wasn't about to take advice from a mystery man. Besides, he was wrong about going easy on the recruits.

After a half hour of decadence, her body was relaxed and calmer. Her irritation at John Mason had diminished. As she got out of the bath, she thought about dinner. She'd picked up pizza from a local place, along with a gooey chocolate-chip cookie. She dried off, dressed in a red, one-piece pajama thing she could live her life in and had reached the living room of her patio home when the phone rang. She checked caller ID and smiled at what she saw.

"Hello, favorite aunt," she said.

"Ha, *tesorino*, I am your only aunt. How is my girl tonight?"

"I'm fine, Aunt Sabina."

"Are you liking the Fire Academy any more now?"

"A bit." She could hear the sadness in her own voice.

"You are still sad because of your ankle?"

"Uh-huh. Because it's not healed enough to go back on the line."

"For me, that is a blessing. I worry enough about the other three."

The other three, Mitch, Zach and Jenn Malvaso, were firefighters downstate. "How are my cousins this week?"

"Mitch is very busy. They keep giving him more and more responsibility."

"He probably loves it."

"I took care of Genevieve's Angel yesterday. She is growing so much."

"I love the pictures you sent."

"And Casey's girls spent last night with me."

"You have a lot of grandchildren now. From all your kids."

"Not the one I am speaking to. There should be a nice man in your life who gives you babies."

Because Tess had lost her parents when she was fourteen, Sabina and her kids were the only family she had. She and her brother had gone to live with the Malvasos for six years after the accident that took away their mother and father. Since then, Sabina viewed her as another child. Sabina was her mother's sister, which was why Tess didn't have the same last name. "I don't think I'm cut out for marriage."

"Bless your heart, you don't know anything, Teresa."

Again, Tess laughed. "Maybe not."

"Tell me about the teaching."

"You know, I like it. I can contribute to the department by training the best recruits." Contrary to what Mason thought. She spoke more of the fire department, which was her life.

Before Sabina disconnected, she said, "Zach has reserved a house for all of us next summer in the Finger Lakes. We hope you can join us."

Images of the Malvaso clan and their kids made her smile. "Oh, Aunt Sabby, I'd love that."

"Good." She gave her dates. "Meanwhile, stay in touch. And remember what I said about men. I still miss my Angelo."

"I know you do. I miss him, too." The patriarch Malvaso had treated her and Joey as he had his own children.

"Goodbye, dear. It is your turn to call me next week."

"I will. I promise."

Tess hung up, feeling nostalgic. After rocky beginnings in their relationships, all her cousins had gone on with their lives. She must not have gotten the gene that enabled a person to pick up the pieces and go on. Or maybe those pieces were permanently broken. On that negative thought, Tess sought out her pizza.

CHAPTER 2

After the morning inspection, half of the recruits went with another instructor and the rest stayed with Captain Righetti. Unfortunately, Jack was assigned to her. But maybe he could help out the kids without antagonizing her.

She tugged on one of the braided coils hanging from the ceiling. "This rope will hold three hundred pounds of weight, and at least you all appear to be in shape. The task today is to climb to the top and shimmy back down."

Jack scanned the recruits. Their faces were blank, and some jaws dropped.

She noticed. "You've had classroom instruction in this technique. You'll be asked to do this in the practical exams you take at the end of the fourteen weeks. What's the problem?"

"We've never seen anybody do it. Could you demonstrate, Captain?" Jordan, one of the twins, made the request.

For some reason, she hesitated. Hmm. Couldn't she climb the rope? Jack doubted that. She was definitely fit, not too thin, no fat on her, and she sported a strong set of muscles—everywhere. He'd noticed how she'd filled out those jeans the night she'd called him into her office.

"Fine." She toed the mound of mats. "Note there's padding if you fall. You could still get hurt if you go down fast, but you won't die."

A gasp from the small girl, Mae. Hell!

Jack asked, "What if we get partway up and can't finish?"

"Come back down. But you won't pass your practical test until you can go all the way up and down."

"Today's our first time," he added.

She looked up. Seemed to think about it. "Yeah, okay. Go only halfway today." She scanned the group. "But remember what I said. You'll have to climb the whole thing eventually. Like this."

After she donned gloves, Tess grabbed on to the rope and hauled herself up until her feet also touched the hemp. Putting one hand over the other, she began the climb. From his viewpoint, he saw her wince after she got about a third of the way up. But she continued her ascent. Sensing something—a firefighter's best weapon against the Red Devil was his intuition—Jack moved closer to the rope. The thing didn't sway because it was rooted to the ground. Still...

After she made it to the top, her descent was slow, and he could see the pain on her face as she reached the halfway point. She kept going. At about three body lengths above the ground, her foot slipped. She cried out and fell. Jack caught her and fell backward onto the mats. She sprawled on top of him, every single inch of her aligning with his body. And holy hell, if he didn't get...aroused. Trying to ignore his reaction, he held her and whispered, "You okay?"

"No."

"You can lie here awhile. I don't mind."

"Can't." She rolled off him and onto her back on the mats. "Everybody, come over here."

Now the recruits were white-faced. "Listen up. What happened to me just now is due in part to arrogance, the fatal enemy of a firefighter. I wanted to show you how it's done, but I should have called in someone else to do the exercise. I fractured my ankle a year ago, and apparently rope climbing is too stressful for it."

The damn fool woman.

"I should have been more careful today. So take that lesson from me. If you're hurt, tell someone. And don't overdo it."

Jack thought of the time he'd broken his hand in a fire but didn't exit the building. It still ached sometimes. She gave good advice and he was surprised at her candor, her humility. Admired it.

Rolling to his feet, he took control. Someone had to. "I'm going to help Captain Righetti to the training office. Here's what the rest of you can do. Get your firefighting text and, as a group, review the rope-climbing techniques. Someone will be back to conduct the drill before you finish."

It said volumes that Tess didn't balk. Until he went to pick her up.

"No! Just get me up and I'll walk."

He understood she didn't want to appear weaker than she already had. "Hanley, come give me a hand so we can help Captain Righetti to the office."

Her look was grateful. Warm. Feminine. Huh! He liked it. A lot.

o0o

"Sit down, Captain Righetti."

Furious at herself for showing off for the recruits, Tess did as she was told. Damn it all, she should have paid attention to her ankle. It had begun to ache partway up. But, she'd been too proud to quit and she was going to pay dearly for it.

Mason said, "Thanks, Hanley. I'll take it from here." The recruit nodded and left; he must sense Mason's authoritative attitude, too. She remembered his words the other day.

In my other life, I was the boss. I know how to treat people who work for me or who I'm training.

"You don't have to stay." Her voice was low, whispery.

After he dragged a stool from the corner, he put a nearby blanket on it and lifted her foot to rest on the soft fleece. "Where's the ice?"

"Really, Mason. I can take care of myself."

"I know you can." He winked at her. "Not sure I'll make it up the rope, so I'm actually doing this for selfish reasons. Ice?"

"There's a fridge in the bathroom." He left the office, and Tess closed her eyes. For twelve months she'd been taking care of her foot in hopes of getting back on the line, despite what the doctors warned…

The ankle's weak, Righetti. You're going to have to work hard and be sensible at the same time if it's ever going to be strong enough… And I'm not sure even that's going to allow it to heal enough.

Tess had said she'd prove them wrong. And now she'd gone and done something idiotic. Anger at herself swelled like a fire gone wild.

"Here we are." Mason came back in and knelt before her. He had a full head of dark hair, but she could see some strands of gray in it, more at the temples. All of it looked soft. Sexy.

Hell, what was she thinking? Especially after his reaction when she'd sprawled on top of him. He was a recruit, for God's sake.

He packed her foot with ice, then wrapped a large ace bandage around it. "This has to be elevated higher than the stool."

"I can manage by myself."

"I'll help you to the couch."

When she was settled with pillows beneath her feet, he went into the bathroom and returned with a glass of water and a bottle of pills. "Ibuprofen. It'll counteract the swelling."

"Thanks. I'll rest. You can leave."

"I could." He dragged a chair over to the couch. "Now, what's this all about? You had a previous injury?"

Shaking her head, she sighed. "I broke my ankle when I fell through the floor of a burning building and my foot crumpled."

"Prognosis?"

"The docs say it's healed but weak."

"I see."

For some reason, she wanted to confide in this man. So she told him their concerns about her ever being on the line again. "But I'm going to prove them wrong."

"Not like this, you're not. What you did was foolish."

She bristled. "Thanks for pointing out my flaws when I'm at my worst."

He recoiled. "If I did that, I'm sorry. Your actions were foolish but human. I understand wanting to be good at things. To be able to show you understand what you're trying to teach others."

A thought struck her. "Is that why you're here? Were you a teacher before?"

"In a way. But this isn't about me."

"You're right. I don't want to know any more about you."

His smile was uber-sexy. "Afraid you'll warm up to me?"

"Not a chance." Time for comeuppance. "*You* were the one who got aroused in front of six recruits."

"When you sprawled all over me. Plus, you're a beautiful woman, though I think you try to disguise that."

"Aren't you embarrassed?"

"Not like when I was in high school, and all it took was a glimpse of the head cheerleader to make it necessary to carry my books in front of me all day."

She laughed, despite the pain. "You're hard not to like."

"Why would you want to dislike me?"

"Because you've disrupted my equilibrium in the class."

"Then, again, I apologize."

"Gonna tell me what your story is?"

"No."

"You could. It wouldn't hurt anything."

"I'm not sure why." He shrugged his shoulders. "Maybe I'm enjoying being a mystery man."

"You enjoy being maddening."

"I never have before." The corners of his mouth turned up. "You must bring that out in me."

She moved on the couch, and pain shot up from her foot. She cried out.

"You're hurting, more than those over-the-counter pills can cope with. We have to call the fire department doctor."

"I don't want to do that."

Drawing in a heavy breath, he stood. "I don't think we have a choice. You're too involved to know if your foot needs attention, like a splint or something. Giving it a few days could make it worse."

He drew out his cell phone, entered in numbers, and Tess shut up. Actually, her foot was throbbing, so he was probably right. The last thing she needed was to be foolish again and do more damage.

Because no matter what anybody thought, she *was* going to get back on the line, regardless of how long it took or how many setbacks she had.

o0o

"Where's Captain Righetti?" Jill asked.

"Her EMS buddies took her to the hospital. The fire department doctor ordered her there—for X-rays and further treatment. She's in a lot of pain."

Jill frowned. "She going to be all right?"

"Yes. She may require some time off, though."

"Who'll take her place?" Jordan wanted to know.

"Me." A man spoke from behind them. A tall, redheaded guy had approached them. "I'm Captain O'Leary. I'll be taking Captain Righetti's place until she comes back." He scanned the recruits. "Now, what's this about ropes?"

Jack sighed. He was going to have to climb the damn thing after all.

Later, he showered, then left the gym, his thoughts whirling in a million different directions. He'd gotten only two-thirds of the way up the rope—Hanley had aced this one—but Jack had learned something vital. Rope climbing was going to be a stumbling block for recruits, and best he know that before April.

He bumped into the fire chief in the corridor. "Hey, Chief."

Bob Lincoln was a big black man with a shaved head and an easy smile. He carried an air of command. "Hey, Mason. You still giving Righetti trouble?"

"No." He recounted what he'd done for her. "I was hoping you could tell me how she is after her fall."

"Let me make a call." Pulling out his phone, he spoke with whoever answered. "Yeah, uh-huh. Yep. Okay." Then to Jack he said, "She's been admitted to the hospital. Since this is a workplace accident, and she previously injured that ankle, the doctor here didn't want to take any chances." He checked his watch. "I wish I could go see her, but I've got a shindig with the mayor to attend."

"I could visit her."

"We don't want to upset her even more, Mason. Besides, you're supposed to be a recruit."

"I know. But I'm older and have a different relationship with her. I'll just check in."

"Hard to believe you can pass for a recruit. You just take charge."

"I'm not doing such a good job of passing. I'll have to reconsider my options."

"Mitch Malvaso said you were a great guy. I wish all of my people were so dedicated that they'd go undercover, so to speak, to be better at their jobs."

"You've got a good one there in Righetti. She goes the extra mile." Despite his reservations about her, he didn't want to share his concerns with the fire chief. Yet, anyway.

"Yeah, I know." He glanced at his watch. "Would you call and leave a message on how she is? When she's going home?"

"Of course."

As he drove to the hospital, Jack thought about what he was doing. He didn't even know if he liked Tess, at least he didn't like how she treated the kids. Their professional philosophies were diametrically opposed. But she seemed different when she wasn't on stage with them. Vulnerable. Reasonable—taking the blame on herself for being careless with her foot, using it as a teachable moment for the recruits.

He'd had clients who were injured in a fire and the hardest thing to deal with was the threat of losing their position on the line.

Twenty minutes later, he knocked on the door of Room 215 and heard a cranky "Come in."

Tess lay in the bed, her foot elevated and bound by what looked like one of those removable casts. She was pale and appeared listless. When she saw him, though, instead of annoyance, her expression lightened. "Hi."

"Hi."

"You didn't have to come." She frowned. "You shouldn't have."

"I wanted to see how you are. What the diagnosis is."

"I bruised my ankle bone, the one that had just healed. Ordinarily, it wouldn't be a big deal, but because I broke the bone once, this is a problem."

"May I sit?"

"Yeah, go ahead."

Pulling a chair around, he focused on her. "How big of a problem?"

"It's going to take a lot longer to get back on the line."

"I'm sorry."

"If ever." Her voice came out in that hoarse whisper. Again, he got a glimpse of her vulnerability.

"Don't live the trouble before it comes."

Her brows knitted. He hadn't noticed how delicate they were before, how fine boned she was. "You sound like a shrink."

"Just a concerned friend."

"We've only known each other seven days. I'm your instructor. We're definitely not friends."

"Back to your ankle. You'll be more careful, train wisely, and maybe you'll only lose six months on the line."

"You think so?"

"It's a strong possibility."

She eyed him as if he were an enemy combatant. "You're a good guy, too. I saw that before."

"My bet is you're a whole different person when you're not yelling at the recruits."

"I am." She sat up straighter. "Let's not talk about recruits, or it'll remind me I shouldn't be with you right now."

"It's a deal."

He checked his watch.

"If you have to go, I understand." Her voice had taken on an edge.

"Go? Hell no. *Cleveland Fire* is on tonight."

"Ah, my fav."

"Mine, too." He picked up the remote. "Shall I?"

"Yep."

They watched for thirty minutes, commenting on what was real, what was so outlandish, it'd never happen in a firehouse. Halfway through the program, though, Tess dozed off. Jack watched her, admiring the delicate sweep of her dark lashes on her face. Tonight, she had a loveliness about her that he'd not seen before. Then again, his reaction to having her plastered all over him might have changed the way he was looking at her.

He had to smile. He hadn't lived like a monk after Elizabeth died, except pretty much for those first few years when he was trying to raise twins on his own and get his degree, then hold down a full-time job. Thank God for his grandmother, who'd still been young enough to move in with him and watch the kids. Since then, he'd dated, but nothing serious had developed between him and any of the women he saw. Today, he'd had a surprisingly strong physical reaction to Tess Righetti, and tonight, something inside of him shifted. Hmm, could there be something between him and this woman? The question was, did he want it?

oOo

Tess awoke with a start. The room was dark, and it took her a few seconds to realize where she was. Something moved off to the side, frightening her even more than her fuzzy brain.

"Tess?" A deep male voice came out of the shadows. "It's me, John. Are you all right?"

Her heart beating at a clip, she managed, "Yeah, bad dream."

Some rustling, the he switched on a small light off to the right. He moved to the bed and sat down on the side of the mattress, facing her. He seemed bigger, stronger…and safe. "Was it about the fire you got hurt in?"

"Uh-huh. How'd you know?"

"Common reaction after an injury. Your unconscious is

remembering what happened to you previously as it tries to deal with this latest blow."

She leaned back on the pillows. Her eyes had adjusted to the dimness and she could see his hair was askew and his shirt rumpled. "What time is it?"

He glanced at his wrist. "Around four."

"In the *morning?*"

"Yeah, you fell asleep during *Cleveland Fire.*"

"And you stayed?"

"Not intentionally. I dozed off in that lounger." He gave a self-effacing chuckle. "Must be climbing that rope tuckered me out."

"How far did you get?"

"Two-thirds up."

"How'd the rest of them do?"

"Hanley starred. The blonds about the same as me. Mick didn't do well." He studied her. "Now that you're updated, you should try to rest."

"You can go home."

"I might as well stay. You'll be getting out in a few hours and I can take you to your place."

"You'll be late to class today."

"Yeah, I will."

"Why are you being so nice to me?" Now that her head was clearer, she tried to conjure her annoyance at him.

"There's a question for another time."

She watched him.

"Lay back and shut your eyes. You might be able to catch a few more z's."

"Okay." Her lids closed. For some reason, she felt more optimistic. She drifted off.

CHAPTER 3

Two days later, as he pulled into Tess's driveway, Jack shook his head, chiding himself. He didn't know why the hell he was doing this. He'd talked to Tess earlier in the day and she was fine—except Fire Chief Lincoln had told her she couldn't come back to the Academy until next week. Her tone had been so depressed, Jack felt sorry for her. So he'd grabbed a bottle of his favorite merlot on the way to his hotel, and once there, he showered, shaved, put on jeans, a zip-up sweater, a quilted vest and headed out.

He sat in his vehicle, staring at the house. Once again, a feeling of connection, of perhaps speculation that something was happening—or might happen—infused him.

Finally, he exited the car. The brutal February wind hit him in the face as he made his way over the sidewalk, which was slick from the snow that had started to fall again. Once on the stoop, he rang the bell. She'd said she was getting around, so she could make it to the door. Then it opened and she stood before him, dressed in a pink sweat suit, her hair sticking up every which way and a scowl on her face. "John? What are you doing here?"

He held up the bottle. "I brought wine. You can have some because you're off the strong pain meds. I thought we might order dinner." He peeked inside. "Unless you have company?"

"Look at me," she said, her tone cross. "Do I *look* like I have company?"

He bit back a grin. "You're not at your best."

"Don't laugh at me. I haven't had a shower in two days. My hair's stringy and I probably smell. You don't want to come in here."

"I do."

She leaned on the edge of the door. "It's unethical to be fraternizing with a recruit."

"Let me in and I'll tell you why that's not a problem."

Her eyes narrowed, she moved back. "That's intriguing."

Once inside, he asked if they could sit. When they were on the couch, he faced her directly. "Tess, I'm not a recruit."

Those pretty brown eyes widened. Tonight, they were liquid looking in the lamplight. "I don't understand."

"I'm already a firefighter and a psychologist. I'm here to go through the recruit class's practical end so I can get a better idea of what my guys and gals go through on a call." He sighed. "I didn't take the first half of the course elsewhere. I wanted to be part of just the practical activities."

Now she stiffened. "What? Why wasn't I told this?"

"I asked it to be kept quiet so I could experience the reality of how the recruits feel about officers, what fears they have. I also was worried if I disclosed my identity, I'd be treated differently."

Her face flushed, and he could tell she was calming herself.

"I'm sorry if that upsets you."

"In some ways, it does." She leaned back into the pillows, seeming thoughtful. "But I understand your thinking. How long are you staying in Rockland?"

"I can only take two weeks from my position. Then I go home."

Her brown gaze narrowed on him. "I knew something was up with you." She glanced to the ceiling. "At least I'm not fraternizing with a recruit."

Leaning over, he tipped up her chin; she didn't seem to mind that he touched her. "What do you need tonight, Tess?"

Her eyes closed briefly and she sighed. "Damn it, I'm afraid to shower alone. My best friend is in Europe, and two of my female colleagues are at some kind of special training this week. I don't have any family here." Her voice hoarsened on the last statement. "There was no one else in town to call."

"Well," he said, his eyes dancing, "*I'm* here."

She blushed. "Oh, yeah, sure. I'm gonna let a stranger help me in the shower."

"Tess, we're adults. And we can do this modestly, if that's what bothers you. You got underwear on?"

"Yeah."

"I'll help you remove the pants to your sweat suit and then the cast."

"I was thinking of cutting the material up the side."

"No need. I'll set up and get you into the shower—in your underwear—then I'm sure you can manage by yourself. I'll come back to help you over the tub and be right outside the door in case you need me."

"You won't peek?"

"Scout's honor. Not that I wouldn't mind seeing…"

"Oh, flirting will make me a lot more comfortable." Her tone was an attempt at sarcasm, but it didn't quite hit the mark.

"Seriously, let me do this for you."

"I am desperate. Okay. There's a shower chair in the basement that I bought when I first got injured. I'll go into the bathroom and you can get it."

While she went down a long corridor, he sought out the chair in a very tidy cellar and headed back to the first floor. He found the master suite, then the attached bathroom, where she was sitting on the toilet seat. Still in her sweat suit. "Why the hell I put on these sweat pants is beyond me. I can't even roll them up to take off the removable cast because the legs are too tight. I forced them on, I guess."

"Let me. I've had experience with these casts."

"Yeah, when?"

"My twins broke quite a few bones."

Her eyes widened like moons. "You have kids. Um, a wife?"

"Twins, one of each. I'm a widower. Elizabeth died in childbirth."

"Oh, John, I'm sorry."

"Yeah, me, too. It was twenty years ago, but it still stings sometimes."

"I imagine." She squeezed his arm gently. He liked the feel of it. And the gesture was spontaneous, revealing who she was inside.

He knelt before her.

"Scootch up and pull down your pants to your knees."

She did and he eased the sweats off, nearly tearing the material, it was so tight. Then he removed the cast. Her ankle was swollen but not as bad as when she hurt it. His hands went for the zipper of her top.

Tess shook her head. "I think I can manage this."

"Sure." He stood, set the seat in the tub and turned the shower on to just below hot. When he faced her, he saw she wore a serviceable sports bra and plain white panties. She had beautiful shoulders, toned biceps and a flat tummy. All a golden brown.

"You're staring."

"I'm not," he lied and moved closer.

She slid her arm around him so he could help her get her legs over the tub. When she settled, he said, "There you go." His voice was husky from the feel of her silky skin. "I'll be right in the bedroom. Don't get out by yourself. I put a towel within arms' reach."

Jack left the bathroom, closed the door and leaned heavily against it. Holy hell! He *had* been staring. He'd wanted to touch more, much more, of the skin she'd bared. And he felt like a peeping Tom.

On the other hand, she didn't seem affected at all.

oOo

Tess let the water sluice over her like a gentle waterfall. She'd removed her underwear because John had indeed left a thick towel next to the tub for her to wrap herself in after this. The hot water felt wonderful; soaping up her body and hair was a tiny miracle and she took joy in the sensations. When she was clean, she just sat there a minute. And was hit hard in the face by what had happened to her in the past few days.

No, don't dwell on it, she told herself. *You're going back to the line. This isn't final, no matter what the doctors said.*

To defer the notion that she was at fault, she thought about John. Who wasn't a recruit. Instead of anger, she'd felt a sweep of relief when he told her he wasn't her student. And now, she thought about him helping her undress, the way his calloused hands felt on her skin. The images made her heart beat faster.

"Hey, you okay in there?" His voice came from the other side of the door.

"Uh-huh."

"It's been twenty minutes."

"Oh, sorry. You can come in soon."

Retrieving the towel, she managed to wrap it around her naked body. Then she called out, "Come on in."

He did, carrying a pair of gray yoga pants and a long-sleeved top and undies. She stared at the bright yellow lingerie. "You went through my drawers?"

"Guilty as charged. I picked the most comfortable-looking ones."

She felt herself blush.

A sexy brow arched. "Not all of them were made for comfort, I don't think."

"I have a fetish. Underwear."

"It could be worse." Leaning into the tub, he turned off the faucet. "What do you need now?"

"Help me to the seat again and put the cast on. The yoga pants are wider legged, so I can manage after that."

"Oh, hell."

Tess felt her face redden and not out of pique. "Cut it out. You're making me nervous again."

Once he'd gotten her seated, he asked, "Lotion?"

She scowled.

"My daughter, Sara. I buy her different kinds to put in her Christmas stocking, her Easter basket. One of the times she had a removable cast, she liked the feel of the lotion on her first."

Why not? She wouldn't have bothered because it would be too hard to reach by herself. Nah, it wouldn't. But she let him do it anyway. "Yeah, there's some in the vanity."

He retrieved a big pink bottle from a drawer and knelt again. She was mesmerized by how he opened the lid, sniffed it. "Mmm." Taking a dollop, he rubbed it between his hands, then on her leg. Her entire calf. A jolt of desire shocked her system. When was the last time she'd felt something that intense? She didn't date much. Sure, she'd had some recreational sex, but she couldn't remember the last time she was with a man.

"Tess?"

Oh, God, she'd closed her eyes. Had she moaned?

"Are you feeling weak again?" He sounded only concerned.

"Some."

He didn't respond, just clipped the cast back on and stood. "I'll be out here. I ordered dinner from a menu on your fridge. I picked the things that were marked."

"Thank you," was all she could manage.

He left and Tess took deep breaths to calm herself. Geez, she'd responded to him like a Victorian bride. This kind of thing *never* happened to her.

Okay, Teresa, she told herself. *You're being foolish. Nothing was said, or done, really. He doesn't know you wanted to jump his bones. Calm down.* Her other half responded, *But you could jump his bones.*

I could, she thought mischievously. He wasn't a recruit. And she was attracted to him—a lot. His wide shoulders and long lean torso all appealed to her. Some casual sex with a stranger sounded pretty damn good right now. And he'd be leaving town at the end of his two weeks, so choosing him for a partner wouldn't have any long-term complications.

Once she had the idea, it wouldn't go away. So she just sat there and pondered what to do.

oOo

His back to the bathroom, Jack stood staring out at yet another February snowstorm in upstate New York. The bedroom window was crystalized with ice, making squiggly patterns on the panes. Every now and then, a tree limb knocked against it. But the weather didn't concern him. All he could think about was how Tess looked in plain white underwear, how she'd trembled and drew in a breath when he massaged her leg, how her eyes had glittered with interest. He'd never been into sex with someone he didn't have a standing relationship with, someone he hadn't gotten to know, but right now, he was up for it, literally.

Weren't you embarrassed? she'd asked when she'd fallen on top of him in the gym.

Nope, not then. And not now. He just didn't know what to do about his attraction to her. And something else—he was having trouble reconciling the woman in the tub with the tough recruit trainer. Tess Righetti was a paradox. And Jack liked paradoxes.

He heard the door to the bathroom open. "John?" Her voice was stronger this time, but husky.

Pivoting, he faced her. And his jaw dropped. Nothing unusual about her damp hair prettily messed, her cheeks red from the shower, her full mouth. No, what stumped him speechless was the towel she wore. Only the towel.

He warned himself, *Don't be presumptuous.*

"Do you want something more?" he asked in what came out as a croak. And thought, *Please say yes, you want me.*

Her hand was at the knot. "Now, there's a question." Her tone was flirty.

A grin spread across his face. "What exactly do you need, Tess?"

She started toward him. "First, call me Teresa."

"A beautiful name. Your given one?"

She nodded. "Tonight, I want to be a mystery, like you are."

It was his turn to nod.

"Do you want mystery, John?"

"Right at this moment, I want a hell of a lot more than that."

This time, her laugh was sultry.

Another step. And another, until she was so close he could see the drops of water still on her shoulders. He had a slicing urge to lick them off. His gaze lowered to the towel. "You gonna drop that thing, darlin'?

Another step, until she stood so close to him that he could see her pupils were dilated. She said, "You want me to?"

"No."

A frown.

"Let me do it." His hand went to her chest, wrapped around the knot. But he didn't undo it. "Tell me, Teresa, is this a good idea?"

"Who the hell knows? We're both adults. Unattached." A frown. "You are unattached, right?"

"There's no woman in my life."

"No man in mine now, either. So what would be the harm of two strangers in the night, like the song says, having a little fun?"

Jack swallowed hard. The feeling that this was going to be more than *a little fun* caused him to think twice. For about ten seconds.

Then he unloosened the knot.

oOo

She lay on the bed, like some naked harem girl sprawled out before him, while he looked his fill and slowly disrobed. Desire, thick and steamy, hummed in her blood—and it felt so good, especially after her depression the past few days. He slipped the sweater over his head to reveal a black shirt.

"Hmm," she said as he grasped its hem. "Double hmm," she added when he shrugged it off. His chest was sprinkled with dark hair, perfectly placed across his pecs and abdomen, as if by some deity who'd taken his time to do it right. She tracked his hands to his belt, which he unbuckled.

"Shit," he said unexpectedly. "I don't have condoms."

"I got some out of the bathroom and put them on the dresser next to the door."

Making quick work of retrieving the box, he dumped the protection on the bed and resumed his disrobing; it amused her. The actions looked practiced, but she bet they weren't. He wasn't a player. She knew that instinctively. When he was fully naked, he cocked his head. "And no, I'm not embarrassed this time, either. You're an alluring woman, Teresa, when you want to be. And I'm very much looking forward to this." He rolled on a rubber as she watched.

"So am I, John."

His knee pressed into the bed and, bracing his arms on either side of the pillow, he covered her body with his.

"Ahhh," he said hoarsely.

"Mmm," she moaned.

Locking his gaze with hers, he asked, "How shall we do this?"

Her smile came easily. "Surprise me."

o0o

Jack lost himself in the sensations of this woman's body, one he did not know but had all night to discover. He started at her jaw and kissed his way down to her waist. Then over to her navel and back up the other side. He cherished the goose bumps when they rose on her skin. Stopping at her breasts, he took both in his hands and kneaded them.

"You're so gentle, yet so strong. I noticed it when you touched me before."

"Well, right about now, I'm exercising Herculean control over myself." Leaning in, he whispered, "It's been a while."

"For me, too."

He smiled against her skin. "Then, let's make it good, Teresa."

"I agree, John whoever you are."

His mouth found hers and he brushed his lips back and forth, back and forth, until he probed them with his tongue. She opened willingly, and he explored her. She tasted so sweet. So sensual. So womanly. His mind began to cloud as the kiss got very wild, very fast.

oOo

"There?" he asked, his body outlined by the small lamp in the corner.

"Oh, God, yes. Right there."

He pushed harder. Stopped. Pushed some more.

"John, please."

"No, no, not yet. It feels too good."

"What are you doing with your hand?"

"Can't you feel it?"

"Hell, I can now. I'm going to…"

But she lost control of her speech. Lost control of everything.

oOo

He woke to the heavy feel of someone behind him, her arm sliding to his chest. She tangled their legs, her cast scratched him, then she kissed his shoulder. Jack hadn't slept with anyone in a long time and had forgotten the tender excitement of being awakened for sex. His hand went to hers. He picked one up and brushed her knuckles with his lips.

"So sweet, Teresa. So very sweet."

"Teresa is sweet. Certainly not Tess."

"Good thing I'm with the right woman."

She stilled for a moment and he wondered, too, at the intent of his words.

Then she began again, her hand roaming over his chest, tickling his belly, and inching down to his groin.

"Arrgh…" His moan was long, lusty and…frustrated. "You're missing your mark, woman."

"No, I'm not. I'm doing just what I want to do."

She teased him until he grabbed her wrist. "Do something now, or I'm flipping over and…."

Her hand closed around his erection. When she began to massage him, pleasure flooded his whole body.

oOo

"Here, take these."

She lay with the sheet halfway up her body, her breasts showing, feeling totally unselfconscious. "I don't need pain medicine. You're my elixir."

"You cried out when I bumped your ankle—the last time, when you were on top."

Sitting up, she took the medicine and water and downed them. He set the glass on the table, then climbed in next to her. "Turn over on your side. I want to hold you while we sleep some more."

"Sounds wonderful."

"I'll fix you breakfast in the morning."

She smiled. "I'm addicted to coffee."

"Whatever you want."

Tess steeped herself in his body as it aligned with hers. He buried his face in her neck, and soon her breathing evened out.

oOo

Jack heard the buzz, and it awoke him immediately. Old instincts from raising kids died hard. Drawing away from Teresa, he slid out of bed and picked up his pants. When he retrieved the phone, he exited the bedroom, closing the door behind him.

He heard, "Dad, it's Seth."

"Seth. Is something wrong?"

"Yeah, or I wouldn't have called you in the middle of the night. It's Sara. She, um, Dad, she got arrested."

"What?" The kid was a straight-A student and good girl. But she had a side to her that worried him.

"You're gonna find out anyway." The twins rarely tattled on each other, so this must be serious. "She got caught smoking pot. Listen, I know you're close by in Rockland. State College is only an hour from there. Can you come down here?" Jack recognized the edges of panic in Seth's voice. Despite their different sexes, his twin children were so close it was almost spooky.

"I'll be right there, but first tell me if she's hurt. Or you are."

"No, nobody's hurt. We're at the police station."

When Jack disconnected, he inhaled and let it out slowly. The breathing made his nerves settle. He had to concentrate on getting to the small town where the kids both went to college. Hell, they'd just gone back from winter break. Quietly, he snuck into the room and saw Tess hadn't moved. She was sleeping soundly. No way would he wake her up.

He dressed in the bathroom, took a minute to throw water on his face, and another to scribble on a pad by her bed: *I've been called away on an emergency. I had a wonderful time.*

How inadequate those words were. But he didn't have the clarity of mind to create any flowery prose. His baby girl was in trouble and he had to get to her.

CHAPTER 4

Six weeks later

Tess stared at Dr. Tim Leone and bit her lip so she wouldn't cry. "You're sure?"

"We are." The doc's face was somber, fitting his message. "The latest X-rays reveal the second injury made your ankle a lot weaker. I believe loss of strength and stamina in your leg won't allow you to work actively on the line again."

"So I caused this?" Tess could barely tolerate the thought.

Leone, who was a great guy, touched her arm. "I wouldn't jump to that conclusion. You know how uncertain I was before the accident with the ropes. I told you that your ankle might never heal properly. Or enough. Actually, Tess, I was pretty sure of that, but I didn't want to jump the gun."

Chief Lincoln straightened. "This isn't the end of your career, Tess. You're a perfect role model for women in the department. You can teach. Or work in PR, recruiting female firefighters. There are a lot jobs you can do here."

She stared at him blindly. The words wouldn't register. She couldn't picture her life without actual firefighting: the camaraderie among people who faced death together, the rush of adrenaline as they entered a burning building, and okay, saving people's lives. After Joey died, she'd withdrawn, and though she had friends, she didn't have deep commitments. Except to Sabina and her family. Her career was her life.

"I'm so sorry, Tess." The chief again. "Is there anything we can do on our end?"

"I... The recruit class just finished. Can I have some time off? To decide what to do? I have furlough coming."

"Take what you need."

Tess managed to get out of the doctor's office, out of the Academy and into her car. Once seated, her breath hitched and then she couldn't take in enough air. She'd had panic attacks before, when her brother died, when she first broke her ankle, so she gripped the steering wheel and forced herself to take deep breaths.

When her phone rang, she tried to ignore it, but remembered Aunt Sabina was due to call this morning. With a shaky hand, she pulled out the phone, confirmed the caller and clicked on.

"So, how is my niece this lovely morning?"

"Not good, Aunt Sabby. Not good."

oOo

"Morning, Daddy." Sara kissed his cheek, grabbed coffee and stood by the counter, dressed in girly pink pajama bottoms and a white T-shirt.

Jack smiled at his daughter. He was still pissed as hell at her for the pot incident, but God, she was in his heart. "Hello, young lady." Arching a brow, he nodded for her to sit. The twins had come home for three days and gotten in too late last night to talk. "Daddy, is it? I'm not letting you off that easily. We have a lot to discuss."

"I wish we could just have a good time this weekend." The girl knew how to pout. Sometimes it drove him and Seth crazy.

"We will, after. Did you think about what happened in February? And my comments on it?"

Sara donned what he'd come to call her *Elizabeth Look*. "I only smoke pot once in a while. Everybody does. I thought about what you said." Here she raised her chin. "*I* still think it's no big deal."

"To me it is. And you got caught. Don't downplay that."

"In a stupid attempt by the police to appease the town council. They had to let us off because the search and seizure was illegal. Nothing's on my record."

"This time."

Silence. So, okay, Jack knew kids smoked pot. Hell, he had when he was younger. But it was frightening when your children were breaking the law.

"Last word on this. I promise. If you do something illegal again, and it gets on your record, you won't be accepted into Cornell for grad school."

She mumbled, "No one would get in if they kept all pot smokers out."

Knowing when to stop with his little rebel, Jack let the griping go. They had a quiet breakfast, and Seth came ambling in when they finished. "Coffee, I need coffee."

Sara got up, poured him a cupful and kissed him on the cheek. "There you go zombie-man. You're addicted to caffeine."

I'm addicted to caffeine, Tess had said weeks ago. An image hit him of what might have happened when he and Tess awoke that morning if he hadn't had to run out, or even after that, if he'd called her. He hadn't, for a very good reason.

The morning after he'd been with Tess, Jack had brought Sara home. While she took a nap, he'd gone into the office to check his messages, intending to call Tess and tell her why he'd left so suddenly. That he planned to return to Rockland in two days to finish out his time in the class. That they could be together again. Before he left her house, he'd gotten her number off her cell phone. He'd just punched in a few digits when Mitch knocked on the open door. Jack never finished the call...

Mitch had come through the doorway, so Jack disconnected. "You're back early. I saw you on my way in for a battalion chiefs' meeting."

"It's a long story."

"Anything serious?"

"Yeah, we can talk about it later."

"Anytime." He cocked his head. "Was Lincoln helpful up there?"

"Uh-huh. Thanks for paving the way for me." He was anxious to make his call. "Do you need anything from me?"

"No, I just stopped to say hi." He started to leave but turned back around. "There is one thing. Did you meet my cousin at the Academy?"

"Your cousin?"

"Yeah, remember when I said I had family in the Rockland Fire Department and asked if you wanted to connect with them?"

"You didn't say your cousin taught at the Academy."

"No?"

"In any case, I wanted to be anonymous to everybody except the chief."

"I know. But you're done now."

Jack wasn't, but he didn't correct Mitch.

"So, did you meet Tess?"

Stunned, Jack stared at Mitch.

Mitch stepped farther into the room. "Jack, are you okay? You just went white."

"I'm okay. I, um, Tess?"

"Righetti."

"*She's* your cousin?" He barely got the words out.

"Uh-huh. My mother's sister's daughter. But she's like another sibling. Her parents died, so she and her younger brother came to live with us for six years." He snorted. "She was fourteen then but gained three older brothers who still watch out for her."

Jack swallowed hard. "W-watch out for her?"

"Yeah. Monitor boyfriends. Set them straight. Make sure nobody takes advantage of her. What we did with Jenn and Connie."

Holy hell!

"So, did you meet Tess?"

"Yes, I did." And more. Much more. He'd done things with Mitch's cousin that would make his friend's toes curl.

"What'd you think? She's a spitfire."

"I agree. But, if I can be frank, I also thought she was too rigid with the recruits."

He hadn't expected the light to go out in Mitch's face.

"Mitch?"

"Her brother was killed in a skiing accident. He was being reckless and went off course. He hit his head hard and never woke up." Mitch sighed. "We were all devastated, but Tess was inconsolable. In some ways, she never got over it."

Oh dear God in heaven! "I'm so sorry to hear that."

"At the time, Tess told us her parents had coddled Joey too much. The only boy in an Italian family. I happen to agree with her. He was ten when we got him, but he already had that sense of entitlement. We tried to straighten him out, but nothing worked. It got worse when Tess took over raising him and Joey badgered her into moving back to

Rockland. When that recklessness caused his death, she was leveled."

Jack wanted to weep for her. He remembered asking her, *Would you like to talk about that? Maybe there's a root cause for your rigidity.* He'd been on the money.

"But she's a good girl at heart, if you got to know her, which you didn't…"

"Dad?" Sara's voice intruded on his memory. Looking around, he saw the kids had finished cleaning up. "Where'd you go?"

"Nowhere. What's on for today with you guys?"

"We're seeing our friends, then tonight we're cooking dinner."

"Great. I might go into work for a little while."

Happy his children were in town, in his house again, he put negative feelings about Tess, and Sara, aside and drove to the Academy. Not long after, Mitch Malvaso came into the office—again—to talk about the new recruit class starting in two weeks. "Hey, Jack. You ready for me?"

"Yep." Jack pulled out a folder from his bottom drawer. Before they could begin, Mitch's phone rang.

He checked the ID and grinned. "My little girl. Sorry, I have to take this." He clicked on, said, "Hi, Trish" and walked out of the office.

Jack called up his email, but he stared blindly at the screen. Mitch had reminded him again of his earlier thoughts about Tess and why he'd left her alone after lovemaking that had blown his mind. Life certainly had a way of biting you in the ass when you least expected it.

When his buddy returned, Jack asked, "Everything okay?"

"Couldn't be better. Trish is pregnant and she calls to relate all the details."

"Sounds great to me."

"Me, too." He got a goofy smile on his face. "Especially after all the trouble we had with her. Remember?"

"I do. But she turned out fine." He smiled. "Sara will, too, I guess."

"How is she after her escapade in February?"

"Sassy about it."

"Ah, a teenager's second-best weapon after silence. Luckily, Sara dodged a bullet."

Jack ran a hand through his hair. "I know, but what happens the next time?"

"You hold your breath and hope she comes through it." He took a bead on Jack. "As a matter of fact, I think you gave me that exact advice about Trish *and* Bobby."

"Probably. Physician heal thyself."

They exchanged a knowing smile, reminding Jack that Mitch was pretty much his only friend, the one person he could share his personal life with. Losing Tess because of that friendship was worth it. Wasn't it?

And did it even matter now? She probably hated him for running out on her without a word and, worse, never calling.

oOo

Tess wandered around her apartment for a day and a half. Her female friends had come over last night, bearing wine and snacks, and talked endlessly to her about the vagaries of life and why she should stay in the department, even after the devastating news. But their visit hadn't clarified anything for her.

She didn't want her life upended like this. She'd already had a close call with John Mason just six weeks ago. After a night of mind-boggling sex, he'd left her in the early hours of the morning, without waiting for her to wake. Worse, he'd never contacted her, never called. Her disappointment had been grave and she'd had trouble getting back to herself. She'd enjoyed him, liked him, hoped to see him more than that once. But it wasn't in the cards and she'd managed to put the whole experience behind her. Most of the time, anyway. Now she had more bad news to deal with.

The front bell rang. She hadn't showered or even combed her hair or brushed her teeth this morning. Who cared? She pulled the door open.

And found her cousin, Zach Malvaso, standing on the porch stoop. His rakish hair and arrogant stance were familiar. And his blue eyes were filled with understanding. "Hey, baby. I heard you're not doing so good."

Of course he had. Sabina had sent in the cavalry. "Your mother shouldn't have called you."

"She's worried about you." He nodded to her coffee. "Got any more of that?"

"Yeah, come on in. I'm a mess, though."

"You're beautiful to me." He kissed her cheek. "And it's been too long."

"I know." She felt her voice crack. "I meant to come to Hidden Cove sooner."

She poured him coffee and they sat in the sunny breakfast nook, which overlooked her small back yard. A rabbit raced across the grass, and it made her think of the fact that she wouldn't ever be racing into any fires again.

"I'm sorry, Tess. I know the final diagnosis must be hard."

"Fuck!" She felt her eyes mist. A few tears trickled down her cheeks. "I don't know what I'm going to do now. Being a firefighter was all I had."

"But it's not all you are. And anyway, you don't have to leave the department."

"How can I stay, when every day I'll be faced with the one thing I want and can't do?"

Leaning back in his chair, Zach watched her. "I ever tell you about Ian Woodward?"

"The name sounds familiar."

"He's the firefighter who lost the use of his legs in 9/11. He said almost the same words at a support group for PTSD survivors several years ago."

"What happened to him?"

"He teaches response-to-terrorism tactics at the Anderson County Fire Academy. He's the most in-demand teacher there."

She sighed. She knew this was a good lesson, and she should listen to it, but it was too soon. She told Zach so.

"That's what I figured. So you're coming home with me."

"What?"

"Mama sent me up here to fetch you. Pack up for a few weeks and take some time in Hidden Cove to decide what to do."

It sounded like heaven, being surrounded by family. But...

"I can't Zach. I'll be terrible company. I don't want to impose that on your mother. She's been wonderful to me all my life."

"As if all of us haven't been basket cases one time or another. Mama works her magic on that, too. She did it with Casey when we broke up."

"I remember that. You were stupid."

"Yep. But I'm wiser now and I'm not taking no for an answer. Mama would kill me. So go take a shower, get your things together, and I'll take care of anything in the house that needs to be done before we head back."

"I want to say yes."

He stood. "Then, as far as I'm concerned, it's a fait accompli. We love you Tess and want to help."

She was too weak to resist. "I love you, too. Okay, I'll come."

He dragged her up. And hugged her. "Great. Now scoot so we don't hit too much traffic on the drive back."

oOo

Two nights after Tess got into town, the Malvaso sisters and brothers insisted they take her out to dinner. They'd invited Sabina to come along, but she had a meeting for an upcoming church bazaar. Megan and Grady were working.

"This is a pretty place," Tess said when they entered the Hidden Cove Inn.

"Yeah. It's quiet, too, so we can talk some sense into you about staying in the fire department." This from Zach. "Later, we'll go to Taylor's and let off some steam."

Jenny, on one side of her, and Connie on the other, both nudged her. "Don't let him bully you. Even in his forties, he's a brat."

"I am not." Zach lifted his chin. "I'm a fine, upstanding man, now that I'm married and settled."

Mitch gestured for the waiter. "Let's get some drinks before we start fighting."

"We're not going to fight." Paulie, the second oldest brother, was more soft-spoken than the others. "We're going to enjoy having our cousin with us."

Tess gave a him genuine smile.

After they ordered drinks and a pitcher of beer, Mitch turned to her. "Honey, I'm sorry about what happened to you. But this is a chance to have you back with us again—for good. Why don't you move down here?"

"*What?*" She hadn't considered the idea of living permanently in this town.

"Move to Hidden Cove. You can live at our house with Mama, Megan, Sabby and me until you want your own place."

"I'd never impose on you like that. Besides, I have roots in Rockland."

For a moment, no one spoke.

Then Connie said, "We talk to you enough to know your job is your life."

"I have friends there."

"And no family." This from Mitch. "When things are tough, you need family."

She glanced at Jenn, who was often more reasonable than the guys. Jenn held up her hands, arrest-style. "I'm with them. You could live with us, too, if you want. Get to know Angel, Bella and Ben."

All of the family reiterated invitations.

Tess looked around, realizing how much she missed them: Mitch had taught her how to ride a two-wheeler; Jenn and Connie had told her about boys; Zach had been her partner in childhood crime; Paulie had been the first one there when her parents died. When Joey died, she'd already moved back to Rockland. Now, the longing to be with these people for more than just a few weeks poleaxed her.

"She's weakening." Zach grinned. "I can tell. I always could."

Tess raised her chin. "This is too big a decision to make spur-of-the-moment."

Mitch nodded. "If you need help figuring things out, you should talk to somebody. A professional."

"You mean a shrink?" She thought immediately of John Mason, who was a psychologist. But she shouldn't be wary of all therapists just because he turned out to be...so shallow.

"Don't knock it." Zach emphasized the statement as he poked her in the side. "Me, Grady and Mitch saw one routinely when our lives were underwater."

"I didn't know whether to go back to the line again when I had kids," Jenn added. "I saw the department psychologist a few times. He really helped."

"I usually deal with my problems alone."

"Not this time. Get some help." Mitch reached across Jenny and covered her hand with his. "And stay."

"I'll think about it."

"Which, getting help or staying?"

"Both."

Mitch's gaze strayed over her shoulder. "Hmm, here's a sign from the Almighty." He stood and motioned to whomever was in back of her. "Good to see you, Jack. We have somebody here you know."

Pasting on a smile, despite the pressure they'd put on her, Tess looked over her shoulder.

The world blurred.

She couldn't speak.

She could barely breathe.

Because there, dressed in a taupe sports coat and a brown shirt beneath it, was the man she'd shared more of her body with than any other lover. Unfortunately, the same had obviously not been true for him. He'd left her without looking back, and now on top of everything else, she was going to have to deal with him.

oOo

Jack's jaw dropped, and his heartbeat began to thrum in his chest. All he could see was Teresa Righetti standing before him—and superimposed over her were images of her, in a towel when she came out of the bathroom. Her, kneeling between his legs while he sat on the bed. Her, looking up from under him. It took him a few seconds to get his vision under control. He was in a restaurant, with his kids, for God's sake.

She recovered first. "Hello, John." Her tone was neutral, as if she was meeting a stranger.

"No, honey," Zach said, unaware of what was between them. "It's Jack. Jack Harrison."

"They already met upstate," Mitch told his brother. "But Jack was incognito. Right, Tess?"

"Yeah, we met."

"Dad?"

"Oh, sorry, honey. Tess, this is my daughter, Sara, and my son, Seth. Guys, Tess Righetti, a woman I worked with in Rockland when I went upstate."

Mention of upstate made Sara blush. As it should. She'd been responsible for a lot more than she knew. Had he stayed at Tess's apartment six weeks ago, who knew where the two of them would be today.

Mitch circled around the table to the kids. "Hey there, you two."

"Chief Malvaso." Seth extended his hand. "Good to see you again."

Sara hugged Mitch, then in typical Sara-mode blurted out, "We had fun at your house last time we were home. Maybe we can do it again?"

"Mama would love to cook for you two. You were so appreciative."

"That'd be cool." Sara grinned. "How about on Sunday before we go back to school?"

Jack touched his daughter's arm. "Baby, don't invite yourself to someone's house. Besides, I have some things I already set up for us."

Pivoting, she frowned. "No, not for Sunday."

Mitch grinned. "Why don't you plan on it? We always have Sunday dinner together unless one of us is working. And Meg and I are both off this weekend."

Jack caught Tess's gaze. Her arms wrapped around her waist in a classic self-protective gesture, but he couldn't read her expression. Then she turned away. "Excuse me, please. I need to use the ladies' room." With that she stood and took off.

"Is she okay, Daddy?" Sara asked. "She looked pale."

"I'm not sure." He faced Mitch. "We should let you get back to your party." He told the kids, "Go to the table." Then to his friend, "Mitch, a word."

They stepped off to the side. "Look, Tess and I… We didn't exactly hit it off at the Academy." They had in bed but not at work. "I never told her who I was. And I imagine she's royally pissed about how I criticized her treatment of the recruits."

"No big deal. She'll get over it."

He glanced to the restrooms. "I'm not so sure. Maybe we should wait on dinner at your house."

"I'll smooth things over with Tess. See you Sunday."

Torn about what to do, Jack made his way to the kids. They were seated and reading the menu. "I'm going to the restroom. I'll be right back." He couldn't let this go. He just couldn't.

When he arrived at the ladies' room, Tess had just come out. He blocked her way and eased her back inside, then closed and locked the door. When he turned around, those eyes were blank again. "What are you doing in here?"

"I've got to talk to you. *Now*, Teresa."

"Don't call me that. We're not those people." He couldn't tell from her tone if she was sad or angry. Maybe a little of both. "That night was all smoke and mirrors."

"You have every right to be upset with me."

"I got over being upset with you. And wanting a relationship with you. The fact that you snuck off in the middle of the night told me everything I needed to know."

"I—"

She didn't let him finish. In the same tone she added, "Besides, you never contacted me. Since you didn't give me your number, I couldn't get in touch with you. I didn't even know John wasn't your real name." The last was said with disgust.

Nothing short of the truth was going to work here, so he said simply, "In the middle of that night we were together, Seth called. Sara had been arrested."

Her whole face fell. He remembered Mitch's words.

Her brother was killed in a skiing accident. She never got over it.

"She got caught smoking pot at school."

"I...I'm sorry." Tess gestured to the restaurant. "She seemed all right out there."

"Yeah, a little too all right. They had to drop the charges because of some technicalities. I'm afraid she got off scot-free."

Tess watched him. "I'm sorry your daughter had problems. But you could've come back after you took care of her."

"I brought Sara to Hidden Cove for few days."

"Still, at least a phone call was in order." She ran a hand through her hair, messing it. "You know what, though? It's water under the bridge. Let's forget anything ever happened between us."

He went on as if she hadn't spoken. "I was going to call you as soon as I got Sara settled, but I, um..."

At his pause, she asked, "You got cold feet?"

"No, I had a visit from Mitch."

She frowned.

"He asked if I'd met his cousin."

"So what?"

Raking a hand through his hair, he shifted his stance. "Hell, Tess, I had a hot one-night stand with a woman who's like his baby sister. He'd kill me if he found out what I did."

"Why? We're both adults."

"You don't know these guys as well as you think you do, if you believe that. Zach decked Grady, his best friend, when he found out Jenn was pregnant. And they knew each other all their lives."

Her face flushed, and now, fire lit her eyes. This time, he could definitely read what she was feeling. "Let me get this straight. You cut me out of your life because you were afraid of Mitch?"

"You've never been out of my life. I've thought of you every day since then."

Closing her eyes she shook her head—in disbelief?

There was a loud knock on the door. "Hello, is somebody in there?" Man, Jack had really blown this. "We have to go."

"Good." She backed away from him. "Don't worry, *Jack*. I'll keep our secret. Just stay away from me."

"I didn't say I wanted that."

"Yes, you did, when you called what happened between us a hot one-night stand." Opening the door, she walked out, leaving him chagrined at facing an angry woman in the doorway.

And about how badly he'd handled seeing Tess again.

oOo

Zach convinced Tess to go with him to karaoke night at Taylor's. Mitch went home to Megan. Paulie had an early trial the next morning, but Jenn and Connie decided singing would be fun, so they agreed to tag along. As the group was heading out of the Hidden Cove Inn, they passed Jack's table. Tess was hoping to avoid him. But Zach stopped, so Jenn and Connie, ahead of her, did, too. Tess was trapped.

Zach put his hand on Seth's shoulder. "Hey, you two. Want to come with us to Taylor's? Tonight's karaoke."

"Sorry," Jack said sternly. "They're not twenty-one."

"On karaoke nights, underage kids can get in. They wear a bracelet that shows they can't drink." Zach socked Jack in the arm. "You come, too, old man, so you can watch them."

Old man, she thought, remembering how she used to call him that. But that was before…

Tess ground her teeth so tight they hurt.

"You're right. I'm too old for Taylor's."

Sara slipped her arm through his. "We won't go without you, Dad. We came home to spend time with you."

Seth agreed.

"But you wanna go, right?" Again, Zach wouldn't give in. Tess wished he'd let this one go.

"Yeah, I do."

"It'd be fun."

Jack looked to Tess—for approval—but she turned her face away.

And heard, "We'll talk about it."

Finally, Zach led them away.

The four Malvaso relatives arrived at Taylor's, a popular place for the over-thirty crowd. Off to the side was the karaoke room. The place was filling up with people, but Zach managed to snag a table for seven. Tess inserted herself between Connie and Jenn so if the Harrisons did show up, she wouldn't have to spend the night next to Jack.

The three of them arrived a half hour later.

"We talked Daddy into coming," Sara said.

Seth shot his sister a sideways glance. "You can talk him into anything."

Just like Joey, who could charm a stone.

A waiter approached the table. Tess, Zach and Connie and Jenn were nursing beers. Jack ordered a pitcher of soda for him and the kids.

Connie addressed Seth and Sara. "You know, Jenn and I are twins, too. We don't look as much alike as you guys do, but we are womb sisters."

Her face bright, Sara bestowed an affectionate look on her brother. "We love being twins."

"Speak for yourself, sis."

She ignored the comment. "So, who's singing?"

"We'll surprise you." The mischief in Zach's eyes reminded Tess of how much trouble they'd gotten into when she lived with them. Nothing as serious as being arrested, though. They'd had the fun kind of trouble, like hopping the fence at the public pool and swimming late at night. Jack didn't seem to have much control over his children. Once again, the notion brought memories of Joey. It was vitally important for adults to protect kids. Tess knew that only too well.

Unable to prevent herself, Tess took surreptitious glances at Jack. He was seated across from her; his hair was a little longer, she noticed now, his gaze still direct and intense. She remembered vividly having all that intensity focused on her.

The karaoke DJ announced, "Next up is Martin, and on deck are Zach, Tess, Jenn and Connie."

"Hey, I never said I'd sing." Tess had been okay with the idea that Zach would force her up on stage, until Jack had arrived.

Literally, her cousin dragged her out of the chair. Scrambling for a way to get out of this, and finding none, she followed him to the front.

While they waited, out of the corner of her eye, Tess saw Sara perusing the list and elbowing Seth.

When the Malvaso cousins finally took the spotlight, Zach stood in the middle of the girls as they belted out Journey's "Don't Stop Believin'." Though she was self-conscious, Tess could sing, and sure enough, she got into the moment. She took a solo part, and the guys at one table stood and cheered. She sashayed over to them and bent down with the mic so they could sing into it. Laughing, she flirted. They flirted back.

When they finished and returned to the table, the kids were laughing. "You guys are good," Sara said with awe. "I'm afraid to go up there now."

"I'll sing with you." Though Seth teased her, they seemed genuinely close. Had Joey lived, would he and Tess have shared this kind of bond? They were four years apart, but the Malvaso siblings had a wide age range and that didn't keep them from being tight.

When Seth and Sara left the group to submit their songs, Jack, who'd been quiet, braced his arms on the table. "You know, there's a whole psychology to which tune people pick for karaoke. I read an article about it in the *Journal of Psychiatric Medicine*."

Zach elbowed Tess. "I know. That's why I picked Journey for all of us to sing."

"What's the significance of the song?"

"We're trying to talk Tess into moving to Hidden Cove."

His eyebrows skyrocketed. "Why would she do that?"

"Oh, that's right. You don't know." Zach's voice was somber.

"I'd prefer not to spread my woes around to everybody," Tess told Zach with more curtness than she intended.

Like a lot of things, the objection simply rolled off Zach's back. "He'll know eventually, when you stay." Zach looked at Jack. "She can't go back on the line in Rockland. When we found out, I went up and got her."

"Was it from your fall, Tess?" Jack asked.

A quick vision filled her mind of him tending to her ankle in her office, then it switched like a camera to him rubbing lotion on her calf. When she started to think about what happened that night, her body reacted the same as it had then. She had to clear her throat to speak. "Yes, it was from the fall. But I haven't given up on my ankle yet. Mitch arranged for me to see your department doctor in a few days."

Reaching across the table, he grabbed her hand before she could pull it away. And squeezed. The gesture sent sparks up her arm and simultaneously made tears prickle behind her lids.

"I'm so sorry, Tess."

Thank God Zach interrupted the moment. She'd had the absurd urge to throw herself into Jack's arms. "We want her to transfer to the HCFD, and I just had a brilliant idea. She could work at the Academy here, with you guys. There's usually openings."

Jack looked as if he was about to swallow his tongue. He wouldn't like having her in Hidden Cove because of their past. But there was more. Her teaching at the Academy would bring back his objections to her methods. Tess ignored the hollow feeling in her stomach at the notion that he wouldn't want to work with her.

CHAPTER 5

The fire chief's office was big, bright and filled with a warmth that most official surroundings lacked. Its plush leather couches, wide expanse of windows, oak desk and conference table were part of the reason. But mostly, Jack attributed the atmosphere to the fact that Noah was such a happy guy now that peace and contentment exuded out of him and into the space he occupied.

Jack stared over at the chief. "What do you think?"

Noah looked up from the outline he'd been reading. "It's great. I told you before I was on board. But I still have concerns about the teachers' reactions to the program."

"Olive Hennessey is supportive of the new class." A battalion chief, Olive ran the recruit classes. "I wouldn't have brought it to you without consulting her."

Leaning back, Noah seemed thoughtful. The chief's hair was grayer now but his face remarkably unlined. "You know some of the fire house guys are going to balk. They'll say running a support group for recruits babies them, when the program should toughen them up."

Those would be Tess's objections. He could still see her face reddening as she shouted at him in her office in Rockland, saying trainers shouldn't coddle recruits. But Jack knew he was capable of walking the fine line between coddling and helping where needed. "If I worried about what the staff says about me, I wouldn't get anything done."

They both laughed. Then Noah asked, "Now, for the big question, should it be mandatory, or just an option?"

Jack frowned. "Olive and I went back and forth on that. But ultimately, we decided if we think the class is valuable enough to offer in the first place, it should be mandatory."

"And what about privacy? For the recruits and the teachers."

"In order for the class to be successful, the recruits will have to share their feelings. If they're shy or fearful, there are ways to make their comments anonymous. But I was hoping for a more freewheeling discussion."

"Will you inform the teachers what they say?"

This was a hard one. He'd struggled with whether he should let the teachers know when the recruits thought they were too harsh or demanding, mostly for the teachers' to monitor their own behavior. "After much forethought, I decided not to tell the staff anything, even anonymously, at least for this first time around. Like for everyone else I treat, what's said in my office is confidential, unless I think they're going to hurt somebody or themselves."

"I trust you on this, Jack." He leaned forward. "Anything else?"

"Nope."

"Then, I'm off for lunch with Will Rossettie." The former police chief who'd retired.

"You thinking anymore about joining his ranks?"

"I am. I'd like more time with Eve and Iana." Noah's child had been named after her brother, and Ian's daughter was Evie.

"How's Ian doing?"

"Super. I can't believe he's turned our terrorist training into a nationally known program. Fire departments from all over the country want him to come and train their people."

"His experience in 9/11 made him understand the concept of preparedness better than anybody. But his real talent is his ability to reach seasoned firefighters."

"Because they respect him so much."

They left the room together and strolled down the hall to where Jack worked. They passed Ian's office on the way. Outside in his waiting room sat Tess Righetti.

Jack halted. "I'm going to step in here a minute. Tell Will I said hi."

Tess didn't see him until he reached her. At first, when she glanced up, there was pleasure in those dark eyes. Then she doused it like foam on fire. She stood and he noticed right away how the stretchy beige slacks and a navy blue blouse fit her…nicely.

"Good morning, Tess." He hadn't seen her since the dinner at the Malvasos. The kids had a blast but Jack and Tess had tiptoed around each other and there'd been no moments of privacy.

"Hello, Jack." Her nearness affected him. He'd been thinking about making love to her ever since he'd seen her again.

"Let's sit." When they did, he asked, "What's happening with your ankle and your plans?"

"I'm bummed. More after this morning."

"What happened this morning?"

"I met with the HCFD physical-fitness trainer. He agrees with the diagnosis that my ankle will never be strong enough to go back on the line. One false move could endanger my crew."

"Which you wouldn't want."

She stared at him, and again, a deep sadness claimed her face. "You know, you always did talk like a shrink."

"Let's talk about *you*." He hesitated. "Are you still thinking the rope-climbing incident caused the final result?"

"No. Both the RFD doc and Cory say it was the original break, received in the line of duty."

"Cory?"

"The new trainer here. He's a sweet guy." She lifted her chin a bit, and something feminine flitted across her face. "I like him."

Jack remembered now. Cory Cameron was about Tess's age, and Jack had heard the females at the Academy call him *yummy*. He'd also heard some of the male officers say the guy was a womanizer.

"Keep your head on straight about Cameron, Tess." The words came out more clipped than he intended.

"My head on straight?"

Even as he gave her the scuttlebutt, he felt like a jerk. He never participated in gossip.

Her eyes flared. "*That* is none of your business."

"Isn't it?" he blurted out, his tone rife with meaning. Damn it to hell, this woman was still in his blood.

"Why would it be? We had *a hot one-night stand*—your phrase. That's all."

Before he could tell her that wasn't what he thought, the door to Ian's office opened and he wheeled out. "Sorry to keep you waiting, Tess."

"No problem. I'm early anyway."

Ian gave him a bright smile. "Jack, hello."

"Hi, Ian. Doing well?" He certainly looked it with his relaxed posture and calm demeanor. It had been a long road to get there. He wondered if Tess would be able to accept the loss of her physical ability to do the job. If anyone could help her do that, it was the man before him.

"Couldn't be better." He motioned to Tess. "Come on in."

She walked away from Jack without saying good-bye. Ian's interruption was good fortune, though. Jack had been about to broach dangerous territory. For days, he'd been thinking about this whole thing with her—the lovemaking, the separation and her ending up in Hidden Cove, maybe permanently. He'd finally admitted he had strong feelings for her. He just didn't know what the hell to do about them.

oOo

"I was emotionally immobilized for a long time. I couldn't get my bearings." Ian Woodward stared ahead, and Tess regretted causing the pain in his eyes. "I'd lay in that bed at the rehab center and think about the life ahead of me. About never being a firefighter again. I believed I couldn't live without the job, the use of my legs. I didn't want to."

"What happened?"

Ian gave a small smile. "A volunteer in the center straightened me out with some tough love, and also real understanding. When I couldn't sleep, he'd stay up with me and talk. He made me get out of bed during the day, and before I knew it, I was racing with other wheelers down the corridors."

"I admire you so much, Ian." Tess meant that. "And I feel like a jerk that I'm bitching about something so small in comparison."

His blond brows knitted. "Don't say that. You have to give up line firefighting. I know how hard that is."

"Yet you surround yourself with what you can't have."

"That was my exact sentiment to my brother-in-law. In some ways, it's still hard. But I'll tell you one thing, I've found such profound meaning and satisfaction in working here"—his hand encompassed the

room, the Academy—"that my life would be incomplete without it."
He took a bead on her. "You can have that, too."

She felt her eyes sting. "It would be so hard to teach others to do what I want to do so bad."

"At first. But I got over it rather fast. Teaching them to survive out there has its rewards, Tess."

"I did like teaching." She thought of Jack. "But I was tough on the recruits."

"We need to be tough on them. Within reason."

She drew in a breath. "Thank you for sharing your experiences with me."

"One more thing. Firefighting used to be my life. It isn't anymore. I have a wife and baby girl, and I'm happier than when I could still walk. Remember that, too."

"Thanks."

"I hope I see you again."

Giving him a grateful smile, she left the office. She had some thinking to do about the first part of their talk. Maybe she *could* teach recruits and be fulfilled, but she'd go back to Rockland to do that. She didn't think she could work with Jack.

It was too dangerous. Since Joey died and she'd lost the most important relationship in her life, she never let anybody in but the Malvasos, and even that was hard for her to do. But seeing Jack again made her realize he threatened those barriers, and she was afraid to have them knocked down. If he hadn't loved and left her, so to speak, she might have trusted him, might have taken a chance. But no, not now.

She was glad Ian had a spouse and a child, but she never would. And so her choices about her career had to be made carefully.

o0o

Right after lunch, the instructors for the next recruit class met with Noah in his office. "Olive, you're on."

Olive Hennessey, the only female battalion chief in the department, was a force to be reckoned with. Smiling, she addressed the group. "We're here to discuss an addition to the upcoming recruit class which starts in nine days. You all have your assignments, and this won't add to your load." She turned to Jack. "Do you know everyone here, Captain?"

The group included Captain Ian Woodward, Lieutenant Quinn

Frazier, Captain Haywood Jenkins, all officers permanently stationed at the Academy. Line firefighters, a necessary part of training, were Lieutenant Jane Phillips, Firefighter Tom Senate and Lieutenant Tony Ramirez. Mark Lucas, who ran EMS, was the medical representative.

"I know you all." His expression was quizzical. "I'm surprised to see you back, Tony."

Tony's laugh was deep and from his belly. "Yeah, I volunteered. Grady O'Connor made captain, and so I'm letting him take over my officer spot at Quint 7 for a while. Besides, I wanted to teach again."

Tony's story was vastly different from the last time he'd come to the Academy. His wife had become unable to deal with the dangerous job he performed. The couple was doing fine now; Jack knew, because he'd had lunch with Sophia last week. Though her therapy was over, they still kept in touch. And he'd also cooked for Tony's crew in the recent past. Jack made a point of visiting firehouses periodically to stay in touch with firefighters. That he also cooked them a meal went over big with the crews.

Olive continued, "Jack is here because he'll be running a workshop entitled Recruit Concerns."

Tom Senate, a tall guy with a buzz cut was a firefighter at Engine 5. He moved to the edge of his seat, a sign that he was troubled by the announcement. Word on the street was that he was a good guy, but strictly by the book. "There's been rumors about this class."

"Jack?" Olive gave him the floor.

"The workshop was my idea, Tom, but approved by Olive and the chief. The class is intended for the recruits to work off some psychological stress, much like they work off physical stress in fitness training."

"So they'll talk about what's stressful for them in the training they get from us?"

"Yes."

He shrugged. "That's good, I guess. As long as we're told of their concerns."

Jack was prepared for it. "No, you won't be notified, unless I suspect they'll harm themselves or others."

The man's dark brows knitted. "*Any* stress they experience can harm others who're fighting fires next to them."

"That's true on the line. But while they're training, the issues won't affect what you and the other instructors do with them."

"Will you talk about us?" Tom asked.

"Probably." He thought of Tess and how the young recruits in Rockland complained about her toughness. He was grateful she wasn't part of this group; he didn't want to deal with negative things said about her.

Tom shook his head vehemently. "This isn't okay with me. Not unless the instructors are included in the loop."

Leaning over his desk, Noah braced his arms on the surface. "We want to give these kids the best opportunities they can get. Admitting their dissatisfaction, discomfort and fears will give us insight into what we might want to improve for future classes, as well as helping the recruits deal with their concerns."

Tom was still scowling. "I don't like the idea of this goin' on behind my back. It'll create paranoia." He turned to Jack. "No offense, Doc, but who's to say if we're tough on them that they won't go cryin' to you and we'll…I don't know, get in trouble somehow?"

"You're looking at everything negative that can happen, Tom. I'm sure I can handle whatever I hear from them in a constructive way."

Tom faced Noah. "Sorry, Chief. I volunteered to help teach recruits because I thought we should all do our part. But I didn't sign up for fifteen kids takin' potshots at me. I'd like to be returned to the line."

Noah's brow furrowed. "I can't guarantee you'd get your spot at Engine 5."

"I'll do my four months somewhere else, then, and go back to my station house after my time's up."

"You feel this strongly about Jack's workshop?"

"I'm afraid I do. Sorry to upset the balance of things, but I don't wanna teach under these circumstances."

"And we don't want you here if you feel that way." Olive's voice was stern but not hostile.

"Go ahead, Senate." Noah's tone was also grave. "I'll have Battalion Chief Malvaso take care of reassigning you."

Once Tom left, all eyes focused on Noah. "So," he said to them. "What do we do now? I hope it's not too late to get someone else."

Mitch leaned forward. "I might have the answer to that. My cousin Tess is visiting Hidden Cove." He explained her injury. "But she got glowing reviews from the RFD where she was training recruits.

She's here for an indefinite period of time. Maybe she'll take the job. You'd have to interview her, of course, but it would solve our vacancy problem."

Olive gave a sly smile. "That'd even this up, three women, three men. What does everybody think?"

Everybody agreed to at least interview her.

Except one person. "I object, Mitch." Jack's voice was firm. "I'm sorry. I know you care about her." *I do too,* he thought. "But she isn't a good match for us."

oOo

Tess asked Ian to let her into the Academy gym to work off some of the tension that coiled inside her like a knot. Ian had told it to her straight, and she'd listened—with a heavy heart—but she'd heard what he said: she had to accept what had happened to her and do something else with her life.

She'd brought a workout bag, changed into bike pants and a tank top and started to walk the track, which formed a perimeter around the gym. The place would be the home of the recruit class in nine days. They'd treat the space like a firehouse: they'd train in here and outside all day. Ropes would hang from the ceiling, and the maze on the left side of the stage was ready for them. One corner near the kitchen would be set up for lunches and dinners. She remembered one time in the RFD class, the kids had cooked a big dinner of fried chicken, fancy potatoes and salad. They'd just sat down, when the chief in charge sounded the alarm for a call over at the smokehouse. Except for two teachers who went with them, the staff had stayed behind, laughing at the traditional initiation every recruit class experienced. Now, when she smelled chicken cooking, she remembered that night.

As she sped up her walking, she remembered other things: the joy at seeing every single recruit graduate, the pride she took in herself for being part of their instruction. One small eighteen-year-old, whom she thought maybe wouldn't make it, had come up to her after graduation and hugged her.

Thanks for being tough on me, Captain Righetti. Nobody is, because I'm so small, but keeping on me helped me make it through. I won't disappoint you.

"Take that, Dr. Harrison!"

Tess had been trying to keep thoughts of him at bay, but it was hard, because he was tight with her family and seeing him made her remember their time together. No matter, she'd go back to Rockland soon. Maybe teaching up there, and being away from him, would make her forget what it felt like to have his hands all over her.

Buck up, Tess, she told herself now. *Stop the pity party.*

She'd just increased her speed again when Cory Cameron came into the gym. "Lookin' good there."

So was he. His blond hair was longish; he had muscles to die for and killer blue eyes. Right now, wearing a damp shirt and shorts that showed the sinew of his legs, he was very attractive.

Keep your head on straight about Cory Cameron, Jack had said.

Damn him for invading her thoughts.

"Want some company? I got some free time."

"Sure."

Falling in step beside her, he kept his stride in time with hers. "Walking will strengthen those muscles around the ankle."

"You think I'll ever be able to run or at least jog, Cory?"

"Uh-huh. Six weeks isn't that long to recover from the latest injury. So you'll probably be able to jog soon."

When she started to chide herself that she should have been more careful, she stopped. No sense in making the situation worse by blaming herself because she knew all along she might never be ready to go back on the line.

"I know you talked to Ian." Cory's voice was a low baritone. "He's a great guy, isn't he? God, I admire him. Everybody here does."

"There's a lot to admire."

Glancing over at her, he gave her a male smile. "Ever seen his wife?"

"No. Why?"

"She's a looker. A former Broadway star."

"Wow."

"She's the light of his life now."

Again, she thought of how that didn't seem to be in the cards for her.

After an hour, Tess was perspiring and welcomed the simultaneous tired muscles and enervation of her body.

"That's good enough, don't you think?" Cory asked.

"Yeah, I do."

"Come on. There's a spot to get water and juice outside the gym."

Her hair damp, her clothes, too, she said, "I'm a mess."

"Nah, you look beautiful."

They headed to the door, and he pulled it open for her. "Sure wish you were stayin' in town, Righetti."

"Yeah?"

He slid his arm around her shoulders for a friendly hug. "Yeah."

o0o

Jack stared over at a man he admired more than anyone else in the department. A man who'd become a close friend. "I'm sorry, Mitch, but I've had recent experience with Tess's teaching that makes me object to bringing her on board."

"You said that before, but honestly, Jack, I'm flabbergasted that you'd blackball her here because of a brief encounter."

"Blackball?" What an ugly concept, one with strong negative connotations. "I'm not doing that."

Noah got up, circled his desk and leaned against the edge so he was part of the group. "I have to say, Jack, I agree with Mitch about the blackballing—that's what you're doing. But Mitch, if Jack has cause for concern, we need to know why."

"All right. I can't object without reason." Jack chose his words carefully. "You all know I train in firefighting every once in a while to give me insight into firefighters who come to see me as a psychologist. I went upstate to the RFD recruit class, and Tess was an instructor at their academy. I went incognito, I might add, for two weeks. Her attitude toward the kids was…unpleasant. She rarely complimented the good things they did and got on them about their faults."

"*On* them?" Mitch asked. "How?"

"She was sarcastic if one couldn't complete a task. She often said there was a good chance that some of them weren't going to become firefighters. She criticized them for every little infraction." He scanned the group. "The kids need encouragement when they fail, not blame, so they can improve. I stand by that."

Olive sighed. "We criticize them, too, Jack, and are stern." She caught Tony Ramirez's eye. "Well, except for Mr. Nice Guy over there."

Tony grinned. "Remember what you told me when we talked about that?"

"Uh-huh. That the class needed the good guys and the bad guys to instruct them. I was pleased you weren't hard ass but could appreciate the staff who demanded more." She looked at Haywood Jenkins.

"You're tough, right?"

"More than I like to be. But it's necessary."

Jane Phillips sat forward. She glowed these days, her brown eyes and hair reminding him of Tess's looks. "Can I say something?"

Olive gave her a generous smile. "Of course."

"I volunteered now because I'm closer in age to the recruits than you all are. I appreciated guys like Tony when I trained, but I also needed the toughness. One guy was super hard on me because I was eighteen and female. I'll tell you, I hated him, but he made me a better firefighter because I was gonna make it just to piss him off."

"Was he pissed off?" Mitch asked.

"No, he was pleased. He even told me that at graduation."

Noah turned to Jack. "What do you think?"

God, this was hard. He *did* believe Tess was too tough, but as the people in this room, the people he admired, spoke, he knew he agreed with much of what they said, too. That caused him to wonder if his personal relationship with Tess was interfering with his professional judgment. He *didn't* want her at his workplace because he couldn't think straight when she was around.

"Jack?"

"After hearing all this, I'm torn. I agree in part with what you said. But I think you can be *too* tough on recruits."

"Won't your class help with that?" the chief asked.

Oh, man, he'd have to deal with the kids' complaints about Tess directly. "I suppose."

"I say we interview her." Olive looked at Mitch.

"There's another issue," Jack pointed out. "What if this group decides she isn't what we want after talking to her? Can you deal with her on that, Mitch?"

Mitch laughed. "She was fourteen when her parents died and she came to live with us. I was more than a decade older, and I had to deal with a lot of hard stuff with her. We have a bond because of that. I don't think it'll break over this. Besides, you'll love her."

That's what I'm afraid of, Jack thought.

"Jack, are you okay with this compromise?" Noah wanted to know. "Since you're torn anyway?"

"Yeah, I am."

"Thanks, Doc." Mitch's tone had softened. "For giving her a

chance."

He just nodded. He felt out of his depth here, which was something that almost never happened to him these days. It was best to tread lightly.

oOo

The little juice bar sported four tables, and a counter. The lights were bright, despite the gray day outdoors and the mistiness of the air. She smiled over at Cory. "Thanks for the support during my evaluation. I appreciated it."

"So, what do you think you'll do now?"

Shrugging a shoulder, she sighed. "Go back to Rockland. Try to piece my career back together somehow, in the RFD."

"I meant what I said before. I wish you were staying here. You got the whole Malvaso clan to look after you."

"Yeah, that's appealing. But my life's back there."

"Hey, honey."

Tess looked up at Mitch standing over her at the table. Her mood perked up at the sight of him. The fact that she got to see him casually like this was a gift. Once, she'd taken their daily encounters for granted, when she was young, but then she'd left the Malvaso home and was… lonely, she realized now.

"Speak of the devil," Cory laughed.

"What?"

Tess smiled at Mitch. "We were just talking about you."

"Anything good?"

"Actually, for us it would be." Cory's eyes twinkled. "I'm trying to talk her into staying in Hidden Cove."

Mitch nodded. "Can I borrow her for a minute, Cory?"

"Sure, sit here. I have an appointment soon." He looked at Tess. "Think about what I said."

When Cory left them alone, Tess drained what was left of her water.

"Want more?" Mitch asked.

Always the caretaker. She wished it didn't feel so good. "I'm fine, but get some if you want."

Instead, he sat. "We just came out of a meeting about the new recruit class."

"Did it go well?"

"No. Tom Senate, a line firefighter, asked for reassignment."

"Why?"

"Because Jack is holding a workshop for the recruits called Recruit Concerns. Did you know about that?"

"Yeah. He was upstate to get some experience for it." She scowled. "I still think I should have been told about his role." Something occurred to her that should have before. "Mitch, why didn't you tell me he was coming up to Rockland?"

"He asked Noah and me not to let anyone know who he was. When I told him I had family up there, he said not to mention we knew him, he wanted fair treatment. He got it from you."

"Not that he was happy about it."

Mitch shrugged a shoulder. "In any case, Tom didn't want to open himself up to scrutiny by letting the recruits talk about the staff in the RC class. And he was totally against not knowing what they said about him."

"If Senate's doing what he thinks is best, he shouldn't care."

Mitch bestowed an approving smile on her, like the ones she got from him when she'd won the Senior English prize in high school and graduated from the Fire Academy. "That's how I feel. But not everybody has the self-esteem that's in the Malvaso blood."

"You helped me form that."

"We fought, kiddo, remember?"

"I do. I loved you like a brother, though. I knew you had my best interest at heart." She bit her lip.

His brow furrowed, and his expression turned bleak. "Joey didn't take it so well."

"I know, Mitch. He was too spoiled by the time he came to live with you. He never got over his sense of entitlement. Of invulnerability. And it killed him."

"Do you think about him all the time, still?"

"Not all the time. Lots, though. Especially after I visit his grave." She shook her head. "What were we talking about?"

"The recruit class. The team wants to interview you."

She thought about Cory and Mitch both asking her to stay. "Who's the team?"

He told her.

"Jack Harrison won't want me on staff, Mitch."

"You're right. I was gonna tell you that he voiced his concerns. But he agreed that if everybody else wants to hire you after your interview, he'll go along with us."

"I'm surprised he gave in." She sighed. "He's so stubborn and opinionated."

"Jack? Everybody loves him."

"He has good traits, I know." That was an understatement. She knew a great deal about how *good* he was. "But Mitch, I still haven't decided to stay in Hidden Cove. Though I'm giving it more thought now."

"I heard you talking to Chief Lincoln last night. Sorry, I didn't intentionally eavesdrop."

"That's okay. I would have told you if you asked. There's no recruit class until the fall, but I can go back to the Academy. He says I can train seasoned firefighters"—she rolled her eyes—"or do PR for the department."

"Teresa Righetti, the poster child for women recruitment. I can see where you'd like that." His tone was dry.

"I'd hate it. But I do want more women to join the department. I suppose I could tolerate the job."

"What about the other?"

"What other?"

"Having your surrogate mother and brothers and sisters around. Getting to know your nieces and nephews. Doesn't that appeal to you?"

Her heart twisted in her chest. She thought of Sabina fussing over her at home now. Of Zach stopping by to see her during the day. Of their wives asking her out to lunch. "You know it does."

"Then, go for this job, honey. Give us some time together. I'm sure Noah could make arrangements with Chief Lincoln for a temporary leave for you to do this if you want to go back in four months."

"You think?"

Mitch nodded and took her hand. "What do you have to lose, Tess?"

Jack Harrison's face appeared before her. *My heart*, she thought, but didn't say it. She didn't even know him well enough to be thinking that. "I'll need time to decide."

"Meet with the other Academy staff later this afternoon, but tell them you need overnight to consider it."

"You are a pushy older brother, you know that?"

His grin was mile-wide. He'd won this one.

oOo

Three hours later, Jack once again sat in Noah's office. This time, Tess Righetti occupied Tom Senate's chair. Dressed in the same stretchy pants and navy blouse he'd reacted to this morning, *she* didn't seem anxious at all. Then again, she was confident in her profession. Because of that, she'd done a fantastic job with the interview. Olive and Jane had drilled her—female firefighters were a tight bunch, but they didn't let anyone in their ranks without scrutiny.

Olive spoke now. "I guess that's all we wanted to cover, Tess."

"We should discuss something else." She transferred her dark gaze to Jack. He'd noticed she hadn't looked at him for the whole past hour and a half, not even when she described her philosophy about recruits. "We need to address the elephant in the room." The damn woman never backed away from anything.

Noah raised his brows.

Mitch spoke up. "I told her about Jack's reservations."

"He cleared it with me first, Noah." Jack's voice was even. "Everything should be out in the open."

Keeping emotion out of her voice, Tess addressed him directly. "Did you know, Jo—Jack, that everybody graduated from the recruit class you were in?" Her tone was smug.

He grinned, despite being on the hot seat. "Even Mick Riley and Mae—I can't remember her last name?"

"Even them. Can't be I did such a bad job."

"I never said you did a bad job. I simply don't agree with your methods."

She scanned the group. "Could you tell me now if the rest of you agree with Dr. Harrison?"

"I'm okay with being tough, Tess." Olive spoke first. "But if we do hire you, I'll challenge you if I think you're out of line."

"I'd expect that regarding any of my behavior."

Phillips, Quinn, Ramirez and Jenkins agreed that toughness was important in dealing with recruits.

Noah looked to Jack.

Jack nodded. "I withdraw my objection."

"Then, the job's yours." Noah smiled. "Welcome to the Academy."

"Thank you. But I'd like to think this through overnight if that's okay. As I said at the outset, leaving Rockland would be a big decision."

"Fair enough." Noah stood. "Let me know early tomorrow morning. I—"

Mitch's phone rang. "Uh, sorry. I have a specific ring tone for Megan. She wouldn't call unless it was important." He stood and crossed to the side of the room. But they could hear, "What's up, baby?" A pause. "*What?*" Mitch slapped his hand on the wall. When Jack saw him turn white, he rose and went to stand behind his friend. "I—" Mitch cleared his throat. "I'll be right there." He clicked off his phone and stared at it.

Jack settled his hand on Mitch's shoulder. "What's wrong?"

Mitch glanced over at Tess. "It's Mama. She's been rushed to the hospital."

Bolting up, Tess rushed to them. "What's wrong?"

"She had a heart attack." Mitch took her hand. "We have to go to the hospital."

Tess froze. "Aunt Sabina?" Her voice was raw.

"I'll drive you there," Jack decided. "Noah?"

"Go ahead. Let us know what happens. I'm sorry, Mitch, Tess."

Ramirez called out, "All of our kids know each other.

If you need help, call me. I can pick them up and keep them at my house."

Now Tess was white-faced, and her hands shook. Jack ushered her out, with Mitch at his side. No one spoke. In light of Sabina's illness, the previous disagreements voiced in this room seemed inconsequential.

CHAPTER 6

Mitch and Tess hurried inside the emergency-department waiting room while Jack parked the car. "Is there any news?" Mitch asked the question of Megan, who met them at the door.

Her police calm slipping, Megan's lips quivered. "None. The nurse came out and said the doctors were running tests." She put her arms around Mitch and hugged him.

Tess turned away at the emotion between them, because it weakened her even more.

When she drew back, Megan said, "Let's go sit."

As they made their way to couches, Tess tried to curb the fear curling inside her like a snake, ready to uncoil. She adored Sabina but hadn't spent enough time with her. The desperate feeling was exacerbated by the atmosphere of the hospital—ringing phones, the PA calling for doctors, the sense of urgency in this area. Just like before. Her parents had been brought to a hospital after their car slid on black ice and crashed into an embankment. Joey had been helicoptered to one from the ski slope. She remembered the horrific hours of praying and then the hopelessness. People died in hospitals.

The area was empty except for them. About twenty-by-twenty, the room sported a big window and was painted a cheery yellow, which didn't seem right, given the suffering that took place here on a routine basis. When the three of them were sitting on couches, Megan took Tess's hand. "You're pale. Do you need something to drink?"

"No, just tell us what happened."

"Mama was alone at the house. Sabby was in school when Mama had chest pains and called 911. I was at the precinct and the dispatcher let me know, so I met them here."

"Did you get to talk to her?" Mitch asked gruffly. Tess could see the worry etch itself in every line of his face.

"No, she was already in the treatment area."

Mitch glanced toward the ER door. "How long has it been?"

"Not even an hour."

Checking his watch, Mitch frowned. "It's four. Where's Sabby?"

"I called Lisel Woodward because I know she's home with her daughter. Sabby loves playing sister to Iana. They picked her up from school."

Listening to mundane matters made Tess feel worse. The waiting area seemed as if it was closing in on her, so she stood. "I need to use the bathroom."

"There's one in the corner over there." Megan glanced up. "Want me to go with you?"

"No, I'm fine. Stay with your husband." Tess wasn't fine but she needed time alone to process what was happening without the interference of the others' reactions, without them worrying about her. Besides, Mitch was more likely to show his true feelings to Megan if they were alone.

Tess made a beeline to the lav, and once inside, she leaned against the door. The two stalls were empty. Sabina was seventy-four years old. She'd lived a full life. But, oh, God, she didn't want to lose her beloved aunt now.

No, don't think that way, she told herself. Tess had to get a grip. She crossed to the sink, threw water on her face. And stared into the mirror. But she couldn't wash away the worry. The woman who'd been a second mother to her could die today. Tess's eyes misted. The people she loved most in the world would be devastated. She buried her face in her hands.

The door to the women's room opened, and Tess looked over, expecting Megan. Instead, Jack stood in the doorway—big and unbreakable. He took one look at her and snicked the lock. Crossing to the sinks, he grasped her by the shoulders and pulled her to his chest. She went, willingly.

His hand in her hair and his woodsy scent soothed her. "It's okay to be worried, to cry about having someone you love in danger."

She buried her face deeper in his white captain's shirt.

"But, Teresa," he whispered softly, "you also have to keep things in perspective. Sabina is strong physically. Mitch and I were talking about that when we had dinner with you guys when my kids were home."

Wanting to be comforted, she nodded.

"You can let go, honey."

His words of understanding battered her defenses, and Tess burst into tears. He held her tight, kissed her head, kept her close. When she finished crying, she drew back. "I know I don't have the right to break down like this." She swiped at her cheeks. "All her kids...they need you now."

"Hush. Sabina loves you like a daughter."

"She took me and Joey in, Jack. I was fourteen. Paulie and Mitch were out of the house. Zach, Jenn and Connie still lived at home. The whole family supported me until I graduated high school and got a job. Our lives would have been a nightmare without her."

"I'm glad you had that. It must have been tough when your parents died. Then...Joey."

She shook her head. "Did Mitch tell you about him?"

"Yes. You've suffered a lot of loss in your life."

"I can't think about that now. Especially Joey."

"Then, wash your face and we'll go back out."

Someone banged on the door. "Is anyone in there?"

He gave a little smile. So did she. "What is it with us and bathrooms?" he asked.

oOo

Jack returned from fetching nine cups of strong coffee from the hospital cafeteria. The Malvaso family had been at Memorial for almost two hours. "I think I got this right," he said to the group. They'd clustered together, having dragged chairs over to the couches. The entire family, minus children, had arrived, as well as Will Rossettie, who'd been a stalwart friend of Sabina's for years.

While Jack doled out the cups, he addressed them all. "We don't know how long we're going to be here. Let's make sure the logistics are all worked out. Kids, for instance."

Jenny, clutching Connie's hand, looked to Grady. Her husband said,

"Tony called me when you were notified. He's got all three of ours. Indefinitely."

Connie's kids had gone with her husband's family. Her husband, a doctor, was out of town and would fly in if necessary.

Jack's gaze transferred to Casey Brennan, Zach's wife. She'd gotten close to Sabina, something Casey didn't do with most people. Her face was ravaged and her blue eyes bruised. "My ex has ours—my girls and Zach's boys."

"Good all around. If anybody wants them picked up, I'll do it."

"Trish and Bobby don't know yet," Mitch put in. Trish lived in Florida, and Bobby was in college an hour away from Jack's twins. "I thought it best until we get some news on Mama's condition. If they have to come in, maybe you can get Trish at the airport."

Jack saw Tess swallow hard. The Malvaso young adults would head home if Sabina had to have surgery. If she died. Studying Tess, he could practically see the thought flicker across her face. And he wanted nothing more than to hold her hand like the other couples in the room. But he knew he had to stay professional.

"Is everybody's shift taken care of, Mitch?"

"Noah said he'd cover whatever we needed."

"Then, we wait." He encompassed them in what he intended to be a reassuring gaze. "Have hope and hang on to each other."

When the Malvasos were settled, Jack made his way to Will. Though he'd retired from the police department a couple of years ago, he'd stayed fit and healthy. But worry over Sabina's attack accented the lines in his face, making him look older than usual. "How are you doing with this, Will?"

"Hangin' in there." His eyes were filled with worry. "I was cooking dinner for her tonight. She always makes food for everybody, so it was supposed to be a treat." His voice broke on the last words.

Jack stayed with the older man until Mitch joined them.

Zach got up from Casey's side and strode to Tess. Sitting on the couch next to her, he slid his arm around her.

And they all waited.

o0o

At six o'clock, the doctors came out. Jack knew the cardiologist, as they'd done some work together coordinating the fire department's interaction with emergency personnel. "Hi, Ben."

Dr. Ben Black nodded, then faced the rest of them. "We've done an angiogram on Mrs. Malvaso. Her left artery is ninety-five percent blocked, but the right one is mostly clear. We should put a stent in the left to avoid having too much stress on the open one."

"A stent?" Tess could hear the hope in Mitch's voice. She understood it. "That's not bypass surgery."

"No, and since many of you have medical training, you know that this is a good diagnosis. She's lucky we caught the blockage now and that little damage was done to her heart. Since she's only in her mid-seventies, this is the best course."

Tess, who'd stood when the doctor came out, dropped to the chair in relief. *Thank you, God.*

Jack crossed the room, knelt in front of her and took her hands. They were ice cold. "It's good news, Teresa."

"I know. I know." She swallowed hard. "I'm so glad."

The two of them waited in silence while the rest of the group discussed visiting hours. After, Mitch came up to them. "We can go in two at a time and see her, Tess."

"You guys go first, of course."

"No, Megan wants you and me to go in together. She'll come along later."

"No, I—"

Jack interrupted. "Go ahead. Sabina will be worried about your reaction." More softly, he said, "Because of your parents and Joey."

They found Sabina lying in the bed, seeming frail, but her eyes brightened when she saw Tess and Mitch. The room smelled of antiseptic but it was tinged with Sabina's talcum-powder scent. "Oh, good Lord, I have caused so much worry."

Tess held back while Mitch moved to the bed and sat on the mattress. "Mama, hush. We love you. Of course we're worried."

Stroking Mitch's face, she said, "I understand." Her gaze transferred to Tess. "Come here, *tesorino.* I want to see you up close."

Tess approached Sabina and put on a brave front. "Hi, Aunt Sabby."

"Look at you. You have cried. *marone!*"

"I'm just glad you're all right." Even to her own ears, her voice sounded weak. Raw. "And the treatment isn't too bad."

"Dr. Black explained the procedure. I should be all right in no time."

"You'll be all right, but some things have to change, Mama." Mitch's voice had turned serious. "You do too much for all of us."

Sabina eyed Tess. "Some things do have to change. And I am hoping Teresa will help us."

"Of course I will, Aunt Sabby. Anything you need."

"Good. Stay in Hidden Cove for a few months."

Mitch looked puzzled. Then he burst into belly laughter. "If I didn't know better, Mama, I'd think you set up your niece."

"If I had thought of it, I would have. Now I will use a mother's best weapon."

"What's that?" Tess asked, relieved to be joking about this.

"How do you say it, Mitch?"

"You're guilting her into this."

"Yes, Teresa. I am."

"I'll stay. For as long as you need me."

Mitch squeezed Tess's arm. "You've made her a happy woman, honey."

"That's all that's important now."

oOo

At midnight, Jack pulled into the Fire Academy parking lot to drop Mitch and Tess off at their cars. Mitch would go back to the hospital to sit with Mama Malvaso, whose surgery had been a resounding success. Sabina, in her typical caretaker role, had insisted everyone get some rest, so the Malvasos had agreed to take shifts. Amazingly, Sabina would be able to go home tomorrow.

From the back seat, with the lot's lamplights shining on them, Mitch put a hand on Jack's shoulder. "Thanks, buddy. For everything." Then he touched Tess. "Where's your car?"

"At the other end of the lot."

"I'll run her down," Jack told his friend.

"Get some rest, honey."

"I will. My time to come back is ten. I wish I could stay now."

"Everybody did. Mama's out of the woods, but we don't want to overwhelm her with visitors. It's still two at a time."

"I understand."

After Mitch exited the car, Jack turned in his seat. "How you really doing?"

She nodded. "I'm tired, but I doubt I'll sleep."

"You've had a big day. All that at the Academy and now Sabina's problem." He watched her for a minute. "Why don't we go for a drink?" Leaning back on the headrest, she closed her eyes. "I'm trying to stay away from you."

"Given the fact that you'll be working at the Academy, it doesn't look like that will be possible. We should at least talk about it." He waited till Mitch left, then drove to the Hidden Cove Inn. "Their bar is open until two. I doubt we'll run into anybody we know at this late hour."

"We would at Badges." The Hidden Cove hangout for firefighters and police officers. "I always loved that place."

"You'll get to see it more now, I suppose."

Once they were settled at the Inn, she ordered a martini and he, a double scotch. "So," he said turning to her. "Mama Malvaso blackmailed you into staying in Hidden Cove?"

Tess couldn't hide a smile. "I guess so. Who would have thought she had it in her?"

"She's full of secrets."

"My aunt?"

"Yeah. Did you notice how she got rid of everybody but Will Rossettie tonight? He was the last one to go in, and I'll bet he stays until Mitch gets back."

"What are you saying?"

"I think she's sweet on him."

"Seriously?"

"Yep." The drinks arrived and Jack held up his glass. "Let's toast."

"To putting the past behind us?"

He couldn't read her tone. Holding her gaze, he didn't clink her glass. "Do you think we can do that?"

"We don't have a choice." She sipped her martini and sighed. "I'm staying in town, and I'll accept the job with the recruit class. In four months, I'll go back to Rockland. Meanwhile, you and I can maintain a friendly relationship."

"Even though you're still pissed at me that I didn't call you or come back in February?"

Another sip. "I guess I am still upset about that. You could have at least called me to tell me what happened." She shook her head. "Except that you thought it was a one-night stand, so why would you?"

"Calling what happened between us a one-night stand was a knee-jerk reaction. I didn't see it that way."

When she gave him a dark, disbelieving look, he set his glass down, then took hers out of her hand. They were in a very private booth in the back; he turned her to face him. Leaned in. She started to protest, but his mouth was on hers, hard, demanding. He took, partly with anger at their situation, partly with passion. Her hands went to his chest, and instead of pulling away, she fisted them in his white captain's shirt. He moved in closer and angled his head; his tongue parted her lips and demanded entry. She opened like a flower blooming in the sun and seemed to lose herself the contact.

When they drew apart, they were both breathing hard.

"Now, that should answer any doubt you have about how I feel about you."

Tess took a bigger sip of her drink. "All it shows is that we're attracted to each other."

"Are you kidding? I've thought about doing that for weeks. I wanted to call a hundred times. Fuck it, Teresa, I told you all this. I didn't do it because I didn't want Mitch to find out what happened between us."

"Why, Jack? I don't understand that. Surely you don't think he'd beat you up or something like that."

"No. But the reason *is* selfish. I don't have many friends. Because of what I do—counsel so many of the guys—I have to stay professional with the firefighters. But Mitch is different. Since I helped him out eight years ago, our friendship has become very important to me. I didn't want to lose that."

"So you choose him over me?"

Jack ran a hand through his hair. Had he done that? "Hell."

She took pity on him. "Look, Jack. I love Mitch. I want you to be his friend, and maybe what we did together would affect that. But at least admit what you did."

"I admit it. Though I never saw it that way."

"Fine. Now we can go on from here."

"Seeing each other?"

"No. That ship has sailed. I'm not sure I could ever trust you again. In any case, I'm taking the Academy job, so we're bound to clash when you psychoanalyze the recruits. A relationship between us would compromise us both."

She made his head spin with her comments about choosing

Mitch and now the language she used about the recruits. "I won't be psychoanalyzing them!"

"Whatever. Either way, we'll be at odds. You're going to have to settle for being friends."

"And at work, if we disagree?"

"Friends can disagree. We'll be mature."

He didn't want to accept that. But what choice did they have? She was right.

When he let her off at her car later, and she looked over at him, Jack was hit by a premonition: that they were letting go of something that might have been very rare and very precious.

oOo

Sabina's bedroom smelled the same as it always had—sachet made of rose petals. The scent brought back memories of when Tess had first come to live in this house. She'd been a distraught teenager who'd lost her rudder. How many times had she laid in this bed and cuddled with her head on Sabina's bosom and cried about her parents' death? Joey had isolated himself, but Tess took comfort from others. Then, at least. After Joey died, she shied away from getting too close to people.

"What are you thinking, *bambino?*"

From her place on the other side of the bed, seated cross-legged, Tess smiled at the old name. "How you took care of me after Mom and Dad died. You'd lost your only sister, and you helped *us.*"

"As Rosa would have wanted." Sabina took her hand. "You were so sad it broke my mother's heart."

Glancing out the window, Tess hoped the warm April breeze would soothe her, but it didn't. "I should have paid more attention to Joey."

Shadows darkened Sabina's face. "I could not reach him. Gus and the boys tried, too."

Tess couldn't speak around the lump in her throat.

"You were different after he died."

"I know. I'm sorry I wasn't here to see you more."

"None of that. Except to say I am so happy you will be with me now."

"Me, too." She glanced at her watch. "You need to rest."

"I would like to help you cook."

"No way on earth are you cooking this week. I'll be taking care of you until I start at the Academy."

A broad smile from Sabina. "I love you, Teresa."

The use of her full name reminded her of Jack. And how he'd kissed her senseless in the bar two nights ago. She stood. "I love you, too. I'll call you when supper's ready."

"Can I see my little girl when she comes home?"

"Sabby? Of course. You just have to rest, not sleep."

At three o'clock, Tess met Sabby at the school bus stop. As she descended from the vehicle, Tess realized this was another thing she'd missed out on—her cousins' kids. Sabby was seven and tall for her age. She had that lovely combination of Megan's steel-blond hair and Mitch's dark eyes. When she saw Tess, her face lit from within and she raced over.

Sabby reached for a hug, and Tess bent down. Having her own flesh and blood's arms around her felt good. "Hi, honey. Have a good day at school?"

"Hi, Tess. I got an A on my spelling test."

"Good for you." They strode up the walk. "How's Nana?"

"Resting. You know she's going to be fine, right?"

"Daddy told me that. He never lies."

Hmm. "Maybe not now. But I could tell you some fibs he told when he was little and I used to play with him and Uncle Zach and your two aunts."

A devilish look on Sabby's face reminded Tess of Zach. "Cool."

"Come on." Tess tugged her faster. "I made you cookies. After you visit with Grandma, I'll have one with you and we can talk about Daddy."

o0o

"What do you think, Jenn? Her sauce as good as Mama's?"

Mitch, seated at the head of the table, winked at his mother. Tess had offered to cook for all the siblings, but only Jenn and Paulie could come over. Grady, too, who right now was busy in the living room settling a dispute with their twins, Bella and Ben. Their other daughter, Angel, was at the end of the table, whispering in cahoots with Sabby.

Jenn sneered at her brother. "It's wonderful, Tess. I hate to cook but love this sauce." Its spicy scent filled the air.

"I think it's terrific." Paulie held up a fork of rigatoni and shot Tess a sideways glance. "Maybe she defrosted some of Mama's."

"I won't even deign to answer that."

A high-pitched scream from the twins. Jenn started to stand. "I'll go help Grady."

"No, you worked all day. I just watched the soaps with your mother." Tess rose and headed to the living room.

Ben, who looked like Grady, with dirty blond hair and blue eyes, and Bella, with Jenn's dark looks, were seated at a table for tots, glaring at each other.

"What's going on in here?" Tess asked.

Grady looked up from where he knelt down with them. His face was lined with fatigue; she knew his house had four fires today.

"Children aren't allowed at the dining room table if they're mad at each other or their parents."

Hunching down next to Grady, she zeroed in on the kids. "Did you guys know that was a rule when I lived here?"

"It's stupid." This from Ben.

She hid a smile. "Go, eat, Grady. I'll arbitrate."

He didn't have to be asked twice. Grady bolted up and strode out.

Bella said, "Brothers are stupid."

Out of nowhere, acute pain gripped Tess's heart.

As if the little girl read Tess's mind, five-year old Bella asked, "You got a brother, Tess?"

"I, um, did."

"Where is he?" Ben asked.

"He, um, went to heaven." It sounded dumb, but she wasn't sure what Jenn had taught her kids.

"You mean he died?" Ben again.

"Yes."

"Daddy says death might not be so bad. Everybody dies."

"I think that's probably true, Bella."

"You feel bad he's dead?" Again the girl showed remarkable insight.

"I do. I wish I could see him again."

Ben stared at Bella. Bella stared at Ben. Tess hadn't meant to teach them a lesson, just give Grady a respite. But Bella apparently took her situation to heart. "Sorry, Ben."

"Sorry." Ben's words were begrudging, but they were said.

Tess stood. "Good, let's go eat now."

oOo

Feeling restless, Jack rang the doorbell of the Malvasos' house. He hadn't seen Tess since Sabina came home four days ago. Since he'd kissed Tess in the restaurant. Since she'd said they should just be friends. Problem was, he'd admitted to himself he wanted a relationship with her, despite how Mitch might react. But in some ways, she was right. There could be professional issues because of his class with the recruits. As he waited for her to answer, he recalled what he'd told patients to do in circumstances like this. Accept it, and move on. Date others.

But the thought of dating anyone else fled from his mind when the door opened. Tess wore a simple pair of gray shorts, a white T-shirt and sneakers. Nothing fancy. And her hair was a little damp. Acute desire shot through him at the sight of her.

"Hi," she said easily. "Did you come to see Sabina?"

"And to find out how you're doing."

"I'm good. You?"

They sounded like strangers who'd met on the street. He shifted on his feet. "I hate the stilted tone between us."

"I know. Come on in. Being with Sabina will make you more comfortable."

When Sabina saw him, her eyes brightened. "My favorite doctor."

"My favorite woman in the world."

They smiled at each other. He'd come to love Mama Malvaso, too. Sabina said, "Sit with us, Tess."

"No thanks. I'm going for a run."

"I'll be here when you come back." Jack took a chair next to Sabina and opened a bag he'd carried inside. "I brought you some mysteries to read."

"My favorites."

"Let me tell you which ones I like best."

By the time Tess returned, Jack and Sabina were talking about books and characters and plot lines. For an uneducated woman, Sabina was one smart cookie. He was in the kitchen, waiting for Tess, when he saw a list on the table.

Get groceries.

Clean Sabina's room.

Get gas for drive to Rockland.

The back door had opened and Tess came inside. "Hi, again."

He looked up from the list. "You going to Rockland tomorrow?"

"Uh-huh. I'll need my uniforms for the recruit class. And some clothes, other personal stuff. Zach's off and he's going to stay with his mother."

"Anyone going with you?"

"No. Casey offered, but I said no."

"Why?"

She bit her lip. "I, um…" She shook her head. "Personal stuff to take care of."

A very unpleasant thought came to his head. "You aren't…you aren't seeing some guy, are you?"

"I told you in February that I wasn't seeing anybody."

His relief was intense. "Yeah, that's right. In any case, I could go with you, honey."

Her eyes widened, and he realized what he'd said.

"I'm sorry. I shouldn't have called you that. But honestly, Tess, I can make myself free."

"Are you always this protective? I'm a grown woman and can drive four hours up to Rockland."

"I'm not protective of everybody." Even as he said the words, he knew them to be mostly untrue. "I have feelings for you, Tess."

"Thanks for the offer, but no. I can do this on my own."

"Friends help friends."

"Will you stop?"

He should. He was being stupid. "Just be careful, then."

oOo

Since the weather could turn on a dime in upstate New York, Tess had left Hidden Cove in the sunshine and hit drizzle halfway up. Now the air was misty and gray. No matter. She'd held fast to this ritual for years.

The headstones read: Rosa Campisi Righetti. Anthony Righetti and Joseph Anthony Righetti. Dates of birth and death. Beloved mother, wife, father, husband, son, brother. Joey had never gotten married. He'd died at twenty-four, but he'd *been having too much fun* he'd said, to find a woman to share his life with.

With a heavy heart, Tess rose from the bench and knelt in front of her parents' graves. Starting with her mother, Tess cleared away the old flowers she'd put there two weeks ago and set out a pot full of daffodils. "You would love this, Mama. I'm staying with Aunt Sabina for a while. She's so nurturing and kind, like you."

"Hey, Papa." She rubbed a white stain off the stone with a cloth she'd brought with her. "Remember how much you always liked Mitch? I've spent time with his daughter Sabby. She's a doll, like her dad."

Last, she moved to Joey's plot. A heavy sigh escaped her and she sank back onto her heels. "Oh, Joey, why did it have to be this way?"

Up until this visit, she hadn't voiced that question for years. The pain hadn't been as acute. But being back with the Malvasos, talking about him with Bella and Ben, made her miss him more. She plucked some weeds around the headstone. "Never mind, Joey. Rest in peace."

Closing her eyes she said the prayer she always did here: "Dear Lord, thank you for these wonderful people in my life, for the time I had them. I hope they've all found joy with you and maybe even each other. I love you all."

Getting up from the grave, Tess felt a bit foolish. She didn't know if she believed in God anymore, but her parents, at least, would like for her to say a prayer over their graves. And who knew, anyway, what people had in store for themselves—now and in an afterlife?

CHAPTER 7

Danny Mauro sat on his bed, leaning against the headboard in a room he used to share with his brothers but now occupied alone. At eighteen, he was still living at home. In his hand, he held two acceptance letters; both came a while ago.

Letter #1

"Congratulations. You've been accepted into the Anderson Fire Academy for the class beginning April 15. You are being recruited to one of the finest organizations in existence, the fire department. Pick up your uniform and information packet at the Anderson Fire Academy before the above date, and come dressed in daily blues, shoes shined, tie in place, hair combed. We will welcome you then.

Noah Callahan, Fire Chief

Letter #2

"Congratulations! You've been accepted into the next graduating class of Notre Dame University. We have reviewed your transcripts, recommendations, SAT scores and essays and find you are the type of young man we want to educate. Also, because of your situation, a financial aid package is attached. Welcome to our distinguished university.

The president of Notre Dame had signed this one.

"Be careful what you wish for," his father always said, and Danny now mimicked aloud. "You might just get it."

Danny had wished with all his heart and soul to be a Notre Dame man. His father had wished with all *his* heart and soul for his youngest son to become a fireman. Like Dad. Like his two brothers. It was expected.

Because you let it be expected, he admitted to himself.

He hadn't been able to disappoint his father. Not that his dad would want him to do something he didn't enjoy. But in the Mauro family, it was simply assumed that you'd want firefighting. How could he do anything else?

A knock on his door. "Come in."

His mother poked her head inside. "Hey, buddy. I came to say good night." She smiled down at the letters. "That your acceptance letter for tomorrow?"

"Yep."

She studied him, and Danny was terrified she saw behind his mask, like she'd done when he'd hid frogs in his pockets or had a fight with one of the guys or was afraid to ask Sally Slattery to the prom. "You okay, Danny?"

"Sure."

Unconvinced, she came into the room and he slid the Notre Dame letter beneath the fire department one.

She sat on the bed. Still pretty at fifty, she had soft brown hair and hazel eyes. God, he loved her. And his Dad. "You've been quiet lately. Reflective."

"Just pondering my future, Mom."

Again the scrutiny. "I'm not sure you're telling me the truth. If you ever want to talk to us, your dad and I are here for you." She squeezed his other hand. "Always."

"Thanks, but I'm good."

"Okay." She headed to the door but turned back before she left. "You know, no matter what you do with your life, we love you to pieces."

"I love you to pieces, too, Mom. And thanks."

After she left, Danny berated himself. She'd given him a perfect opening, had even suspected something with her mother's intuition, but he hadn't taken it. Maybe he did want to be a firefighter after all.

So not true, the voice in his head echoed. *So freaking not true.*

oOo

Tess stood before the stage at the side of the gym, among the instructors, in front of the fifteen recruits. They came to the Anderson County Fire Academy from all the neighboring towns, including Hidden Cove. She studied the young group—no grandpas among them like Jack had been—and listened to Chief Hennessy tell them about the fire department. It was a paramilitary organization... members were expected to follow orders, dress correctly...be punctual. The first seven weeks would cover classroom work and the second half would be practical hands-on training. Those who made it in this class would start out as rookies and rise as far as their talents allowed.

Turning to the side, Olive gestured to the instructors. "These are the people who will teach you how to become a firefighter and an EMT. After your induction into the fire service, you'll need to complete the EMS certification, but you'll receive first-responder training along with firefighting techniques."

Olive went on to introduce the teachers. One was new—the EMS instructor, Larissa James, who was employed by the city, not the Fire Academy. Tess hadn't met her, nor had she been in any of their previous meetings because Larissa was recently appointed. The former EMS guy, Mark Lucas, had quit to take another job in a bigger city. It was unexpected, but Noah said they were lucky to have been able to draft Larissa. Not a firefighter but a paramedic, she was tall and lithe, a bit delicate. She wouldn't be here full-time, but would cover the EMS segments.

"Now that the preliminaries are over," Olive told the recruits. "Go into the large classroom on this floor for instructions on what we'll study the first weeks."

They headed to the large classroom off the gym. Once inside, the recruits sat down at a desk that had been designated for each of them by a tented name card.

"The *Essentials of Firefighting* text in front of you will be your Bible during your training," Olive told them. "You'll not only read it but mark it up, study it and make the knowledge in it your own. Now turn to the table of contents." Pages ruffled. "Each of you will read aloud an area of study."

Tess watched as the recitation began. Firefighter Safety...Rescue and Extrication…Building and Construction… It wasn't until halfway through that she realized why Olive had started the class this way.

Recruit Liam Murphy read the title and blurb of his area with confidence. Anita Cruz's energy and enthusiasm was palpable. Robert Johnson sounded nervous. Daniel Mauro read in monotone. Their recitation gave insight into their personalities.

Tess scanned them. They looked a bit shell-shocked. The book contained a huge amount of information, but if they didn't learn it, they wouldn't become firefighters. When her gaze landed on the back of the room, she saw Jack leaning against the wall. At his nod, Olive added, "I want you to meet one last person from the Fire Academy. Dr. Jack Harrison."

Looking very professional in the navy pants and white shirt of an officer, Jack strode down the side of the room with an easy gait. She'd never watched him walk much and hadn't realized even his stride was attractive. He joined the others up front. From where she stood, Tess could see a little nick he'd gotten from shaving. "I'm Dr. Harrison, or Captain Harrison, if you prefer. I'm the Academy psychologist."

No one even moved. The recruits remained stone-faced.

"I'm sure that even in the first hours of training, you're overwhelmed. Know that is common. You'll feel that way until you get your fire legs." Here he grinned broadly, and the gesture made Tess's stomach contract. "That's our equivalent of *sea legs*. Meanwhile, I'll help you navigate these new waters. Every Wednesday and Friday afternoon, you'll come to me at four p.m. We'll share some food, my treat, and then we'll talk about your experiences here."

Again, Tess scanned the group. Now they looked confused.

"I'm conducting this Recruit Concerns class because the fire department wants you to have a place to share your feelings."

A couple of recruits sighed heavily, stiffness leaving their shoulders. Hmm, Jack's statement made them less worried. Tess wasn't sure that was a good thing. But Jack seemed confident about the rightness of holding the class. Tess hoped it didn't come between them too much. Though they agreed to be just friends, she didn't want to go into combat with him.

As planned, Tess stepped forward. "I'll be leading you in your first fitness event. Go to your assigned lockers, get dressed for physical training and store your stuff. You have five minutes to accomplish all that. Don't make me start without you. After PT, you'll shower, dress in your uniforms again and be back here by eleven hundred. Pronto. Lateness will not be tolerated."

She'd made her voice purposely stern. Jack could coddle them all he wanted, but she wouldn't and hoped the other teachers were closer in stance to her.

o0o

Jack's intentions were good. He was going to leave the classroom without talking to Tess. She'd turned to him during the ordeal with Sabina, but she'd made it clear when he visited the Malvaso house a few days ago that they were back to square one. He needed to respect Tess's wishes. But today, when he got to the exit after the recruits went out, Tess reached it simultaneously. Kismet or bad luck?

"Good morning, Captain Righetti."

"Dr. Harrison."

He studied her face. "You look rested." She did. Her hair shone in the overhead lights, her eyes were clear. Even her skin glowed.

"Sabina is an easy patient, as you might guess."

"How is she?"

"Chomping at the bit to babysit the grandkids. Mitch is having a hell of a time convincing her not to do that anymore."

"Was it fun spending so much time with her?"

"Yeah."

"Good." He squeezed her arm and said, "See you later."

As he walked away, he pondered the two sides of Tess. From her behavior up front, she was establishing a firm tone with the recruits. But in her interactions with Sabina and the rest of the Malvaso family, she turned into a vulnerable woman. He knew, of course, people had many facets to their personalities, but he was having trouble reconciling these diametrically opposed traits in her. He was still thinking about that when he reached his office and found a tall, blonde woman at his door. His smile was immediate. "Hey, Larissa. Good to see you again."

"Same here. I've come for advice."

Jack had worked with Larissa on city projects at various times; she seemed confident enough, so he wondered what she referred to. He opened the office door. "Come on in."

Once they were inside, they took seats on a couch. "So, what can I do for you?"

"I wasn't prepared for this job. I've never been in charge of EMS in a recruit class. I helped Mark over the course of the years with different segments of the medical training, but that was mostly during practicals. I'd like some advice on how to approach them as students."

"Hmm." He was thoughtful. "I don't hold the tougher-you-are-the-better-teacher-you-are philosophy."

"Me, neither, but…" She shrugged. "I don't look much like a teacher. What I mean is…"

"You're young and beautiful and are worried they won't take you seriously."

"I'm not that young. But essentially, yes."

He cocked his head. "I've always found you to be professional and strong on knowledge. Let them know that you're in charge, that you know your stuff, and what you expect from them. Those traits should go a long way in establishing your authority."

"Good advice." She stood. She *was* beautiful with that blond hair and those light blue eyes.

"Jack, can I ask you something personal?"

"Sure."

"Would it be unprofessional to have lunch together sometime? Get to know each other better. I'm working here, but it's only temporary."

He thought of Tess's argument that seeing each other would be unprofessional. "Well, I do have that Recruit Concerns class. They might talk about you."

"That's a good point, but I'm not worried about it."

"All right, let's do it sometime."

She left the office, and suddenly Jack realized he was flattered that he'd been asked out on a date.

oOo

The morning was warm and no mid-April breeze cooled the air, as had been the case all week. A savage sun beat down on them as the trainers and recruits headed out to trails behind the Academy.

Cory Cameron joined the group today. When they gathered together, he introduced himself. "Hi, guys. I'm the physical therapist/trainer at the Academy. If you get hurt, I tend to you. If anyone needs more physical training than you're getting, I run a class at six a.m. Monday, Wednesday and Friday."

No one moaned. No one even moved a muscle. Either these kids were scared to death, or they had a lot of self-control.

Because she didn't know what they were feeling, Tess added, "It won't be held against you if you need more fitness training. You all passed the initial physical exam, but you have to be in top shape, very soon." Fitness was always an issue at first. "Remember you can't be a firefighter without stamina and strength. So take Mr. Cameron up on his offer if need be." She thought of her ankle. "Let me tell you this now and get it over with. I'm off the line because of a weak ankle that I injured in a fire. I can't jeopardize fellow firefighters by going into a situation without being in top shape. So you have to be, too."

Cory added, "If you injure yourself, come to me. Don't tough it out. Something could be wrong and you could make it worse."

Tess purposely looked her nose down at them. "I might add that I can probably still outlast you all today, but give it your best shot. Let's go." She'd offered to take the first, easier exercise, to do exactly what Cory said, take care of herself. She'd learned her lesson.

Falling into step at the head of the class, she asked Cory, "Think they'll keep up?"

"They will today. Wait until they get to the Confidence walks." The recruits hadn't been told yet about the grueling biweekly walks they'd be taking, in hot weather, in full gear. They'd know soon enough. Olive didn't want to shake them up this soon, and though Tess hadn't necessarily agreed with waiting, it was a small compromise to make.

"So, the ankle good?"

"Yeah, I'm wearing the brace you gave me. It feels better than any I've ever had. Almost makes me forget it's injured."

"Don't overdo."

She smiled at him. "I won't."

They walked for ten minutes, then they sped up. At a half hour they went as fast as walking would allow. She slowed at fifty-five minutes to cool down. Before they were completely finished, Olive, who'd been at the back so she could observe the recruits, blew a whistle. Everybody halted. Turning around, Tess saw the BC wending her way through the fifteen bodies.

Cory and Tess met up with her in the middle. Tess was shocked to find a recruit—Anita Cruz—on the ground, gasping for breath. Cory dropped to his knees. He placed his hands on the side of her neck. "Pulse is racing. Recruit, try taking deep breaths."

"I…I can't."

"Sure you can. Close your eyes. Do it with me. Breathe in… Let it out slowly."

After a few minutes, Tess could see Cruz's chest rise and fall more slowly.

Olive knelt down, too. "Head back to the training hall. Sit down, have some water. Someone will go with you."

She glanced at Tess, then nodded to Cory. "You go, okay? Captain Righetti, stretch out the troops."

Huh! That was interesting. Had Jack's warning about her strictness affected Olive's decision to let the trainer go with the recruit instead of her? Did she think Tess would be too hard on Cruz? She'd ask the BC later. Right now, she had the rest of them to lead.

oOo

"Thanks for coming in to see me before lunch, Cruz."

Feeling flushed and clammy, Anita stared at Chief Hennessey, wondering if she was going to get kicked out of the Academy on her first day. "Yes, ma'am."

"Sit." When she did, the chief held up a manila folder. "Department physicals show you passed the test to become a recruit. Yet on the first day, you practically faint. Did you eat breakfast?"

No. "Yes."

"Did you sleep last night?"

Hardly. "Yes."

"So what happened?"

Since she couldn't tell the truth, she averted her gaze. "I don't know. I feel fine now."

"*I don't know* won't cut it. You're scheduled for another physical exam with the department doctor this afternoon. If you don't get a clean bill of health, you're out."

She couldn't be. She had to make it in this class. So she looked the woman in the eye. "I passed everything once."

"Maybe you've got a bug."

"I don't have any symptoms."

"Somehow," the chief said, "I don't think you're telling me everything." Hennessey's statement had a note of sympathy in it, and the woman's hazel eyes had a ton more warmth than Captain Righetti's. Thank God *she* hadn't left the trails with Anita.

Anita struggled to keep her voice from trembling. "I'm telling the truth."

"All right. Go to lunch. Eat plenty. Visit the fire department doctor, then come back to the classroom. I'll see you at the end of the day."

Shaken and afraid, Anita left the office. She barely made it to the locker room, then dropped down on the bench and put her face in her hands.

"Hey, Cruz. You okay?"

Her head snapped up. She was relieved to find another recruit in the locker room instead of a teacher. And who wasn't Mauro, who was acting like a zombie. "Yeah, Murphy, I'm fine."

He dropped down next to her. "What's goin' on?"

"I don't know. I got weak all of a sudden."

"It wasn't that hot."

"I see the doc this afternoon."

"You, um, wanna talk?"

She stood abruptly. "Nah. Nothing to say. I'm sure it's a fluke."

"Yeah, okay."

"But thanks for asking."

Murphy nodded and strode out of the locker room without waiting for her. Which was good. She needed to keep to herself, stay focused. She didn't have time for friends.

o0o

"Hey, there, Doc." The voice came from behind Jack as he stood at the stove of House 7, Group 3.

Pivoting, he smiled at Grady O'Connor, who'd taken over for Tony. "*Captain* O'Connor, good to see you." Jack wiped his hands on his apron and held one out to him. Instead of shaking, Grady gave him a bear hug. Jack had spent a lot of time with this man, and now he could see those results in Grady's sparkling eyes and relaxed stance.

Grady glanced at the counter. "You making steak for us today?"

Jack enjoyed these excursions, when he got to go to the firehouses to cook. And he especially liked House 7 because it was home to the Quint and Midi and a Rescue truck. This way, he could see a lot of the guys at once. Today, he'd come while the Rescue Squad was at a call and started the meal alone in the house.

"Everybody loves steak so, yeah, I'm spoiling you today."

"And since you're here we won't get another call during lunch."

"Shh. Don't jinx my record."

By some freak of fate, every time Jack visited a firehouse to make lunch or dinner, the group didn't catch a fire, or any other call, until the meal was over. An interruption was bound to happen, and Jack had a plan for that: he'd either go on the call just to experience one again, or he'd stay and wait for the guys to come back, nosing around the firehouse, reading their literature, straightening up, until the meal was cooked. Sometimes, too, only one truck went out, so he got to spend time with those on other rigs, at least.

"I'm going to shower," Grady told him. "Be back soon."

"Fine."

When Grady left, Jack put the chuck steak in a pan to brown and opened cans of tomatoes. Reaching up into the cabinet, he found the vinegar, oregano and bay leaf. He'd brought his own fresh garlic. As he prepared the meal, he savored the scent of cooking meat and spices and tried not to think about Tess. But she was never far from his mind. Today, he was remembering that night at the Inn, her mouth swollen from his, telling him there could be no relationship between them.

"Son of a bitch!" he said aloud. Maybe it couldn't go further, but she was still attracted to him.

Disgusted with himself, Jack finished the meat and took a seat at the table. On it was a copy of *The Heart of Hidden Cove*. The magazine was put out by the husband of a firefighter on a different group in this house. He read about Parker Allen Erikson and Lisel Woodward's plans for the Hale's Haven camp this year. One of Jack's favorite things about working for the HCFD was the camp they spearheaded for the children of slain firefighters and police officers, and now the kids of veterans of war. Mitch and Megan Malvaso started the project almost a decade ago, and a huge number of fire and police members had helped make the camp grow and flourish.

"Hey, Doc."

Looking up, Jack smiled and stood. "Riley Gallagher. One of my favorite people."

"Ha! It wasn't too long ago you knew what a jerk I was."

"Yeah, but you came out of it."

Riley and Jane Phillips, who was teaching with Tess, had a rough time after years of being together. Riley had sought help from Jack to reconcile with his estranged father. Things must have gone well all around, because his dad had been best man at his son's wedding to Jane not long ago.

"Janie doin' good at the Academy?" Riley asked of his wife.

"When has Janie ever not done good at something?"

"She's a gem." He got a faraway look in his eyes. "I can't believe I almost lost her."

"Don't forget it, but don't dwell on it."

"Okay, Doc."

"Did somebody say Doc?" Nick Evans entered the kitchen. Dressed in blue sweats, he was barefoot. And looked a lot younger than he had last year. Nick's story had been sad, and he'd come to Jack when he wanted to marry Stacey Sterling but didn't feel worthy.

"Hey, buddy." Again, Nick enveloped Jack in a bear hug, too.

"Jack. Good to see you."

Riley snorted. "Everything's good to you these days."

"Yep. I caught some of that fairy dust here at Happyland."

"How's Stacey?"

"Good. She's five months along. Hell, I'm going to be a dad again."

Jack knew he'd help sprinkle some of the dust. All these hugs, the relationships he'd formed over the years made him forget his own issues for a while.

When the crew came to the table, Jackson McCabe sat next to O'Connor. The paramedic had had some trouble with alcohol but he'd been clean and sober for ten years. And he appreciated the meals probably more than anybody. "This is so damn good it makes me wanna cry."

"Baby," Lisa Beth, his partner, said.

The meat was tender, the noodles perfectly done and the bread crusty. And no calls came in until just after lunch was finished.

"Your timing's impeccable," Nick said to Jack. "Come on, the rest of you. Let's get to it."

He followed the firefighters out to the bay, watched them jump into the turnout pants and boots, which were lined up, ready to be filled. They hopped on trucks, where they'd don their coats. At the scene, they'd get the SCBA masks on.

After the rigs left, Jack went to the kitchen and began clean up. He'd been soaking pans, so he scoured them mindlessly. Until Tess took center stage.

What was she doing now? Was she being hard on the recruits today? Just from observation, he could tell they were intimidated. He could help them with his class; he knew it in his gut. But as he rinsed pots and put them in the dishwasher, he wondered how he'd feel when they said negative things about Captain Righetti. He wasn't prejudging, he just knew there'd be some fireworks with her.

Then his mind turned to a different kind of fireworks with the woman, and he forgot all about the recruits.

o0o

Tess and the other instructors laid out fifteen sets of firefighter gear on the stage of the Academy while the kids ate lunch. Each set was labeled with one of the recruits' names, as they'd been fitted for size when they came to pick up their uniforms a week before class started. The students filed onto the stage, looking a little less overwhelmed than they had all morning.

Tess said evenly, "Find your name on the equipment that's been assigned to you." She waited as they sought out their spots. Tess nodded to the gear she'd set out for herself. "Let's start with the bottom up, because that's how you'll put your protective clothing on when you get a call. I'll demonstrate then you follow suit."

She'd set up boots with the pants stuck in them. "First are your boots and bunker pants. You'll leave them positioned like this in the bay first thing in the morning and after every run. When a call comes, you'll jump into both simultaneously."

For effect, she carefully toed off her shoes. "I know you see firefighters kicking off their shoes on TV shows, but don't do it. I worked on a shift once where a smoke eater almost got his eye poked out by someone else's shoe." Stepping into the gear, she pulled the pants up to her waist and fastened the suspenders. "Make sure these fit tightly." She nodded to the floor. "Your turn."

They began the process. When all fifteen had the two items on, she retrieved a turnout coat and slid into it. They did the same and fastened it up. "This was the easy part. Learning how to put on the breathing apparatus is the most crucial and the hardest."

They watched her with owl eyes.

She held up a hood. "You put this on first. It's made of Nomex, a specially engineered material to keep your head, neck and ears from getting burned. You don't want embers getting under it, so adjust it carefully. I hadn't taken enough time once—those little suckers snuck in where skin was exposed. It itched and burned like hell for days."

Next came the tanks for the oxygen. First, she showed them how to check that the thing was full. That took twenty minutes, as she watched each recruit follow the procedure. Next, she inserted herself into the straps that would secure the cylinder. As the recruits tried to emulate her, she, Jane, Olive and Quinn walked around to assist. Tess approached Mauro. Without any help, he'd slid into the straps, buckled each properly and was already adjusting the regulatory device. "Whoa, hotshot, we're not there yet."

His face blanked. "Oh, sorry."

She studied his face. "You know something about gear?"

He nodded.

She arched a brow.

"My father and brothers are firefighters. They already went through all this with me."

"I see. Any of them trained to instruct in proper methods of donning gear?"

"No, ma'am."

"Then, stay in step, Recruit Mauro."

"Yes, ma'am."

Once all fifteen sported tanks on their backs, the instructors went about the arduous task of teaching them to put on air masks. Out of nowhere came an image of Jack, in her class, wrestling with the mask and swearing under his breath. He'd been a firefighter for years. The notion gave her more patience with the recruits.

It took two and a half hours to get all fifteen fully dressed and checked by an instructor.

Olive Hennessey looked at her watch. "Take off the facemask, helmet and hood." She scanned the recruits. "You look worse for wear." Down to a person, the recruits were dripping with sweat. "Go put your gear in the locker room. Lt. Phillips will show you where to stow it. Then hydrate. In fifteen minutes come back here wearing just your uniforms." She smiled at Tony. "Lt. Ramirez will show you what every firefighter should carry in his or her pockets, and he promises it won't be strenuous."

They exited with slumped shoulders and dragging feet. Tess took off the borrowed gear, trying not to think about how good the heavy equipment felt, how its smoky scent was so familiar and the smell caused a spike of adrenaline to go through her. She'd never wear it into a fire again.

That ugly fact stayed with her as she descended the stairs to get some water. By the half fridge off to the side, she found Jack, his stance casual, his face relaxed. God, he looked good like this. She hadn't seen or heard him come in.

She asked, "How long have you been watching me?"

"I got back from the firehouse a half hour ago. I stopped in to see how things were going."

"Why were you at a firehouse?"

When he explained his lunch and dinner missions his face brightened, so he must have enjoyed it. "That's a great idea."

"I have them once in a while, Teresa."

"So, what'd you think of my lesson?" Her tone was challenging.

"It was perfect." He watched her. "Except for one thing."

That annoyed her. "Seriously?"

"Yeah, I've seen other instructors teach this content. They allowed the recruits to take off their turnout coats and pants for the time you have to spend on the SCBA."

"Why would they do that? Recruits have to learn how to put on the tank and face mask fully dressed."

His expression was one of...pity? What the hell? "Seasoned firefighters have mastered how to get into gear quickly; they aren't learning. You know as well as I do, it takes them minutes to suit up. For first timers, it takes hours to learn how."

The knowledge that he might have a point niggled at her, but she ignored it. She'd taught this lesson before in the same way. "Criticizing me already, Captain?"

"You asked."

"My mistake, then. Do me a favor and stay out of my instruction until the recruits come to complain about it to you." She started away. He grasped her arm, but she shrugged him off.Damn him. He was finding fault, and it was only day one.

While she was talking to Jack, Tony Ramirez had come into the gym and was distributing papers on two tables where they'd eaten earlier. "Need help, Tony?"

He glanced up at her. For the first time, she was struck by his appearance, which everybody teased him about—they called him and his wife the Beautiful People. "Yeah, sure. Put some paper on the second table and add the magic markers."

After she checked out the material, she gave him a quizzical look. "I thought you were going to teach them what to store in their pockets before they went into a fire."

"I am. This is a game to learn about the tools."

"It looks like a puzzle."

"More of a picture find. They have to search out and trace the tools and other things that they could or should carry with them into a building."

"Why don't you just tell them?"

"Because kids learn by doing. And it's a good idea to make lessons fun." He added, "Especially after such a grueling afternoon session."

Still stinging from Jack's comments, Tess snapped, "You have something you want to say about my instruction, Lt. Ramirez?"

His brows rose in an innocent look. "Not a thing. I don't judge others' teaching methods."

Left unsaid was *so don't judge mine.*

Tess took in a deep breath and let it out. "You're right. I'm sorry for questioning you. Maybe I'll play the game, too."

Tony gave her a brilliant smile.

After distributing the papers, she sat down and picked up a marker. Hell, she didn't see anything at first. Then the wire cutters came into focus, the screwdriver, the knife and a light. It was kind of fun outlining each one.

"Done," she said, making Tony cross to her.

He picked up her paper. "Nope, you're not. You missed some." He winked at her. "And you're a seasoned firefighter. Not so easy, is it, Captain?"

"I hear ya, Tony," she said good-naturedly, and went back to the game.

It wasn't until later in the day, she wondered why she could take Tony's implied criticism on the chin but prickled when Jack expressed something similar.

oOo

Tess leapt out of bed, wearing the T-shirt and shorts most firefighters slept in at the firehouse. She pulled on pants and socks and hurried downstairs.

Grumbling from the rest of her team about being awakened so abruptly was minimal. They all knew the job of the night shift.

She dove into her boots and bunker pants and adjusted the straps, then climbed onto the truck. Ramirez was the officer, so he sat shotgun, Frazier drove, and next to her were Chief Hennessey and Phillips.

Tony read the paper he'd torn from the computer about the call. "Blaze on Avenue D." Which was downtown Hidden Cove. "The just-built skyscraper in town, which means we'll have excellent water usage from a brand new standpipe to attack the fire."

Soon the rig screeched to a halt in front of the scene. Working standpipes were a necessity as they funneled water from the hydrant or pumper up several floors. Three trucks were on site—Rescue 7 and their Quint and Midi. Tony hopped off the rig while the others donned their Nomex hoods, snapped on the backpacks, adjusted the breathing mechanism and secured helmets.

"Don't forget pocket tools," he told everybody.

Their job, Ramirez reported, was to go to floor five, where the fire had started, carrying a heavy hose to hook up to the standpipe. He led the way, and Tess was right behind him. Halfway up, she began to sweat. Then her ankle started to ache.

"What's wrong, Righetti?" Ramirez asked.

"Nothing."

He said, "I don't judge."

They kept going. It was hotter than hell on floor five as the fire blazed before them. Ramirez stopped. "I don't have a good feeling about this."

Grabbing the hose, Tess limped over to the standpipe, and went to turn the valve. She needed purchase on her legs and…couldn't get it.

She glanced over her shoulder and saw her crew, standing stock still waiting for her.

Their faces began to melt.

Their shoulders drooped into the bunker pants. Soon they'd be a puddle on the floor…

Tess awoke with a start. She was roasting in her gear, covered with sweat, and her breath came like bellows. But, looking around, she realized she was in the Malvaso home, on the second floor in Zach's old room. Swinging her feet off the bed, she tried to calm herself.

But she couldn't. If she kept breathing like this, she'd hyperventilate. She tried slow ins and outs and calmed some. But her hands kept shaking. This kind of thing hadn't happened in a long time, but she'd had several attacks after Joey died. Often, she'd call Mitch or Zach. She could get someone in the house now. But she didn't want to disturb them. Anyway, she knew who she wanted to talk to. Unable to squelch the need, she picked up her phone from the night table, got into her contacts and punched in Jack's number.

He answered on the third ring. "Harrison."

"Jack. It's Tess."

Calmly, he asked, "What happened? Is someone hurt?"

"Um, no."

"Teresa, it's three o'clock in the morning. Something must be wrong for you to call me."

Her whole body was tight as a whipcord, making her muscles hurt.

"No, nothing life-threatening." She ran a hand through her hair. "God, this is embarrassing. I had... I...I had a nightmare. I couldn't catch my breath. And I'm shaky."

"All right." Some rustling. "Lie down on the pillows and get under the covers."

Scooting back on the bed, she rested her head and pulled up the quilt. She was no longer warm.

"Take some deep breaths."

Already she was settling from the sound of his voice. But she took three more breaths. After about ten seconds, she said, "I feel better. That didn't work well when I tried it alone."

"Glad I could help. You were having an anxiety attack from the dream."

"I used to have them all the time."

"Tell me about this one. Talking will dilute its power."

She turned on her side. "I was in a fire. I endangered my crew. But they weren't actually my crew. They were instructors at the Academy."

"Think back. What were the similarities in the dream to what happened today?"

"I was overheated and dizzy before we got to the fire. Sweat dripped in my eyes."

"I think we both know where that came from."

"Oh, yeah, probably."

"What else?"

"There was something about tools in it. I discussed what firefighters carry inside in their pockets with Tony today."

"Harmless enough."

It wasn't, but she didn't mention the discussion she and Tony had had and what wasn't said but recognized.

"They all were dying, Jack. Melting away. Fuck, like the witch in *The Wizard of Oz.*"

"Why?"

"Because I couldn't open the standpipe. I couldn't get a good stance to turn the wheel."

"Honey, you're mourning the loss of your position on the line. You're trying to work out in your dreams what you just lost."

"You think so?"

"Uh-huh."

"Thanks." She picked at the bedspread. "I didn't expect a therapy session."

"What did you expect? Naughty talk?"

A shiver went through her. "Um, no." Though right now, trading sexy quips seemed a lot better than delving into her psyche. His husky voice reminded her of their night together, how he kissed her, touched her, moved inside her. "Maybe just a friend."

"We said we'd be that for each other."

"I guess."

"Anything else?"

"No, I'll let you go."

"It's all right if you want to talk about mundane things. It's going to be a while before your body catches up with your mind on the nightmare. You won't sleep right away."

"I'd like to, Jack." She wanted to call him John. She wanted to be Teresa tonight. The picture he displayed on his desk came to mind. "Tell me about your kids."

"They're almost done with the second semester."

"This early?"

"State college has three summer sessions, so regular classes end in April."

"What kind of people are they? Tell me how you raised them."

"You sure?"

"Yep. It'll calm me, like you said."

"Okay."

She listened to the sexy timbre of his voice. Then she felt her eyes closing. Soon, blankness enveloped her.

CHAPTER 8

Day two of the recruit-class training began with roll call, then classroom instruction. Ian Woodward sat in his wheelchair up front, sporting a serious expression on his face. Tess stood in the back, anxious to see him in action.

"I'm Captain Woodward. I'll be training you on the fire department's response to terrorist attacks locally. An entire unit will be dedicated to this later on in your course work, and the same goes for EMS safety. Those classes will cover using universal precautions, aka suiting up in protective gear, like facemasks and gloves for medical calls. I'll also go into what you're to do when you arrive at a site which might have a dirty bomb.

"But today, Chief Hennessey asked me to talk about the first two areas of safety listed up here."

Clicking into PowerPoint, Ian called up the first slide on the screen behind him.

1. 1.Fire ground Safety
2. 2.Vehicle Accident Safety
3. 3.EMS and universal precautions—to be included in EMS classes
4. 4.First Responders at Terrorist Attacks—to be included in another unit

He wheeled closer to the recruits, who sat like good little soldiers, stiff and attentive. The April sun slanted in through the big windows, casting their young faces in sharp relief, and for a moment, their vulnerability shocked Tess.

"I'm going to call on people to answer some questions. Relax. Having no idea of what I'm talking about or incorrect answers won't work against you." Ian gave them a genuine smile, then peered down at his list. "Recruit Murphy, what would you guess are the dangers at a fire ground?"

Murphy thought for a second. "Going into a building when it's too far gone to do any good. The text said the term is being *fully involved.*"

"Right on both accounts. It's a strict code of the fire department that you listen to the officer in charge about when to go into a fire and when to come out." He picked up a horn that sat on the desk and blew it. Everybody jumped, including Tess, then the recruits laughed nervously. Ian chuckled. "That's the evacuation sound."

When they settled down again, he focused on a different person. "Recruit Cruz, give us another thing that would be considered a safety issue on the fire ground."

"Gear. Wearing it right. Maybe making sure you have enough air." Which Tess had just taught them. *Good girl* that she remembered.

"Those are definitely things to watch."

Before Ian could call on the next person, Danny Mauro raised his hand.

Ian said, "Yes? The recruit in the back."

"My brother's buddy is a firefighter in upstate New York. Some guy torched his sister's house to lure firefighters there and shoot at them. Two firefighters were killed."

From the back, Tess heard gasps go through the group as a whole. Another recruit called out, "Yeah, but that was a fluke. Wasn't it?"

Ian shrugged. "That particular incident *was* unusual. But there *have* been shootings at firefighters of some form in Dallas, Kansas City, Austin and other cities.

"Why?" another recruit asked.

"Because we're authority figures. Remember that, too, when you enter buildings. Anyone inside could hold a grudge against you and what you symbolize. Early in my career, we went into a house, on a call to pump out a basement. A woman was in the living room, but there were four doors around it, and I had the thought that we could be ambushed easily if somebody wanted to hurt us."

"Did they?"

"No, but the officer in charge was worried about the gas and electric. We could have been killed if the captain hadn't been so circumspect."

Ian looked to her and Olive. "Captain Hennessey, Captain Righetti, do you want to add anything to this part of the discussion?"

Olive sighed. "Unfortunately, it's a fact of firefighting today that someone might take out their issues, real or imagined, on us. This new phenomenon is just something else we have to deal with."

Tess strode to the front of the room so she could see the kids face-to-face. "I'm in Hidden Cove temporarily, but I live in the same county as those Webster, New York, firefighters who were killed. The guy who shot them was disturbed. Yes, he set fire to his sister's house, and to her, too." Tess remembered those dark days of feeling so bad for her comrades and scrounging for things the department could do for the ones affected. "Truthfully, it was horrendous. All firefighters in the county mourned what happened for a long time. The Webster crews still aren't over it."

Olive stepped up to Tess. "There's only so much you can do to protect yourself from this kind of thing. Being aware and watchful for strangers near the fire ground is the first step."

Tess didn't let this go. Best they know everything now. "I'll bet you're thinking there's already too much to deal with when you reach a fire, get ready and go inside. But believe me, shootings are a real danger." At their horrified expressions, she added, "If you can't handle it, you shouldn't be here."

Ian took over again. "Well, to be fair, eventually arriving at the fire ground and going into a fire will become second nature, and you'll use muscle memory to get ready. You'll actually have time to assess the situation. Any more questions?"

Somebody raised his hand. Mauro again.

Tess had a feeling Mauro was going to muddy the waters. "Yes?"

"Can I ask Captain Woodward a question?"

Ian nodded. "Of course."

"You obviously weren't safe on the fire ground. That's why you're in that thing." He pointed to the chair. "How can you tell anybody they can be safe?"

"You're out of line, recruit," Tess snapped.

"No, that's okay." Ian's voice was calm. "I'll answer that. What's your name, son? I can't see your tag."

"Dan Mauro."

"To be blunt, Dan, you're right. You'll be walking into burning buildings, so you'll never be safe in the role of a firefighter. And if bombs fall from the sky, we're all at risk. But there are precautions you can learn about ahead of time and take at the scene. But to answer your question about me, I've studied first responders' procedures during terror attacks, which were developed by national experts. However, it was experiencing them firsthand that gave me insight into what to do, as well as making me highly motivated—that means pissed as hell—so I'm probably better equipped than anyone else to prepare you. One thing you have to learn is to benefit from the experience of those who've come before you. And be cautious with your safety. You can't save anybody if you're dead."

Unnerved by the boy's rudeness, Tess didn't address him further. She'd ask Olive if they should do anything about the boy's attitude.

Ian motioned to Tess. "Captain Righetti will now cover safety on heavily trafficked roads when there's been a car accident."

She took the clicker from Ian. "Here's a scene I want you to ponder." She put up on the screen the video of an accident. "An SUV had T-boned a sedan, and the vehicles were entwined." The sound of cars whizzing by was deafening, the speed of them, too fast. "Watch the firefighters and how they're forced to work on the road…"

o0o

Every year, Olive Hennessey held a gathering for the instructors at her house at the beginning of the recruit class. Since she'd had plans with her son last night, the shindig took place on day two. Jack rang the doorbell of her home in a regentrified part of the city, appreciating the brick and mortar that had gone into the place.

Olive smiled when she saw him on the stoop. "Hey, Jack." She nodded to what he carried. "You're such a doll, Doc." She accepted the scotch and sniffed at the pretty yellow daisies. "Thanks."

"Thank you for having us all. I'm sorry I'm late."

"No worries. Some others just got here."

He stepped into the foyer. To the left was a large living room with built-in bookshelves, a high ceiling and plenty of windows, where the

Academy staff mingled with each other. He scanned the group and zeroed in on Tess, talking to Quinn Frazier. Jack hadn't slept much after she called him last night, because he couldn't stop thinking about her.

Tonight, she wore a pretty two-piece red dress that swirled at her knees. Her high-heeled sandals made her bare legs look a mile long. Hell, she was feminine as all get out! He'd better be careful he didn't ogle her in public.

"We're having drinks in here," Olive told him. "The enclosed porch in the rear is set for dinner. There's a cross breeze between the back and front."

Jack sniffed. "Is that barbeque I smell?"

"Yep, from Sticky Lips."

"Man, I love that place."

"Go ahead, mingle. I've got to make sure everything's ready at the same time."

From across the room, Larissa glanced over, and he waved but went to get a drink at the bar in the corner. Tess left Frazier and came up to him.

"Hi," he said as easily as he could. Damn it all, she had makeup on, and her eyes glimmered with it.

Her face was flushed. "Hi."

He took in the red dress up close. It hugged every single curve she had. Clearing his throat, he asked, "So, did you sleep the rest of the night?"

"Yeah. I dozed off while you were talking."

"I know. I heard you snoring."

Her mouth fell open. "You did not."

"Scout's honor." Another grin. "I'm glad you called me."

"I shouldn't have."

"Why did you?"

"When I wake up from a nightmare like that, I'm unsteady and I feel…alone, I guess. It's happened since Joey died."

"I'm always here if you need me."

"You're a nice guy, Jack. I said some *not* nice things to you in the past and you're still kind to me."

"I care about you, Tess." Reaching out, he squeezed her arm. Which was a mistake. Her skin was as soft as down. "I've tried to tell you that."

She just nodded. "I'm going to go see if I can help Olive."

As she walked away, he couldn't help but notice the feminine sway of her hips. Turning away from her, he poured some scotch and downed it.

Dinner was called soon. When he reached the porch, he saw the backyard garden, the crocus and irises blooming in a myriad of colors.

Once people were seated, Olive lifted a glass of ruby red wine. "Okay, here's the rules. No talk about the recruits tonight. We're going to binge on fatty foods and get to know each other better or catch up with those you've worked with before. No work stuff."

Jenkins murmured, "Thank God. It's only day two and I already feel inundated."

"As they say, eat, drink and be merry."

Jack would try to follow Olive's advice.

oOo

Because Wednesday afternoon turned out to be balmy, Jack led the recruits out the back of the Fire Academy to a pavilion that held picnic tables. He'd ordered pizza and soda for them, and it waited on the tables under the roof, out of the sun. Quiet as usual, they found seats in an orderly fashion. He took a place in front of them, sitting on a tabletop so they could all see him. "Hi, everybody. As you know, I'm Jack Harrison. You can be informal and just call me Doc or Captain." He nodded to them. "And take off your ties. Loosen your collar. Let down some."

Blank looks. When one finally followed his suggestion, the others did, too.

"You're here because the department thinks you should have a place to talk about your training experiences and ask any questions you have or share concerns that might arise about your future as a firefighter."

Some nods.

He told them how he saw the group running, then asked if they had concerns today. None. Expecting this, he said, "Get in groups of five at a table, talk to each other." They moved, but when no one started a conversation, he handed out slips of paper.

"Since you seem reluctant to speak today, I'd like you to write down one thing you think will be easy for you in your training and one thing that you might have difficulty with. Don't put your names on the papers. I won't try to decipher your handwriting, so no worries there.

I'll collect them and read them aloud. If you want to talk about what you said, then we will. If you don't, at least you'll know how the rest of you are feeling. Deal?"

Most of them nodded.

"For those of you who haven't agreed, I'll tell you right now this is an order."

They wrote, and after five minutes, Jack collected the sheets.

"Sight unseen, I'm going to read them so you'll know I'm not censoring anything. First, 'I was blown away by the discussion of people shooting at firefighters.'"

Jack paused. "Of course you were. It's a grim reality of the job. Maybe we can discuss that more in here."

Many of the kids eased back in their chairs, shoulders relaxing. Jack read another. "'I'm not fit enough. I can tell after only three days.'" Jack smiled. "Then, take Cory Cameron up on his offer of classes three times a week. I guarantee he'll get you in shape."

He heard a few sighs.

Other thoughts followed. How they admired Ian Woodward, and if he could still fight terrorism, so could they. Some were worried about the course work.

"You know, learning everything in that monstrous text you're assigned is always a concern for recruits. I'm going to talk to the chief about some tutoring. I should have thought about it before."

By the time Jack got to the last paper, he was relieved. Until he saw what was written. But a deal was a deal. He read, "Captain Righetti seems like a real bitch to me."

And so it began.

oOo

Standing at the edge of the huge indoor pool, Tess grinned. "God, this is fun!"

Beside her, Zach squeezed her neck. "See? You should stay in Hidden Cove forever!"

"Great to have you here, Tess." Jenn stood next to her two brothers. Tess wore one of her cousin's bathing suits, a modest black-and-white thing. Jenn's was red. Zach's trunks, of course, were wild and loud. "We have these fundraisers all the time."

The Hidden Cove Fire Department knew how to have good times as well as fight fires. Since it was too cool yet to swim outside, this fundraiser for Hale's Haven had been planned at the Hidden Cove Y. They had to hold it on Thursday night, though, because the Y couldn't close to their membership on weekends. The pool was Olympic size, with Jacuzzis and kiddie pools surrounding it. For a twenty-dollar donation, families or single people would stream in from six to ten o'clock, eat, swim and support a good cause.

Mitch approached them, and the three cousins exchanged nods—just before they picked her up.

"What the f—"

"One," Mitch yelled as they swung her back and forth over the water.

"Two." Zach now.

Even Jenn participated. "Three."

She went flying through the air and hit the water with a big splash. Zach cupped his hands. "Your initiation, babe."

She came up sputtering from the unceremonious dunking. "I'll get you all back."

Mitch guffawed. "Just like old times."

Only it wasn't. She'd missed *years* of this camaraderie. The strong chlorine scent reminded her of swimming with the Malvasos at the neighborhood pool when she'd come to live with them. Their antics made her remember how they treated her like a little sister. How she liked it.

Tess swam to the side of the pool, braced her arms on the concrete and observed one of the kiddie areas. She loved watching the little ones. Zach and Casey's kids, Jason, Nicky, Lindsay and Shannon, had volunteered to be in charge of them. "Geez, Zach, your kids are so grown up."

"That's what I been tellin' ya, girl. You missed too much."

As she watched the smaller ones, Bella and Ben caught her eye and waved. A little girl clung to Zach's son. She was about two. "Who's the tow-headed one? She's got eyes for Nicky."

"That's Beck and Lela's daughter, Cami. Not sure if you met them, but you should."

Watching from the pool, Tess wondered if any of the others had lost a parent and would be going to the camp Tess had heard so much about over the years.

"Come on," Jenn yelled around cupped hands. "Let's play volleyball.

I'll be a captain of one team."

"Me, too," Grady offered. "You're on, sweetheart. We're gonna whomp your butts."

They decided on eight people per side. Four teams agreed to play. Tess found herself with Connie, Paulie, Beck and Lela, whom she *had* met, Cory and a couple of others she didn't know.

Against her team were Mitch, Zach, Jenn, Noah and Eve, Quinn Frazier and two others.

In the server's position, Zach tossed up the ball and punched it over the net. Right to Tess, who jumped up and popped it back into the air. Paulie slapped it over to the other side. He high-fived her. Connie served next. Right into the net, unfortunately. "Get the hook," Mitch called out.

Connie stuck her tongue out at her big brother.

They batted the ball back and forth until the score was tied at fourteen. "Win by two," Noah announced as he served. The ball went high and was coming right toward Tess, who'd moved to the front line. "Mine," she yelled and spiked it down to the water of the opposing team.

"We changed our mind, Teresa." This from Mitch. "You can go back to Rockland."

In the end, Tess's team won. She was energized by the play and swam to the steps. Where she found Jack, holding a towel out for her. It was the same color blue as the one she wore the night they made love, and from his expression, he remembered, too. But he said easily, "You looked good out there."

Hell, *he* looked good. He wore a black suit with red stripes and a red T-shirt to match. The color did great things for his complexion. And she'd forgotten how muscular he was. His biceps and pecs and chest were sculpted.

"Like what you see?" he asked, amused.

She was in a good mood; he'd helped after a nightmare, so her smile was broad. "I never made any bones about that, Doc."

His gaze turned hot as he looked down. She wrapped the towel around her waist only. Her chest was exposed, and though the suit was one piece, it was cut high at the legs and low at the top. "Watch yourself, Doc."

"If you don't want people to look, don't wear something like that."

"Touché."

Cory Cameron came up to them. "Tess, want a hot dog? They're cooking them in the kitchen."

"I would." Nodding to Jack, they left.

Jack stood where he was, confounded by his feelings about Tess walking away from him with another man. He couldn't take his eyes off her.

"You'd better stop staring like that, Doc, or somebody else is gonna catch on."

Turning, he found Sophia Ramirez behind him. Wearing a ruffled bathing suit, she resembled a young Sophia Lauren so much she was breathtaking. Jack said, "I have no idea what you mean."

"I've been watching you since you got here. You keep looking for the prodigal cousin, and when you find her, you stare. When did all this happen?"

He wouldn't lie outright to Sophia. "Oh, God, don't tell anybody."

Her laugh was sultry. "I won't."

"I, um, knew her in Rockland when I went to take the recruit class."

"You going for it?"

"No. Professional ethics and all."

"Hmm."

A whistle blew, and Noah Callahan asked for everybody's attention. "Food's on in the other room, but if you want to be in a diving contest, do it before you eat."

A flurry of activity—soon, all the Malvasos were lined up at the diving board, including Tess. The family loved each other but were super-competitive, too. They let Tess go first.

So, as if he *needed* this, Jack had to watch her climb the steps to the high board. Stride to the end, and bounce. Once, twice. She leapt into the air, bent her body in a perfect jackknife, glided downward, then hit the water almost without any splash.

Fuck, was there anything the woman wasn't good at?

"Come on, Romeo, let's go get food," Sophia said dryly and tugged at his arm.

oOo

Tess was familiar with RTE's, Recruit Training Evaluations, though each department did them differently. At the Anderson Fire Academy, the staff would meet on Friday afternoon while the recruits spent the end of the day with Jack. Tess liked the evaluations, mostly because everything was brought out in the open.

Olive nodded to a pizza on the table. "Jack Harrison got some pie for the recruits, and he bought one for us."

Briefly, Tess wondered about the familiarity of sharing a meal with students. It was customary to maintain structure and distance at first. Dismissing the idea, she took a piece and bit into it. Hmm, cheese, pepperoni, spiced sauce.

After everyone had a bite to eat, Olive rose and stood by the white board. "Listed up here are the recruit names. Each of you will give them a grade, on a scale of one to five, five being the best. We'll discuss their ratings. Let's do it orally. Since there's been no EMS, Larissa isn't here today."

The first name up was Anita Cruz. Tony said, "Three."

Jenkins gave her a four.

Tess said, "One."

All gazes focused on her.

"What's wrong?" she asked.

"We don't give ones, Tess," Tony told her.

"She practically fainted on the first day."

He shot her a questioning look. "But she's done well physically the rest of the week."

"Huh. I guess you don't grade as hard here as we do in Rockland."

"As a matter of fact, we grade hard." Olive smiled at her. "But we don't give ones. We found doing that too demoralizing to the recruits. And discouraging."

"Okay, I change mine to a two."

Next up was Dan Mauro. Scores were 4/5/5/4/3/2.

Again, everybody looked to Tess. "Hell." She shook her head. "I just don't get it. This guy, for example. He's a hotshot." Like Joey had been. "He's arrogant."

"He's aced every single written and physical test we've given him." This from Jenkins.

Tony sighed. "I agree with Jenkins."

Frazier shook his head. "I gave him a three. I agree with Tess. Something's off about that kid. When he challenged Ian, it was almost like he was asking to be called out."

"I have a suggestion." Olive spoke with authority. "Let's outline what we're basing the evaluation on."

They hadn't done that in Rockland. Scores reflected more of a general impression.

Olive looked to Tess. "What do you think?"

"I guess so. I'm clearly on a different page from most of you."

"Then, let's see if we can start a new chapter."

CHAPTER 9

At the end of the first week of recruit class, Hale's Haven held its kickoff, cleanup weekend beginning Friday morning. Firefighters and police officers who were off shift worked from nine to five, as well as some veterans in the area. Academy people and those who were on day shift would put in a few hours at night.

Now, at five o'clock, Megan Malvaso smiled at the assembled group. "Wow. What a great turnout. There were a lot of people here today, but I'm surprised to see so many of you giving up your Friday night."

"Did we have a choice?" Zach Malvaso whined. Jack knew he was one of the camp's biggest supporters and spent a lot of free time here, fixing things up.

Casey Malvaso rolled her eyes. The dynamic between the married couple was fun to watch, though there was a time when it was excruciating to observe their dealings with each other.

Megan continued, "You all know Parker Erikson and Lisel Woodward, the duo who are heading up the camp this year."

Both women, dressed in plain shirts and work pants, waved. Jack knew they were as lovely inside as out.

Giving the crowd a huge smile, Parker stood. "Everyone's invited across the lake to our house for dinner at eight p.m., so you only have a few hours of actual cleanup time. We'll begin again tomorrow, early morning. We promise to tire you out this weekend."

Lisel stood beside her. "We're having people for dinner tomorrow at six, when we quit for the day. Across the lake, too, in case you don't know."

After the applause for their hospitality and some shout outs, Megan went on. "I'm in charge of the campers for the summer."

Mitch, standing by her, shook his head and assumed a look of feigned annoyance. "Still!"

As if he didn't work as hard as she did.

"And Jack Harrison's with us tonight. He runs support groups with kids and is often around to participate in activities." She winked. "You should have seen him on the ropes course last year. He was amazing."

A second round of clapping flabbergasted him. He'd helped a lot of these people, but still...

"These are your work assignments." Megan passed out clipboards. "If you don't feel comfortable with what you're doing, come see me." She shot a glance at her husband. "Don't worry, dear, I'm not making you climb any heights." She cleared her throat. "You're a bit past that."

People laughed. During times like this, humor and happiness ran high. Jack wondered how Tess would get along here. She'd come in as he did, but he'd purposely not searched for her in the crowd. Since they'd agreed it might be unethical to get involved—after all one of the recruits had written that she was a bitch—he best stay away from her. He'd dealt with the incident by saying the instructors had the best interests of the recruits at heart but they each went about it differently.

When the clipboard reached him, Jack found he was working with Gabe Malvaso, Rachel Wellington and Larissa James on the caretaker's house, aka where Mitch and Megan lived for the summer. During the rest of the year, others used it for special weekends and events in the fall. The place needed a good cleaning after being closed up most of the winter. Others would work on the outside, emptying the gutters and washing windows. He checked to see who they were. Shit. Tess. And yay! Tess. Obviously, he was conflicted about more contact with her.

"Again, thanks so much for this." Megan's eyes got misty. The camp was named in honor of her dad, Patrick Hale, who'd died in the line of duty. She'd been one of these kids they were trying to help.

Jack meandered down to the water and met up with Noah Callahan. The chief said, "I was hoping to catch you. How did the Recruit Concerns class go this week?"

Sighing, Jack looked out at the lake. The sun was low, sparkling off the water, so he had to shield his eyes from the brightness. "Awkward about covers it. They wouldn't talk at all the first day. I had to *order* them to write out concerns they had, then I read them aloud."

"Did you expect that kind of reticence?"

"Pretty much, after observing them at the beginning of the week. Today was better. One kid asked about confidentiality. We spent the better part of the ninety minutes deciding what that meant. I let them come up with what they wanted, first, and I accepted everything. All I had to add was the part about hurting themselves and others."

Like the friend he was, Noah clapped him on the back. "If anybody can make this work, it's you."

"How you doing, Chief?"

"Good. Closer to retirement, I think."

"Have you talked more with Eve about it?"

"Same old, same old. She wants me to retire. But she isn't pushing me."

"Remember what I said, no option is going to be a hundred percent."

"Yeah, I guess." He turned to face the camp. "Can you believe we did this?"

"Sometimes I can't. You have a lot to be proud of."

"I'm not responsible for Hale's Haven."

"You are in many ways. Without your support, the camp wouldn't have been built or grown so fast. Don't downplay your importance, Noah. Take joy in it."

"You're right. I will."

"How many kids this year?"

"Four sessions. About thirty kids each session. Then, there's Junior Hale's Haven." The overnight camp was set up for kids seven to seventeen. Junior camp was for the three-to-seven age group. Jack had spent time there last year and changed a few diapers.

"I heard Lela and Beck took over the junior camp." Two years ago, Beck Sloan, a retired army colonel turned firefighter, had suggested they include kids of veterans at Hale's Haven. It had been such a success, they'd made it a permanent part of the program. Other war heroes who'd returned home had volunteered.

"People just step up, you know?" Noah mused.

"Give them an opportunity and they do."

Someone across the way yelled, "Jack, you ready to clean up?"

"Oh, Lord, my favorite task. See you later, Chief."

When he reached the caretaker house, Rachel Wellington handed him a pail and sponges. Jack liked the tall, lithe woman. "Hey, Jack. I'm so glad to see you again."

"Same here.

"Which do you want? The kitchen, bathrooms or living space?"

"Anything. Doesn't matter."

"Take the kitchen."

"Yes, ma'am." He squeezed her arm. "How are things going?"

"Good, I'm back full-time. Anabelle went to kindergarten, so it seemed right." Jack had helped her decide when to return to the line and encouraged job sharing—which Noah agreed to—in the department so women like Rachel could work part-time.

On his way to the kitchen, he stopped to say hello to Larissa. "Hi. I'm surprised to see you here."

She looked cute with her hair up in a ponytail and a shirt that sported an ambulance on the front. The slogan read Nobody Calls Us 'Cause They Did Something Smart! So, she had a sense of humor. He liked that in women.

"I wanted to help," she said sweetly. "Maybe we can get more of the EMS workers in the city to support the camp."

"Good idea. Be careful what you say out loud, though. If you suggest something, Megan will put you in charge of it—forever."

She laughed and so did he. "Good to see you."

When he reached the kitchen, he whipped off his overshirt, so he wore only a black T-shirt with jeans. He was already hot, so he opened the kitchen window. He filled a bucket and began with the exterior of the cabinets. The outside people had set up a radio, and it blasted some god-awful heavy metal. So he blanked his mind and scrubbed and washed, scrubbed and washed. When he went to the sink, the music changed, thank God, to oldies. But when Van Morrison's "Brown Eyed Girl" came on, Jack swore under his breath and scrubbed the sink with excessive force.

A ladder had been propped up right outside the window. As he turned on the faucet, he saw shapely legs come down it. He knew, intimately, who they belonged to. They'd been wrapped around him in the not-too-distant past. He took a deep breath and let it out slowly as he watched Tess hit ground level, go to the cooler and bend over to get some water. Fuck! He tried to avert his gaze, but he couldn't. She had a fine ass, all toned. And fine breasts, too. Fine...

"Jack?"

Shifting on his feet, he turned to find Larissa behind him.

"I came to get some water."

"I think the fridge is running. I haven't gotten to clean it yet."

Jack watched her cross to the appliance. "I've been meaning to ask you how your EMS classes are going. You'd voiced some concern before the course started."

"I haven't taught a class yet." She faced him with a bottle in her hand. "When I was introduced, though, some of the guys were rolling their eyes at me. Cory Cameron was with me, and showed me respect so they did too."

Cameron got around!

She sipped the water delicately. "I've been meaning to ask you something, too."

"What's that?"

Her smile was thousand watt. "Have dinner with me tomorrow night?"

Do it, he told himself. Take the advice you'd give anyone else in his situation. He made himself say, "I'd love to."

Before she left, she squeezed his arm. He circled back to the sink to find Tess at the bottom of the ladder, staring through the window.

o0o

The Erikson house on Hidden Lake was a showcase. Dusk had settled, and lights around the water's edge glowed like yellow beacons. Tess had never been here before, and she admired the structure: three levels, beautiful décor—from what she could see of the inside—and the sprawling multileveled decks. Parker had inherited it from her grandparents, Mitch told her, and Cal had moved in after they were married. The Eriksons were showing off their daughter, Madison, to the Malvasos.

Her cousin held out his arms. "Come on, baby, come to Zach."

The dark haired, blue-eyed clone of Parker shook her head. "No!"

"You're losing your touch," Jenn teased her brother.

Jack joined Zach at the front of the group. He'd thrown on a gray

Columbia sweatshirt, but she remembered all too well what he looked like in a damp black T-shirt. "Nah! Come to me, sweetheart."

Madison's face wreathed with a grin, and she reached out both arms. Jack took the child. "You got taste, little one."

"I don't understand. I have a way with women."

So did Jack. Tess could testify to that fact.

"Not this time." Jack kissed Madison's head, and Tess's stomach tightened.

"Want to go for a walk with me?"

She gripped him around the neck. "Me no walk."

"How about if Uncle Jack carries you?"

"'Kay." She laid her head on his shoulder, cuddling into the warm-looking fleece.

"It's amazing," Cal said, sliding his arm around his wife. "Maddie always goes to him like that."

"Does he spend a lot of time here?" Zach asked.

"Some."

"That must be why she went to him and not me."

"Come on, I'll soothe your battered ego." This from his wife, who dragged him toward the bar set up outside.

Tess said to Jenn, "It's wonderful to see him so happy."

"It took a long time for the two of them to get together." She turned to Tess. "Now we gotta find a guy for you."

Tess tried not to look after where Jack had gone. Luckily, someone came up to her. "Want to go down by the water, Tess?"

She smiled at Cory. His blond hair was windblown and his face ruddy. "Yeah, sure." Maybe he'd take her mind off Jack, whom she'd heard earlier make a date with the beautiful Larissa James. Untying her HDFC hoodie from around her neck, Tess shrugged into it and followed Cory down the decks and out to the water. The place had a dock, at the end of which was a covered little gazebo. He said, "Let's go down there."

They took the twenty-foot span slowly. Tess enjoyed the rhythm of the lap of the water on shore, the crickets chirping and the scent of the lake.

When they reached the end, Tess laughed. "You get me out here to sit in that swing with you?"

"Yep."

She chuckled and sat.

He dropped down on the padded wicker, and their legs touched.

"Nice and cozy."

"Uh-huh. Your intentions seem suspect, Mr. Cameron."

"Oh, they are." He slid his arm around her. Then he kicked the swing, and as they went back and forth, they talked of the work they'd gotten done at the camp and how great the concept was.

When they stopped talking, the silence was comfortable. After a while, Cory turned slightly and took her chin. She gazed up into his blue eyes. He must have seen permission in hers, because he leaned over and brushed her lips with his. It was fun, until she started to think about Jack, kissing her senseless in the Inn last week. And in her bedroom weeks ago.

Cory grasped her arms, and she tried to participate. Still, none of the fireworks came.

After he wound down the kiss and drew away, he smiled. "That was nice."

"It was." Only nice. Why the hell kiss somebody if it was only nice? But maybe she wasn't giving him enough of a chance.

They heard a bell and someone call out "Chow's on."

"Hungry?" she asked Cory.

He stood. "Yes, but I plead the fifth on for what. Come on, we'll go eat."

They hiked back up to the decks again. She and Cory got separated in the crowd headed to the food in the house. Tess eventually ended up in line without him…two people behind Jack. Geez. He turned around when the queue stalled. His expression, when it was directed at her, was glacial.

She gave him a quizzical look. He angled his head toward the back. The buffet was on the bottom floor, and darkness lay beyond the setup. When she didn't move, he slipped out of line, took her arm and led her away from the others, down a corridor. They ended up in a large bathroom; he closed the door and locked it.

"You've gotta be kidding me," she said, motioning to the place where they always seemed to find themselves.

He didn't joke.

"What's wrong, Jack?"

His hand came out and he brushed her lips with his thumb. It was calloused, rough, and the gesture made her head spin. "Did you kiss him?"

Had his tone been jealous or angry, she would have fought him. But it was sad.

The room suddenly seemed small, intimate. "Jack, don't."

"I want to know."

"Yes."

"How was it?"

"What do you want me to say? That it was milquetoast compared to your kisses? That I wished like hell it was you?"

A smile broached his mouth. "That's a good start."

Lifting her chin, she said as haughtily as she could, "You're going out with Larissa. I heard her ask you for dinner."

"I'm going because you don't want a relationship with me."

"I said it was unprofessional. And, again as I also said, I'm not sure I could ever trust you again."

"That's bullshit. You know now why I didn't contact you. Don't make me explain it again."

"I know what you said Jack, but the explanation doesn't make what you did hurt less."

Moving in closer, he grasped her upper arms. Squeezed her gently. "I obviously handled that wrong. I'm sorry."

"I know you are."

His gray gaze darkened, making it the color of dangerous smoke. "I hate seeing you with him." His voice was raw.

"We have to forge a life without each other." Even to her own ears, her voice sounded unconvincing.

"Yeah, look how that's working out."

She stepped back. "I should go."

He didn't stop her.

Until she reached the door. Then he was behind her, slapping a hand against the wood when she tried to open it. She pivoted.

"He won't be the last guy who did this," Jack said, just before he took her mouth in a voluptuous, bone-melting kiss.

They didn't get caught in the bathroom this time.

Except by their own feelings for each other.

o0o

"You look lovely tonight, Larissa." Jack smiled over at the woman he had a date with on Saturday night. She was dressed in a sleeveless blue sheath, the kind Elizabeth used to wear. Her blond hair was up in a knot again, this time with loose tendrils around her face. She'd be any man's dream date.

Too bad she wasn't *his* perfect woman. Short choppy dark hair and liquid brown eyes kept superimposing themselves over Larissa's features. Though God knew Tess wasn't perfect.

"Do you think we should have gone to the picnic at the Woodwards' house?" Larissa asked.

"No. I'm fine missing it." And missing Tess, and whoever she was with tonight. Probably Cameron. Because of her, because of them, he was determined to enjoy dinner and the company.

"I like this place." The Hidden Cove Hideaway was an historic building at the edge of town that had been converted to a bed-and-breakfast. Its cozy winter atmosphere had been replaced by an outdoorsy spring one: windows were open and wildflowers perched on tablecloths, which now sported yellow napkins instead of black.

"I like it, too. Its restaurant is five-star, and New Yorkers often come out here." The place had guest rooms, as well, so it was good for a hideaway, as the name suggested.

Larissa sipped the merlot they'd ordered. "Did you pick it because it's out of the way?" At his quizzical expression, she said, "So no one would see us."

"No. I told you I don't think spending time with you outside of the Academy is a conflict of interest."

"Good. Let me say one thing about the Recruit Concerns class. I don't care what the kids tell you about me. And if you have any pointers for what I can do better after the class is over, please let me know so I can improve."

"What a refreshing attitude."

One Tess didn't possess.

They picked up the menu. "Hmm," Larissa said after she perused it. "Do you like chateaubriand?" The dish, using the best cut of beef, was served with an assortment of vegetables and potatoes for two.

"Absolutely. Rare?"

"The only way to cook it."

"Then, it's settled."

After they put in their order, he cocked his head. "Tell me about your background."

"A middle-class life in upstate New York. I went to school for premed, then decided that being a doctor wasn't what I wanted. I liked medicine, though, so I became certified as an EMT, then an EMS instructor with advance training."

"You had a happy childhood?"

"Yes, I did. Fun teenage years. Good college experience. I'm one of the lucky ones." She smiled. "What about you? Are you from Hidden Cove?"

"No, Brooklyn. Middle-class family, too. I went to college at seventeen and graduated at twenty-one. Dad wanted me to be a lawyer, but I'd been enthralled by the FDNY all my life, so I went to John Jay for fire science. FDNY members were instrumental in our instruction, and the fire department psychologist took a liking to me, probably because I was so interested in his job. I got into the department right away. After a couple of years of firefighting, I decided psychology was my calling, so I went back to school for my PhD."

"I, um, heard you'd been married. And your wife died."

"Yeah, it was a fluke." The old pain surfaced. "It's rare for women to die in childbirth in the modern world. Unfortunately, Elizabeth had a bad heart, which no one had caught before she delivered, and the stress was too much." He shook his head. "She had the best care, too, because her father was an ob-gyn and she was treated at his practice by a highly regarded female doctor." He shrugged. "Life and death can be bizarrely random."

"So you came out here to Hidden Cove?"

"For my last semester of grad school. My grandmother had moved here from New York. After I finished school, the psychologist at the Hidden Cove Academy retired. I was young, but I'd interned out here with him and the guys liked me. Elizabeth's parents were good about it, too, frequently coming from the city to stay with the kids."

Reaching over the table, she took his hand. "I wish you hadn't had such a tough life."

"Thank you. I'm happy now with my work and my twins."

He told her about the kids over dinner. They talked of her marriage, and her husband's death. He hadn't known she was a widow.

"We have a lot in common," Jack remarked when she finished.

"Yes, we do."

The night was still balmy when he drove her home after dinner and escorted her to her porch. "I had a wonderful time, Jack. Would you like to come in?"

"I enjoyed myself, too." Which was true. "But we have to be at the camp early tomorrow morning. Rain check?"

"Sure." She stood on tiptoes and kissed him lightly on the cheek. "Good night. See you tomorrow."

Jack waited until Larissa was inside before he left the porch and got in his truck. He liked Larissa's company. And the evening had been blessedly absent of tension and resentment.

A nice change.

If the entire night hadn't been characterized with a lack of passion, the date would have been perfect. But hell, maybe that would come. Couples his age didn't experience a white-hot attraction for each other right away. With *most* people it took time. Maybe he'd see where a relationship with Larissa led.

oOo

Tess had refused to look for Jack at the home of Ian and Lisel Woodward. They lived in the accessible condo where Ian was residing when he met the Broadway star. "Your house is great, Ian," she said from the kitchen where she'd gone to help get out dessert. They were eating outside.

"It's small now, with the baby, so we're moving. We've built a house just inside Hidden Cove, closer to Evie and the Academy. We're keeping the condo, though, as a summer place for us and the Callahans."

"I can see why. If you ever want to sell it, let me know." She was thinking ahead these days? When had that happened?

"So, you're staying in town?" His eyes twinkled. "I thought you might."

"You were very convincing. And then, of course, Sabina's medical issues made me realize I wanted to be here, for a while at least."

"Good for you."

Lisel came in carrying a two-year-old girl, dressed in pink pajamas. "Oh, wow, aren't you beautiful." Her blond hair and gray eyes bore a strong resemblance to her dad's.

"Thank you." Lisel hugged the baby close. "Say hello, Evie."

"'ello."

"This is Tess." Lisel kissed the baby's head. "We're going to say good night to everyone before we go to bed."

"I'll walk out with you," Tess told her. She picked up a cookie tray that she'd arranged.

"Dad-dy!" Evie yelled when Lisel started to walk away. The girl squirmed and twisted to see her father.

"Okay, sweetheart." He nodded to the chocolate ice-cream rolls. "Bring that out, love, and I'll carry the tyrant here."

The *tyrant* was all smiles when she sat on Daddy's lap. Ian looked up at Tess. "This is what I meant when we spoke last week. The fire department is *not* my life."

"I can tell. I envy you."

"Do you? Then, go after it."

Which was why, when Cory Cameron asked to take her home, then suggested she come to his apartment for a nightcap, she accepted. Tonight, she'd take a chance.

oOo

The last day of the work weekend was gloomy and overcast, the complete opposite from the previous one. Workers prayed it didn't rain. Just in case, Mitch and Megan were making lists for tasks they could do inside.

The rain held off all morning. Jack was in the middle of hauling brush to the road at the entrance to camp when the downpour began. With it came a cold breeze off the lake, chilling the air.

"Shit," he said, pulling up the hood on his sweatshirt. He started down the path to the open pavilion where they met in the morning and for lunch. The rain was slanted and spit right in his face. His feet slipped on dirt which was quickly becoming mud, and he fell on his butt. A greasy brown mess splattered on his face and chest. "Fuck!" he said aloud.

From the corner of his eye, he saw someone carrying an umbrella leave the enclosed social hall off to the left. She picked her way over to him. "Hey, you okay?"

Jack smiled up at Stacey Sterling Evans. "Yeah, if a bit wet and sore."

"We'll go down to the pavilion together under the umbrella."

Managing to get to his feet, Jack ducked under the canvas. "Hey, Stacey. How you feeling?"

"Super. The second trimester's a lot easier than the first." She placed her hand on her just-bulging belly. "Twins, like yours."

"Ah, you'll have your work cut out for you."

"I can't wait."

They headed down the path. The ground was getting muddier and muddier. Stacey went ahead of him when the space to walk narrowed. Something began to niggle at Jack. "Hey, Stace, I think we should stop. Wait this out in the infirmary right over there."

"You're probably right." When she started to turn, though, her foot slid out from under her.

She pitched forward.

Jack grabbed her around the waist to keep her upright.

He stumbled backward, and let Stacey go so she wouldn't fall with him.

He hit the ground with a thud, and blistering pain shot through him.

In seconds, blackness came.

oOo

Tess huddled by the infirmary with the rest of the workers. Zach and Casey Malvaso and one other paramedic were inside with Jack. Word had spread he'd fallen and hit his head because he saved a pregnant woman from toppling over. Thank God Stacey Sterling was all right. And how like Jack to have kept her safe at his own expense. But his type of injury sent Tess into a tailspin.

Next to her, Mitch slid an arm around her. "You okay?"

The rain stopped as suddenly as it had come, and a bright sun peeked out of the heavens, warming everyone but her. "Yeah, sure." She wasn't, but she refused to take the attention off the people involved in the accident.

"Hell of a thing, isn't it?"

"I don't know Stacey."

Mitch smiled. "She's a recent addition to the fire department family. You've met Nick Evans, right?"

"Yeah. He's a firefighter. He must have been scared to death when he found out what happened."

"She was a mess. Did you hear she slid on her butt all the way down to the pavilion so she wouldn't fall, but she had to get help for Jack?"

"No, I didn't know that." Tess had trouble following the course of events. He *hit his head hard* was at the front of her mind. "What, um, what were they doing together?"

"They were both working near the entrance to the camp. Stacey came in to cook and serve, to do her part for Hale's Haven, while Nick was cleaning gutters." Mitch nodded off to the side, where Stacey cuddled into Nick's chest, her eyes wide and frightened. "She went out to get him, under the umbrella. When she slipped, he caught her, but they pitched backward. He let go and she stayed upright, but he went down."

Tess bit her lip.

"What's wrong? I know you don't like Jack, but…" His voice trailed off. Mitch slapped his forehead with his palm. "Hell, honey, I didn't make the connection. But you did."

Tess cleared her throat to keep the emotion at bay. "It's never far away, anyway."

"Joey's head injury in the skiing accident was a lot worse than what happened to Jack just now."

"You don't know that, Mitch."

"I watched when they brought him in. He was already coming around."

"The same was true for Joey. They said it was just the bump on the head that killed him."

Tugging her close, he kissed her head. "We'll wait it out, kiddo."

As she had with Joey. She'd never forget her blinding panic on that freezing slope while she waited for the medic crew to get to her brother. He'd hit a tree because he was goofing off. Tess saw the whole thing because she'd gone down right behind him. Then, at the hospital, the hours had ticked by at a snail's pace and she went from hope to devastation every few minutes. She'd been alone when she got the brutal news. At twenty-seven, she could barely cope. And she'd never been the same again.

Again, time crawled by. Finally, Casey came out of the trailer. "He's gonna be all right, everybody. We cleaned the wound, stitched it up and gave him a shot for pain. We're taking him into town for X-rays."

A sweep of profound relief made Tess weak in the knees. She had to grab on to Mitch to stay upright.

Casey skimmed those gathered to hear news about Jack. Her gaze landed on Tess and she threaded her way through the crowd. "Tess,

Jack wants to see you."

"Tess? Why?" Mitch asked.

"I have no idea. He just does."

Not looking at her cousin, Tess followed Casey into the infirmary cabin. Jack was stretched out flat on a cot. He was covered with mud, and the place smelled of it. She gave him a weak smile.

He said, "Can you two leave me alone with Tess?"

"What for?" Zach asked.

Casey pulled at his sleeve. "None of our business. We'll be outside. Call us when you're done."

"Thanks." When they left, Jack said in a gravelly voice, "Come here, Teresa."

Her eyes misted. She'd been really worried about him. She crossed to the cot and knelt down beside him. He took her hand. He said, "Hi."

"Hi." She kissed his grimy knuckles. "You're a hero, you know?"

"I was scared for her, Tess. I was afraid she'd fall on her stomach."

"So you sacrificed yourself."

"Hardly. I hadn't planned to slam down backward."

With a shaky hand, she smoothed his muddy hair from his face. "I...I'm so glad you're all right."

"I thought you'd be worried, so I asked for you."

"It was public. My cousins can't figure out why."

"Yeah, about that. I want to tell them about us."

She should try to convince him that there was no *us*. But when she saw him, bruised and hurting, she couldn't lie to herself. She cared about this man.

"I—"

"Don't decide now. I'll text you when I get home from X-raying my head. You can come to my house."

"Tonight?"

"Um-hmm. Make something up about why you're going out. We'll talk about all this then."

This time, Tess let her heart decide. "All right."

CHAPTER 10

Jack's head hurt like hell, and he did have a mild concussion. So the FD doctor insisted he not spend the night alone…

"I have someone coming over," Jack told the man. Zach and Casey had been with him.

"Who? 'Cause one of us can stay with you." This from Zach.

"Thanks, but I have it covered."

Zach snorted. "You got a squeeze we don't know about, Doc?"

"None of your business. Just take me to my house. I'll make arrangements to get my car from the camp tomorrow."

"Maybe your girlfriend can drive you…"

Now, at home, he waited for Tess to arrive. He'd texted her from the hospital and she'd said she'd be over as soon as she could.

Lying on the couch, he closed his eyes and thought of her. The ice pack on his head was cold and he ached all over, but his heart stirred at the thought that she'd acquiesced. To coming over, at least. But he'd seen something in her eyes tonight that made him think he could convince her to pursue a relationship with him and conflict of interest be damned.

The doorbell rang.

He righted himself and stood. Uh-oh. Dizziness swamped him. Grabbing on to the back of the sofa, he waited for his brain to adjust, then limped to the door.

And there she was, outside on the front porch. The rain had come again, and her hair and shoulders were damp. Her eyes were still filled with concern. "You okay?"

"Yeah. It's a mild concussion. But my head hurts like hell. So does the rest of me. Come in and nurse me?"

A half smile formed on her face. "You're something else. But yes, I'll nurse you. I owe you this."

She stepped inside his house and circled to face him. He noticed she'd changed into plain blue pants and a red T-shirt, over which she'd thrown a cotton hoodie. "You're a mess," she told him.

"I know. I'm dirty from the rain and mud and my hair's grimy."

Her eyes narrowed. "Don't tell me. You need help bathing."

"Fair's fair, darlin'."

"Zach could have come home with you and helped you."

"I didn't want Zach. I want you, Teresa."

Her eyes widened. She was remembering what happened after her shower all those months ago. Good. His words had an intentional double meaning.

"Don't get ideas. No funny stuff with a concussion and a wound that required stitches."

A sudden bout of fatigue came over him. He steadied himself with a nearby chair. "Truthfully, honey, right now, I just want to feel clean and get some rest."

"Of course, Jack. I didn't mean to tease."

She glanced around from the foyer. He tried to see the house through her eyes. The one level structure sported cedar siding. The inside matched the rustic exterior with wood everywhere, high ceilings and windows. "This is beautiful."

"Yeah, I like it. The kids didn't want to move out of the house where they grew up, but when they left for college, I put our old place up for sale."

"Where's the bathroom?"

"There's three. Mine's off the master bedroom."

"Do you need help getting there?"

"Yeah. Wrap your arm around my waist."

Because he was leaning heavily on her, she'd know he wasn't in as good shape as he pretended to be. But he couldn't help it. He *was* weak. They did a slow walk down the long corridor to his wing, which contained his den and the master suite. The kids' rooms were on the other side of the large kitchen and spacious family area. They needed privacy, and so did he.

"Wow, Jack, this is lovely." High wooden ceiling, skylights, lots of windows and a lake of a bed. "Thanks." He nodded to the bathroom. "In there."

They entered another large space. "Double wow." This, too, had a high ceiling, a wall of windows, under which sat a Jacuzzi. There was a separate shower. "I did some of the work myself." He sat down on the john. "How shall we tackle this?"

"A bath with the jets will do wonders for you. Can you get up the two steps?"

"Yeah, but you might have to support me. I think maybe you'll have to get in with me. It seats two."

Tess bit back a smile. "Let's get you out of those clothes."

"I hope this isn't uncomfortable for you."

"I've seen it all before. But if I have to get into the tub, I'm keeping my undies on—again." Her reference to her modesty when she was hurt made him chuckle.

After turning on the tub facet, she drew his muddy T-shirt over his head. He lifted up and she slid down his dirt-caked jeans, his dark blue jockey shorts. He watched her for her reaction to his nakedness, but her face remained impassive.

"I think we better wash off the dirt in the shower, otherwise you're going to have a mud bath."

She ran that, too, and he leaned against the wall under the hot spray and let the dirt sluice off him. She waited nearby, with the door open. When he was clean enough and the tub filled, the jets on, she led him over to it.

Quickly, she shucked off her outer clothing, giving him a view of a pink sports bra and panties. Once she was in the tub, she grabbed his hands. He climbed the first step and moaned. "Arrgh."

"When was the last time you had pain meds?"

"At the hospital. I think it's time for more. Just ibuprofen. They're right there on the sink."

"I'll get some as soon as you're seated."

With great care, they managed to lower him down, but the process was accompanied by more, louder groans. The water came up to his chest and the jets pulsed at his feet and the sides of his neck. "Oh dear

Lord in heaven, that feels so good."

Stepping out of the tub, Tess retrieved the medicine and ran a glass of water. After he swallowed them, she climbed back in. "Don't fall asleep. I'll never get you out of here."

"I won't. There's a washcloth and soap right there."

"You could probably manage yourself."

He sighed. "Okay." He sat up and moaned again.

"Never mind. I'll do it."

She knelt between his legs. Ran the soap over his chest and rinsed it with the cloth. She did the same for his arms, neck and face. "That feels as good as the water." He reached out and brushed his hand down her cheek. "I've missed you, Teresa. A lot."

"We don't need to talk about that while you're hurting."

He lay back and closed his eyes. Sitting on her haunches, she soaped his legs and feet. Then she approached his groin.

She ran the wash cloth and over him. His erection sprang to attention.

"You can't be all that sick," she said with a laugh.

oOo

All right, so it had been fun to give him a bath. And she was relieved to see him well enough to joke and flirt after the fall he took. She'd been unable to stop the memories of Joey and those had made her weak, vulnerable to him. But she didn't examine her other motives for being here. She would, but now, she was glad to be the one to take care of him.

When the water started to cool, she climbed over the edge of the tub and wrapped herself in a towel. But she didn't get dressed right away. She knelt beside on the top step, covered Jack's wound with a cloth and managed to massage some shampoo and water into his thick hair. With a cup, she rinsed his head, careful to avoid the stitches. "It's not perfect, but it'll do."

"It was terrific." He grabbed her hand again and kissed it. "Thanks."

As she helped him out of the tub, he swayed. "Dizzy?"

"A bit. But the pain's diminished. All over."

"I could tell." She nodded to the toilet. "Sit."

Unable to stop herself, she took her time drying him off, because she enjoyed the feel of his body beneath her hands, then she helped him dress in pajama bottoms and a T-shirt. Out in the bedroom, she insisted he get in bed.

"Stay with me, Teresa."

"Let me change first."

She made quick work of putting on her top and slacks, sans underwear because they were wet. Going commando was sexy. Too sexy, probably.

From his bedside, she asked, "Have you eaten anything?"

"No. I wouldn't mind some chicken soup. There's cans in the cupboard."

In a few minutes, she brought him soup on a tray. "I'm not feeding you."

"Sit with me."

She started to get a chair.

"No. On the bed."

"You're enjoying this, aren't you?"

"I am. And we do have to talk."

"Eat first."

He downed the soup, crackers and a glass of milk without help, which indicated he felt better. Afterward, she took a place on the bed, facing him cross-legged.

"I had a date with Larissa James last night."

"I know." She cleared her throat. "How was it?"

"Pleasant. Nice." His gaze narrowed on her. "I thought of you."

Swallowing hard at his last remark, Tess stared at him, knowing what she said right now would be crucial. She wanted to be practical, to tell him they'd fight, ask again about professionalism and the RC class, but all she could think of was how he'd gotten hurt, like Joey had. And she'd lost Joey. "I—I thought of you when I went to Cory Cameron's last night."

"Fuck!" His hands fisted and he raised his eyes to the ceiling. "Did you sleep with him?"

"No! He was a perfect gentleman. He said I wasn't giving out vibes that I was interested."

"You weren't?"

"Of course not. I've tried to put you out of my mind, tried to hang on to my anger about you leaving me high and dry, choosing Mitch over me, and our contention over the recruits. But last night, I couldn't do anything with him. Then, when you got hurt..." Now *she* looked up, as if the answers were in the wood. "What are we going to do, Jack?"

"I know what I want."

Staring directly at him, she arched her brows.

"I want to spend time with you. To make love to you like we did before. Let's see where this goes, Teresa. I'm tired of wanting you and not having you."

"What about the recruits?"

"We'll disagree. We can handle it. But I do think it's probably not a good idea to flaunt what's between us until after the fourteen weeks are up."

"Is there a no-fraternizing policy in the department?"

"Hell no." He held up a hand and counted off on his fingers. "A lot of HCFD couples got together: Grady and Jenn, Zach and Casey, Riley and Jane Phillips, and even Noah. He fell in love with the woman from the Fire Prevention and Control unit who came up to investigate him and eventually married her. No one would care about us."

"I'm tired of fighting how I feel, too. I want to try, Jack."

"Good. So do I." Despite the gravity of their discussion, he joked, "But not tonight. Despite earlier evidence, I'm exhausted and woozy again."

"Scoot down and lie back on the pillows."

"Stay, though."

She hesitated.

"I've got a concussion."

"Waking someone up every hour is old thinking, Doc. You know it."

"Just stay."

"I could." She wanted to. "I picked up my laundry this afternoon so I have a uniform in my car."

"Then, it's settled."

"I have to call the Malvasos. They'll worry."

"More like Mitch will come looking for you."

"That, too."

She thought for a minute. "Maybe I'll text him." She got her phone, sat back on the bed and started to type. "I won't be home tonight Mitch," she said, pretending to type those words. "I'm spending the night in Jack Harrison's bed. See you tomorrow."

"You didn't?" he said, only half joking.

"You'll never know."

He yawned again. "Come here, woman." He pulled back the covers. "I want to hold you all night."

"I want that, too."

After a while, the rise and fall of his chest, the steady rhythm of his heart lulled Tess, and she drifted off into sleep. She knew there would be no nightmares tonight.

o0o

Jack awakened at five. The room was dark and a bit chilly from the open windows. Tess snuggled into the crook of his arm, fast asleep. Easing away from her, he slid out of bed and didn't get dizzy when he stood. His head still hurt, so he went to the bathroom, took some ibuprofen and brushed his teeth. Hmm. It was hours before she needed to go to the Academy. From a drawer, he pulled out condoms.

In the kitchen, he made coffee to bring to her. She awoke when he came back to the room. "Um, hi." Her hair was askew and her eyes sleepy. "What time is it?"

"Five. We fell asleep early."

She eyed the coffee. "Thank God." Sitting up she took it and sipped. "Hmm."

He got hard at that little noise.

"How do you feel?"

"Good enough." Amusement filtered into his tone.

She studied him. "Presumptuous, aren't you?"

"Am I?"

"No." She took a gulp, got out of bed and headed to the bathroom. When she returned, she finished the coffee, then dove onto the mattress. "Make love to me, John."

"All right, Teresa."

It was like before, but it wasn't. This time, Jack was emotionally attached, and every touch was more meaningful. Just the soft feel of her skin as he eased off her shirt aroused him. He'd already undressed and when he lay beside her, he aligned each of his limbs with hers. Their faces so close, their noses touching, he sighed gratefully. "I've wanted this a long time sweetheart."

"Me, too. Take it easy, though. Your body had a shock yesterday."

"I will, but my body has risen to the occasion, so to speak."

She arched her hips. "I can feel that."

Intertwining their fingers, he took her mouth. The kiss was tender and sweet, as he savored the taste of her. He nuzzled her neck, where he indulged in a tiny love bite. His hands traveled down her body to her breasts.

She sighed.

But Tess wanted her turn. She ran her hands over his chest. "I love how taut you are. How your muscles feel." Her knuckles brushed his abs. "Here, too."

Bypassing his groin, she slid her hands to his butt, kneaded him there. "God, Teresa."

She took her time getting to the part of him that was about to explode. After she took him between her hands, she massaged him.

"Don't. I'll come."

"I don't care."

"I do. Please."

Up on her knees, Tess took the protection he'd put on the night table and sheathed him. Then she lay back down; he scissored their legs and entered her. He was so hard, it startled her. But the fullness was wonderful and she was wet and needy. He thrust gently. Again. And again. Spasms started deep within her, making her move faster, faster…until finally everything erupted inside her—and him—and she lost the capacity to think.

They cuddled close on one pillow. He was breathing as hard as she. Chilled, she pulled up the covers and nestled into his side. But reality came, an emotional slap in the face. Tess started to think again about the gravity of what they were facing. She was scared—and not necessarily because of the recruit class. In the early hours of the morning, she admitted she didn't want any more loss, and if she let herself love this man, there was risk involved.

"Don't do that," he said commandingly.

"Do what?"

"Let the doubts in. Later, maybe, we can talk about it, but not now."

"You're right." Her eyes closed. "I'll just think about how sexy you are and that, for now, you're all mine."

"Sounds good to me," he said, kissing her hair.

oOo

Tess swerved her car into a parking space at the Academy, jumped out and raced to the door. Because she was late, she'd already missed roll call but was hoping to arrive in time to help introduce the Hurst tools to the recruits. This was a big lesson, as safety with the giant spreaders, scissors and rams was paramount. When she reached the classroom, she breathed a sigh of relief that they hadn't yet begun the instruction. The recruits were only now settling into chairs, and Olive and Quinn stood up front.

She covered the aisle with long strides. "I'm so sorry, Olive. I overslept." It was a lie, but she wouldn't think about what she'd been doing this morning. She'd vowed to keep Jack out of her mind today, even though now, they were happy thoughts.

The BC gave her a genuine smile. "No worries, Tess. It happens to all of us."

Lucky you, she thought.

Quinn Frazier squeezed her shoulder. "We haven't even started the formal intro, anyway."

Olive called for the attention of the group and was the first to talk to them. "Today, we're reviewing what you studied for homework over the weekend—the Hurst tools used for extricating victims from cars and other tight places, as well as popping doors in houses. We'll spend about thirty minutes in the classroom discussing the way the tools work—which again you've already studied—then we'll go out to a bay and get the equipment donated to us by a Hurst company. Later, during the second half of the class, you'll be able to use them in simulated extrication emergencies."

A soft murmur rippled through the group. Recruits always wanted to get their hands on things before they were ready.

Up front on the screen, Olive showed a picture of the equipment. "First, there are tools powered by hydraulics, then there are newer battery-operated ones called eDraulic. The HCFD has both, but found the latter ones are the easiest to use, as you might guess. We're starting with those. The drawback to this type is they have a shorter use rate because they run out of juice."

Another slide. "These are spreaders, for either pushing or pulling a substance apart. They have a thirty-two-inch reach.

"Next the shears, capable of cutting almost any object that can be fit between their blades. Smaller departments often use the combination spreader/shears but the HCFD has separate ones. And yes, this is what is called the Jaws of Life."

After showing a variety of the equipment, she put up a slide of extension rams. "These come in different sizes and are used to gain forcible entry into buildings or cars. Of note, the FDNY used this tool to open 109 doors in their rescue efforts in the World Trade Center. "We'll save the jacks and air bags and cribbing for another lesson." The recruits were sitting at attention, their eyes focused and... interested. Olive had given them a lot of information, but it was fascinating stuff to anyone involved with firefighting. "One last thing. The noise, from the shears especially, is teeth grating, so don't let it spook you. Meet us in the first bay after a ten-minute bathroom break or whatever you need."

To make up for her lateness, Tess headed to the garage, intending to get out the tools. But she'd missed this, too, as she found them already displayed on the concrete surface. The door was up, and rain slanted down but wasn't coming inside yet. Walking the floor, she fingered the Jaws of Life and picked up a ram to test its weight. A lump formed in her throat. She hadn't used these tools in over a year, but she remembered vividly the first time she ripped open the hood of a vehicle. Her muscles had hurt with the force of the steel on the car and the power of the tool. She'd steadied her stance, though, and did the cutting. Several men had been looking on to see if she could handle the grueling task and she remembered thinking that she'd show them women were capable.

Lost in memory, she startled at the earsplitting buzz of the cutters. Whirling around, she saw Recruit Mauro had come to the bay, too, turned on the tool and was spreading it.

"What the hell do you think you're doing?"

He looked up. "Just trying it on for size, ma'am," he said easily.

Without goggles or any hand protection!

And just like that, Tess morphed from the woman who had been well loved only hours ago into a teacher who needed to discipline a recruit. "Turn that thing off right now, Recruit Mauro. You won't be using any of these this morning."

oOo

He'd done it now, Danny thought, as he sat alone on a bench in the gloomy classroom and watched the rain pelt against the windows. He'd been making mistakes, and this was a doozy.

It wasn't a mistake, his conscience told him. *You knew what you were*

doing. You know *what you've* been *doing for two weeks.*
They'd all been pissed...
Captain Hennessey had flipped. "What were you *thinking*, Recruit Mauro?" Usually calm and reasonable, the woman's voice rose and her face reddened. Righetti had gotten the woman all stirred up.
He'd been belligerent. "I wasn't doing anything wrong."
"If you think that, you need to go sit in the classroom until you *do* know what a grave mistake you made. Read the section in chapter five on tool usage *safety* and summarize it for me in your own words, in writing. Pay particular attention to protective gear that you're required to wear before you even touch the equipment..."
So here he was, being punished like a school-kid for his rashness in starting a tool. Damn, this was so not him. He leafed through the book on his desk until he came to the safety section. He'd just finished the written summary when someone came into the room.
"Hello, Dan." Harrison, the staff psychologist. The guy was okay, but Danny didn't like the class he ran. Too much introspection.
Danny stood. "Sir."
"Sit back down." Harrison dragged a bench across from him and settled on it slowly, as if he was in pain. "I understand you got into some trouble this morning."
He shrugged.
The doc pierced him with a hard gaze. "Do you know what you did wrong?"
"I guess I shouldn't have turned on the Hurst tool."
"Why did you?"
"I don't know," he lied. Down deep, he knew why he was taking all these chances.
"Did you realize your actions were dangerous?"
"No. I've been around fire stations all my life. I've held the Jaws of Life before."
"You're from a family of firefighters?"
"Three—my dad and two brothers."
"Do you think they'd see your behavior as acceptable?"
Of course not. They'd kick his ass. Danny didn't answer.
Leaning back, Harrison stretched out his legs. The overhead light showed lines around the man's eyes and mouth. "Dan, do you want to be at the Academy? In this class?"

"Yeah, of course. I'm going to be a firefighter."

"I read your file. Since you got here two weeks ago, you've said and done things that indicate that maybe your intentions might be the opposite."

"I do, I swear." He heard the panic in his voice. "I've done well in all my tests and physical training."

"I know. Congratulations."

Again, he stared silently at the psychologist.

"So, what should we do now?"

"It's up to you all, I guess."

"Is there anything you want to talk about? What you confide in me will be confidential, I promise."

"Look, I'm sorry for what I did. I'll apologize to the teachers in front of the class. I was stupid. Nothing else is going on."

"Okay. Chief Hennessey said you can go back to the class after lunch. You're supposed to stay here and ponder your sins."

"That's all?"

"Yeah, for now. But if you ever want to talk, I'm available."

Danny stood when the captain did, watched him leave—limping a little this time. He sat down and stared out at the rain.

Why the *hell* couldn't he be honest with the shrink?

o0o

Tess swept into his office at lunchtime—her face flaming. Jack's response to her presence was visceral. She, however, was mad. "What the hell are you doing here?"

Before he could answer, Olive came storming through the door. "Somebody just told me you got hurt at Hale's Haven yesterday. You should be home in bed."

Hmm. He'd been there just hours ago, with the angry Captain Righetti. "Hello to you, too, ladies."

They frowned.

"Jack?" This from Olive.

"I'm fine. I slept until ten and have been back an hour. I feel great."

The battalion chief studied him. "When I left the message on your phone about talking to Mauro, I didn't know you'd been hurt."

"As I said, I'm doing better now."

Tess folded her arms across her chest and glowered at him but didn't speak.

"Go home early, then," Olive continued.

"I will. I promise. So about Mauro. I did talk to him."

"He told us when he came back and apologized. What did he say to you?"

"That he didn't know why he turned on the tool. In the end, he admitted he shouldn't have and said he'd apologize."

"What else did you talk about?" Tess asked, her eyes narrowed. It was as if she could read his mind.

"Pretty much what he told you. I couldn't get a bead on the kid, though."

"Something's going on with him. I feel it in my gut. He suited up in turnout gear without the proper instruction. It's my opinion that he insulted Ian Woodward. And now this."

"I saw the pattern, too, in his file. But he's an eighteen-year-old kid. Being from a firefighter family makes him cocky. Maybe that's all it is."

"Could be." Olive was still frowning. "Except for his attitude, he's one of the best recruits I've ever taught."

"I'll concede to that." Tess sounded reasonable. "But I'm afraid he'll have a negative effect on the others."

Jack dug his hands into his pockets, a nervous gesture, he knew. "It's too soon to cut him loose."

"I didn't say we should. We have to watch him vigilantly."

"Great, then we agree?"

Both women nodded.

"I've got to get back," Olive told them. "I have a meeting."

Jack asked, "Tess, can you stay a minute?"

"I can." He couldn't read her expression.

Scanning her from head to toe after Olive left, Jack gave Tess a sexy smile. "All alone again."

She bit her lip but the grin won out. "Yep." Then her eyes turned dark. "Seriously, should you be back at work so soon?"

"I had a great morning."

"Hmm, me, too. Except for this thing with Mauro."

"Tess, something occurred to me while I was talking to him. Does he remind you of Joey? He's got those strong Italian features."

"I wouldn't say he looked like Joey."

"How about his attitude? You told me your brother was cocky, entitled. Could that be prejudicing you against Mauro?"

Her eyebrows skyrocketed. "Jack, I haven't made up what he's done."

"I know. I'm concerned about you in this, too. Not just the boy."

She pushed away from the wall. "I don't want to talk about Joey."

"Have you ever, to anyone?"

"Mitch and the family."

"No, I mean professionally."

Her whole body stiffened. "Look, how'd we get on this?"

Experience told him it was time to stop. "Tell you what. Let me buy you lunch. There's a great hamburger joint just down the road."

"I'm not sure we should do that."

"Why? It's convenient. Olive knows we're together. We said we wouldn't tell anybody about us, but lunch would be okay, honey."

"Don't call me that at the Academy."

"You didn't mind this morning, Teresa," he said sexily, again.

"Will you stop?"

"Only if you have lunch with me."

They both smiled all the way out to his car.

oOo

Tess conceded to driving in Jack's SUV with him. They should have taken two vehicles, but she succumbed to his request because she was still buzzed from this morning. The tenderness, the closeness had almost eclipsed the mind-numbing pleasure he'd given her. And vice versa, she thought, smiling.

"What's that for?"

"Nothing."

"Come on, baby. You're thinking about me, right? About this morning, because I have to tell you I can still…feel you."

A good description. "It was different from in Rockland, though that was great."

"Different for me, too. I might lose my psychologist card for this, but let's not analyze it to death."

"I agree. Just tell me honestly if you're well enough to be back to work."

"For a while. I'm planning to go home early. Rest. Wait for you to come back and take care of me."

"You're incorrigible."

The diner was large, sporting a black-and-white vinyl floor, booths with paper placemats and plastic forks, and a counter where long-time patrons sat. Jack led Tess to a table, they ordered drinks, then scanned the menu. "I'll have their meat eater's special."

"Seriously, you can eat two hamburgers with everything on them?"

"Hmm. I burned a lot of calories already today."

"French fries?"

"Of course."

When the food was delivered, Tess ate the juicy burgers dripping with hot sauce and relish. Jack had plain beef with cheese but ate heartily. They exchanged small talk only, and the meal was easy and fun…until Tess looked up and saw Mitch walk into the diner. Shit. She knew she'd have to deal with him eventually, but she was hoping for a full day's reprieve.

He spotted her and strode over in that gait he'd used the night he'd come after her when, at seventeen, she went to a bar with an older boy. Mitch had dragged her out and forbidden her to see the guy. Damn, he wouldn't try that with Jack, would he? Mitch was a cream puff until he got riled.

His gaze zeroed in on her. "Fancy seeing you here."

"Hi, Mitch."

"Jack." Mitch said the greeting without taking his eyes off Tess.

The urge to squirm was strong, but she was in her thirties now, not a teen. She bit her lip, too, so she wouldn't laugh. The situation was ludicrous.

Nodding to her meal, Mitch asked, "You done?"

"Just finished." This from Jack.

He faced his friend. And scowled. "What are you doing out and about? You were hurt yesterday."

"I'm recovered enough to work a few hours."

Mitch grunted. "Would you give me some time alone with my cousin? I can take her back to the Academy. And you go home."

A long pause. Then Jack said, "I don't think so, Mitch."

Mitch's brows rose. "Why?"

"Because what you want to talk to Tess about concerns me, too."

It took him a minute. Then his eyes narrowed. "You gotta be kidding me."

"Sit down, Mitch." Jack's voice was full of authority that even a battalion chief recognized.

When Mitch sat, and neither Jack nor Tess offered anything, Mitch finally said, "Tell me what's going on."

Leaning over, Tess took Mitch's hand. "I was with Jack last night. I was the one he called to take care of him."

Again a dark look. "Why would he call you? You don't even like each other."

"Outside of professional differences, we do like each other." This from Jack.

"I don't get it. How do you even know that? She's only been here a few weeks."

Where to go from here? Tess decided on the truth. "You don't know the whole story. We got together in Rockland."

"Define *got together*."

Exasperated, Tess said, "We *slept* together."

His eyes were saucers. "Seriously." Then, "How many times?"

"That's none of your business."

Jack leaned over and braced his arms on the table. "No, Tess, no more secrets." He locked his gaze with Mitch's. She liked seeing him in this role. "Once."

"You had a one-night stand with my cousin?" Now Mitch's face reddened, and a muscle in his jaw bulged.

"Because of unforeseen reasons. I had to come home for Sara."

In careful, modulated tones, Jack explained what had occurred between him and Tess.

To Tess's surprise, the explanation seemed to make Mitch madder. His mouth formed a grim line. But he looked away. Took a few breaths. "I'm gonna leave. I don't want to say anything I might regret. But know I'm not happy about this."

Tess quipped, "Yes, Dad."

The chair scraped back, Mitch stood, glared at them, and walked out.

"You shouldn't have teased him." Jack was smiling, though.

"I couldn't help it. He's acting just like he did when I was a kid." She giggled.

"You're enjoying this."

"I'm sorry, I am. It feels good having him look after me again."

"Easy for you to say. I'm the one that's going to pay for this."

She grinned. "I know."

oOo

The night was warm, and Jack looked around the fire ground. It was good to be here again, which was why he'd tagged along with the crew from Engine 4. His record was still intact for no runs during a meal he cooked. The call had come after they finished a dinner of lasagna and meat sauce. Tess was busy tonight, so Jack accompanied the guys to the fire.

The rig had screeched to a halt, and Jack remembered the sensations of going to fight a fire: the extreme burst of adrenaline he'd always felt before entering the building; the loud noise of the trucks, still running; the scent of gasoline, strong and acrid.

Engine 4 firefighters clambered off the truck, grabbed tools and waited on high alert for their captain to get his orders. Among them was Tom Senate, the man who'd quit the Academy because of Jack's Recruit Concerns class. He'd been pleasant to Jack at dinner, but there had been an air of remoteness about him.

Jack watched the captain trek over the pavement of the parking lot to Incident Command. Thankfully, the convenience store was a single building and not in a strip mall. Then he caught sight of the battalion chief on duty…Mitch Malvaso. Shit. Jack thought briefly of absconding back to his car and hightailing it out of there.

But he thought of Tess's words. *I like seeing you like this. Commanding. In control.* So he couldn't very well let her down on his new image. In truth, he didn't want Mitch to be mad him.

So he strode over to the official vehicle. "Hey, Chief."

Mitch spared him a glacial glance. "Doc." Then, "I thought you were going home early."

"I did, right after lunch. I slept this afternoon then cooked some dinner for Engine 4." Jack nodded to the building, sniffing at the scent of smoke. "Big deal or not?"

"No. Small fire in the back kitchen. The cap could have handled it, but I came because I was…stirred up."

Jack watched the firefighters go inside with hose. Smoke rose, but it was light colored. "About today."

Mitch stared ahead.

"I know my history with Tess must be a surprise."

"You lied to me."

"A lie of omission. I apologize. But I had no idea Tess was your cousin when we…you know…got together." Hell, he stuttered like a teenage talking to his girlfriend's dad.

Another grunt and still Mitch kept his gaze on the fire.

"It wouldn't have mattered. We, um, the attraction was just there." Finally, Mitch pivoted. "I got no qualms about that. But I been thinking about this. Tess must have been upset when you disappeared from her life afterward. When you never went back to Rockland."

"She was. So was I, Mitch."

Dark brows furrowed. He could see them because Mitch wore his uniform and no turnout gear. "Seriously?"

"Honest to God."

"Well, then."

He dug his hands into his pockets. "Mitch, we'd like your blessing, your family's blessing, but in any case, I'm going to keep seeing her this time."

Now Mitch pierced him with a heavy gaze. "Not without preliminaries."

"What are you talking about?"

"You're to come to our house Sunday. For a family dinner."

"Your family already knows me."

"Not as a suitor."

"Hell."

"All of us will be there, so come prepared."

"To find out what my intentions are?"

"Maybe. Be there at three."

Jack shook his head. "All right, I'll come, but Tess isn't going to like this."

"Tough shit."

Jack walked away bemused. He didn't really think the Malvasos would…do anything to him. Yet they were a protective bunch. Hmm. Maybe he better check with Tess.

CHAPTER 11

Tess crouched on the floor behind Mitch and felt her way along the wall of the house. Neighbors reported elderly people in the back bedroom, and her crew had to rescue them.

In her mic, she heard, "Don't be a baby about this, Tess. You have to do what's right."

"I will, Mitch. I promise."

As they crawled at a snail's pace, the temperature rose. Sweat beaded on her forehead, neck and chest. She could hear her own labored breathing. Behind her, a crash, as if timber had fallen.

Mitch stopped and said, "I think we're at the door to a bedroom." They were working totally blind, so they had to go by touch. "According to a neighbor, there's supposed to be another room to the right. Mauro, you go with Righetti."

Tess didn't want to work with the recruit. He reminded her too much of Joey and she didn't want to care about him. Still, she followed orders, and on her knees, Tess felt for the doorway. "In here, Mauro."

She heard him creep inside behind her. Tess knocked her knee on something metal and stinging pain shot through her. "I found a bed. Mauro, see if there's more in here. I can't tell how big the room is."

"Yes, ma'am."

Still kneeling, Tess put her hand on the bed. The mattress bounced, which meant a victim was on it. She felt around...a leg, thin. Arms. Slight. "I got one. You find anybody, Mauro?"

"No answer.

"Mauro, respond."

"What's going on, Righetti?" Mitch's voice.

"Mauro's not answering."

"Did you find anything?"

"Yeah, I got a body."

"Get 'em out."

"And leave Mauro?"

"I'll search for him. Now go."

Tess stood, bent over and picked up the victim. Suddenly, the smoke cleared and she was looking into the blank stare of Recruit Dan Mauro...

Tess bolted up in bed. The air pack was gone and she couldn't breathe. The room was filled with smoke...yet it wasn't. She looked around. Zach's bedroom came into focus. She wasn't in a fire with Mitch. She was home at the Malvasos.

When her breathing evened, she lay back on the pillow. She didn't need Jack to interpret the dream. It was obvious that Tess was worried about Recruit Mauro. Because he reminded her of Joey? Jack had pointed that out, but she refused to see the comparison. Had her unconscious mind made the connection for her in the depths of a dream? Damn it.

Slipping out of bed, Tess went to the bathroom. Her hair was messy and her eyes still sleepy. She'd spent the night alone with Sabina. Mitch had been working, and Megan and Sabby were out. Now she wished she'd stayed at Jack's because he could soothe away the remnants of the nightmare.

That's it, Tess told herself. Think of him. She made her way back to her bedroom and climbed into bed again. This time, she let thoughts of being with Jack, and how different their love making was after they'd begun to care about each other. Her eyes started to close as she could feel his arms around her.

o0o

Anita Cruz held her daughter against her chest and sighed. Charlotte had a cold, so she wasn't sleeping good. Already exhausted, Anita had to get up in two hours for class. As she soothed her child's curly black hair, Anita whispered, *"Shh, bébé, todo será bien."*

But everything wasn't going to be fine. If Anita didn't get some sleep and eat better, she wasn't going to make it through the remaining weeks. Which right now seemed like an eternity.

"*El bébé* up again?" Anita's grandmother stood in the doorway. She was small but sturdy. Still, she was too old to be waking up with babies in the middle of the night.

"We're okay, *Mamagrande*, go to sleep."

"No, you go to sleep."

"This isn't your responsibility."

"*Querida*, we only have to get through this class. You'll be a firefighter, and the three of us will be fine."

Anita's eyes teared. She couldn't tell the woman who'd raised her and sacrificed so much for her that she didn't think she'd ever be a member of the HCFD. "*Sí, sólo por esta vez.*"

When her grandmother took Charlotte to her room in the small apartment, which was paid for by welfare, Anita climbed into bed. And thought of the Academy program. Of Danny Mauro, who ran circles around everybody in PT and in the course work but didn't seem to give a shit. Why was it that the recruits who wanted this job might not get it and the blasé, arrogant ones would succeed? With that ugly thought, her eyes closed and she drifted off.

o0o

All people are created equal, then a few become firefighters.

If you think it's tough being a firefighter, try being a firefighter's wife or husband. ~Author Unknown

Let no man's ghost return to say his training let him down. ~Firefighters Saying

Firemen never die, they just burn forever in the hearts of the people whose lives they saved. ~Susan Diane Murphree

Never fight fire from ego. ~Author Unknown

How important it is for us to recognize and celebrate our heroes and she-roes! ~Maya Angelou

Better a thousand times careful than once dead. ~Proverb

I can think of no more stirring symbol of man's humanity to man than a fire engine. ~Kurt Vonnegut

Seems to me the basic conflict between men and women, sexually, is that men are like firemen. To men, sex is an emergency, and no matter what we're doing we can be ready in two minutes. Women, on the other hand, are like fire. They're very exciting, but the conditions have to be exactly right for it to occur. ~Jerry Seinfeld

The room was cool, creating a soothing atmosphere for the third Recruit Concerns class. But Jack hadn't been able to get them to talk openly. A few had asked questions, and they all wrote when asked, but he wanted freer participation. He watched them as they read what he'd put up on the screen. At least there were a few chuckles for the last entry—a joke he hoped would loosen them up.

"Now that you've had time to read the sayings, I'd like you to pick one of the quotes and write a paragraph about why it's meaningful to you."

A lot of nods. Well, that was progress.

They wrote. He sat on the front table, scanning the group, dying to know which truism each kid had picked, but the anonymity of writing out their responses seemed to make them more comfortable. He gave them ten minutes.

Before he could collect the papers, Liam Murphy raised his hand. "Can I say something, Captain?"

"Yes. I wish someone would."

"I'm twenty-two years old. I don't have to write down what I think. I can say it out loud."

"I'm glad to hear that. I wish everybody would talk about their reactions. You're a quiet group. I respect that. I want you to write things down *first*. That way, you get to articulate what you feel before you hear others' opinions. But after you've formulated an answer, I'd rather you shared aloud. Why don't we try it at least this time?"

Not everyone agreed. Some heads shook.

"Okay, I'll let you pass if you absolutely can't talk openly."

Liam began. Jack smiled at the young man, who seemed more mature than others. His consistent grin and Irish charm made him likeable. "I picked, 'Firefighters never die, they just burn forever in the hearts of the people whose lives they saved.' I chose it because I think it's important to remember what we're training for. To save lives." He went on to talk about why he wanted to join the department.

Another recruit who hadn't said a word raised his hand. "I picked that one, too. But not for the same reason. I'm afraid to die. I wanna be a firefighter but I'm scared, too." He looked around. "Is anybody else?" Several students nodded.

Thinking of the recruits in Rockland who'd said the same thing, Jack smiled easily. "Of course you're afraid. A good amount of fear will keep you on your toes. It's healthy. But too much anxiety over your safety can be immobilizing. I wonder if we might want to go over some techniques for dealing with our fears."

This time, everybody agreed.

Happy with the participation, Jack said, "Next."

A young blond woman waved. She was demure and feminine but strong physically. Briefly, Jack wondered if Tess liked her. "I picked the Maya Angelou quote. All I hear is how sexist the fire department is."

"No fire department is perfect." Though, thanks to Noah Callahan, the HCFD had made more strides than most. "We could get a few women in to talk to you about this."

Ron Johnson asked, "Can the guys listen to them, too? I don't want to be sexist, but yeah, I'm afraid I won't treat women the same as men on the line."

"Done! Next?"

Danny Mauro lazed back in his chair. The kid's eyes were droopy and his shoulders hunched, as if he hadn't slept. He spoke out loud, without raising his hand. "I picked 'Never fight fire from ego.'"

Jack hoped this was a breakthrough with the boy.

"Why did you pick that one, Danny?"

"First, is what we say here confidential?"

"I told you it was. Unless you're going to hurt yourself or others." He watched Mauro. "Why?"

"Because I think our trainers have a ton of ego. Captain Righetti, especially. What the hell's wrong with her?"

oOo

Tess stayed with Jack overnight on Friday. Salmon steaks waited to be grilled, and Tess had brought a salad. They sat on his patio in the warm late-April evening; she sipped a beer and he drank a scotch, both enjoying a companionable silence.

Flowers bloomed and the trees were green, making the backyard homey and pleasant.

"What are you thinking about?" he asked after a while.

"That you still have swings." She nodded to the faux wood play set. "From the twins? No wait, it can't be. You moved here after they were grown."

"It's our second one," he said. "We got it when the twins were ten. Sara wanted me to bring it to the new house for sentimental reasons, I guess. She still uses it when she comes home." He shook his head. "I had a hell of a time dismantling it. I made Sara and Seth reassemble it before they went to school."

Tess set her beer down and stood. "Come on, old man, push me on a swing."

"Old man?" He tugged on her hand, holding her back. "That's not what you were saying"—he checked his watch—"in bed an hour ago."

"Ha. Come on, I'll race you over."

He didn't race. He ambled to the set in that sexy meander he had, and she was sitting on the swing, kicking her feet back and forth when he reached her. He stood behind her and pushed. And pushed. "Man, you're heavy."

"That's not what you said an hour ago." She reiterated his earlier allusion.

"I was in the throes of passion."

"This is fun, too." Back and forth, back and forth. Higher and higher. Tess relished the air on her face and the increasing speed. She felt young again, and…happy.

"You're high enough. When you slow down, don't jump off the swing. You might hurt your ankle again."

"Yes, sir." Her speed decreased and she let her feet drag in the little rut in the grass others had created, to stop her motion. Off to the side, Jack seemed pensive. "What is it?"

"I miss the kids. And I worry about Sara."

"Why is she such a risk taker?"

"Genetics, maybe. You have to have that in your blood to be a firefighter."

Still seated on the swing, she asked, "Do you think you were strict enough with her while she was growing up?"

"Maybe I wasn't. Elizabeth was gone. My grandmother was fair, but everybody felt sorry for them because they never had a mother."

"What was Elizabeth like? I saw a picture of her on the fireplace. She was beautiful."

"Very. Too elegant for me. She was loving and kind, too. A bit spoiled by her parents, sometimes stubborn because of that. But mostly agreeable."

"Huh. So what are you doing with me?" Tess was only half joking. Turning, Jack walked to the set and tugged her up from the swing.

"First off, I like the fact that you can be so tough, but vulnerable and sweet, too."

"Me?" she said. "Hardly."

"You are. I also value your energy, your enthusiasm for the fire department. Then, there's your willingness to help others like Sabina."

"Wow!" She didn't expect all that.

He drew her closer, his hands pressing on her hips. "Is that enough?"

"More than."

He kissed her soundly.

"You make me feel good about myself." She arched a brow. "Want to go back to bed?"

"Nope, we're eating first. Maybe later…"

She smiled.

He smiled.

They walked hand in hand to the patio.

o0o

That night, as they lay in bed, Jack couldn't sleep. Tess was at his side, her head fitting into the crook of his arm. She'd taken a shower and washed her hair, and lotion and some lemony-shampoo scent filled his head. He held her to him, feeling guilty. He knew some things about her work and he couldn't tell her. That led to a thought that had been trying to surface for days. If he'd implemented Tom Senate's request and set up the RC class in a way to let the instructors know how the kids were feeling, would this with Tess be easier? Information could have been transmitted anonymously, in general terms, with no name attached.

She's a bitch, one card had read.

Because I think our trainers have a ton of ego. Captain Righetti, especially. What the hell's wrong with her?

After Mauro made the comment, some of the others had agreed

but spoke of her more gently. Still, the consensus was critical. Even a young woman named Sally spoke then. *Why is she so strict, Dr. Harrison?*

His responses had to be carefully worded. He couldn't slander Tess, but he couldn't let these kids down, either.

People have different philosophies on teaching...you need tough instructors and more laid-back ones. She has the best intentions.

Mauro scowled. *Do you think she's too tough?*

He never lied when asked to give his opinion and he couldn't now. *Yeah, I do, but I'm a softy, so what do I know?*

The entire class had upset him. Now he wondered if he'd betrayed Tess. At the very least, he was keeping things from her. He had no choice, though. He'd just have to handle it. Cuddling her closer, kissing her hair, he tried to blank his mind and will himself to sleep.

o0o

Sunday came all too soon, if you asked Jack. He stood at the door to the sprawling three-story brick house that was home to his favorite people, ready to be interrogated. Or maybe intimidated. Though he knew the guys had to show some bravado simply out of principle, he also sensed they were concerned about Tess and him. And they were right to worry. He and Tess had had a rocky beginning.

Taking a deep breath, he refused to let in the other worry that still plagued him. He'd drive himself crazy thinking about the recruits' attitude toward Tess on top of dealing with her family. And since firefighters were good at compartmentalizing, he stuffed his guilt and rang the bell.

Tess pulled open the door right away. She looked cute today, in jeans rolled up to her calves and a gauzy blouse. Young. Like a freaking little sister.

"Waiting for me, babe?" He mustered some of his own bravado.

"Yeah. I want to see your face again before it's broken and bleeding."

"Not funny."

"They'll be fine."

He stepped inside, glanced around, then kissed her in the foyer. "You're worth it."

"Is that him?" someone yelled out from the kitchen.

"Yeah," Tess called back. "We're coming in."

"No hanky-panky out there." The voice was Zach's.

Hell, they were waiting for him.

When he arrived at the kitchen entrance, he saw he was right. They each leaned against the wall, or the door, insolently. Zach's chin was raised, Connie was glaring at him, and Paulie's face was stern.

Biting back a smile, Jack studied them. "I can't believe you're a part of this, Paulie."

"Family's family," he said, trying to scowl but not quite getting there.

"Where's Sabina? I was hoping she'd referee."

"No such luck." This from Mitch. "Grady and I are cooking."

Jenn pushed away from the wall and signaled Connie to do the same. They crossed to Tess. "You gotta leave, girl."

"No way."

"Seriously." This from Connie.

Tess frowned. "I don't believe this."

"The kids are in the family room with Mama," she said more gently. "Go say hi."

She shot a quick glance to Jack. He nodded.

As soon as Tess left, Zach jammed his hands in his jeans pockets and took a bead on Jack. "So, you're bangin' our cousin?"

"Hell, Zach. That's no way to talk about her."

He and Mitch exchanged a glance.

Jack straightened. "We have a caring relationship. That led to the physical side of things. I'm not going to apologize for being attracted to Tess. We're grownups, guys."

Grady, of all people, stepped forward. "You think tellin' us our cousin is hot will help?"

Stalling and because he was frustrated, Jack ran a hand through his hair. "What do you want to hear?"

"I, for one, want to know why you left her in Rockland and never called again." This from Jenn.

"I told Mitch, and I'm sure he informed you. Sara got in trouble and I had to deal with her."

"Why didn't you go back later to explain things to her?" Jenn was serious. She meant what she was saying. "If it was me, I would've been hurt."

"Right now, the answer isn't going to help."

"Try us." From Paulie.

Patiently, Jack explained about Mitch and finding out he was Tess's cousin.

"Chickenshit." This from Zach.

"Maybe. But when I got a second chance with her, I took it."

Mitch's turn. "Where do you plan to go from here?"

"I don't know, Mitch. I care about her. I want to be with her. We'll just have to wait and see where this leads."

"All right." The man who was his best friend smiled as they broke ranks.

"Want a beer?" Grady asked.

"I'd like something stronger if you have it."

Jenn got out the scotch. Poured him one. Then they formed a circle around him. "This is to you and Tess," Jenny announced sweetly, lifting her can of beer. "Good luck, buddy."

Connie kissed him on the cheek. Grady patted him on the back. Paulie poked him in the arm.

Zach gave him a bear hug, then drew back. "I love you, man. But if you hurt Tess, I'll break your legs."

Jack couldn't help but smile.

oOo

Tess was assigned to help Larissa James in the classroom today. The pretty woman who Jack had dated resembled Elizabeth. The notion made Tess uncomfortable. Sometimes, she wasn't sure she was right for him, despite his compliments Friday night.

"Turn to page twenty-nine in your book and look at the traits of a good EMT." Larissa's voice was strong, and the recruits seemed to take to her. Of course, she was ridiculously attractive with her slim blond appearance. Tess liked her.

As the kids opened their books, Tess flipped the pages of hers and read. She rolled her eyes at the list: pleasant, sincere, cooperative, resourceful, self-starter, emotionally stable, in control of personal habits, able to lead, able to listen and good moral character. Who the hell could fit that bill?

When they'd had time to finish reading, Larissa gave instructions. "Get into groups of five and discuss these traits. Try to come up with examples of each."

Dragging their chairs around the tables, the recruits formed groups. Tess's job was to wander among them and participate in each discussion. She wanted to know what Anita Cruz thought, because the girl was struggling. When Tess reached her, she saw Mauro sitting next to her. Tess didn't leave, though.

"I think it's easy to be pleasant and sincere," Anita said.

Mauro captured Tess's gaze. "Not for everybody."

Anita put down her pen and rounded on Mauro. Her dark curly hair was long, and she had it pulled back, setting her features in sharp relief. "What *is* it with you? It seems like you're being intentionally rude all the time. Do you wanna get kicked out of here?"

For a second, Mauro's face fell; he looked sad and confused. Then his smirk came back. "Nah. They won't kick me out. I'm really good. What about you, Cruz? You good?"

Tess thought Cruz would back down, but the girl leveled Mauro with a glare that could cut glass. "I don't know how good I am. I don't have natural talent like you. But I'm working a lot harder than you are. And I'm not such a jerk." She stood and turned to Tess. "Can I go in another group?"

"Sure."

When Cruz walked away, Tess said, "Go on without her" and left them alone. She approached a second group by the big open windows. Murphy couldn't see her, as she was behind him.

He said, "Man, if EMTs and firefighters have to be emotionally stable and pleasant, half the department would be ousted."

They all laughed. Until they noticed Tess.

The kid asked, "Geez, she's behind me, isn't she?"

"Yes." Tess moved so she was in his line of vision.

"You heard me didn't you?" Murphy's freckled face was as red as the cover of the training manual.

"I did, recruit." She folded her arms over her chest. "And I happen to agree."

They were surprised by her joking. Hmm, maybe she *should* try to lighten up a bit. But it was only the end of the second week, and traditionally, it wasn't until halfway through that the teachers became less strict. More friendly. But her levity put them at ease. And made them more participative. She'd have to think about that. Maybe talk it over with Jack.

When class ended, she went to the front of the room. "How do you think that went, Larissa?"

"Pretty good. I hate this lesson, though. I overheard Murphy. He's right."

"I know. And not just for the emotionally stable and pleasant characteristics."

They laughed together.

Larissa stacked up her things on a bookshelf off to the side. "My turn to eat with the recruits, today."

"Mine, too. Let's go."

The recruits had planned a cookout, so they crossed through the gym to the outside and headed down to the pavilion. Jack stood before a large grill, flipping hot dogs and hamburgers. He was dressed in an apron, and when she got close, she saw the inscription: I'm a Firefighter. What's Your Super Power?

"Boy, he's attractive," Larissa whispered. "Don't you think?"

"Can't say that I've noticed." She and Jack still weren't making their relationship public. "I don't like that gray in his hair." Which was so not true. She loved it.

When they reached him, he gave them both a sexy smile. "Hello, ladies. What'll you have?"

You, Tess thought.

The meal was uneventful, and afterward, as everyone was heading back to the Academy, Jack touched her arm as she passed by. "Captain Righetti, a word?"

Larissa went on.

"How'd the EMS class go?"

"I think it was kind of foolish. The material covered the traits of a good firefighter or EMT." She filled him on the details. "I agreed with Murphy."

"Good for you."

"And Cruz took a bite out of Mauro's ass."

"What do you mean?"

"She told him he was rude and asked him if he wanted to get kicked out of the Academy. He insulted her and she snapped back."

The sun was high and slanted over Jack's face. She caught his frown. "We don't want tension like that among them. Did you talk to her about it?"

"No, she was right."

"Try to go easy on Mauro, Tess."

"Jack, we've been through this. I'll do things my way; you do yours."

Then she remembered the bleak expression in Mauro's eyes. And how her levity made the other group more at ease. "Look, I'm trying to be a little less rigid. But Mauro was way out of line and I wasn't about to punish Cruz for doing the right thing."

"Okay."

"I have to go."

Grasping her arm, he held her back. Now his expression was very male. "My car's in the shop. I need a ride home."

Since everybody had gone inside the building, she placed her hand on his hip, close to his ass, and squeezed. "I think I can do that. And maybe more, if you're lucky."

He winked at her. "Oh, I'll be lucky, and so will you, doll."

o0o

On Friday evening, Jack yanked open the front door as soon as he saw the car pull into the driveway. Though he'd been preoccupied with Tess, he'd missed his kids big-time. When he caught a glimpse of them, a wave of love burst through him.

Sara came running up to the porch and threw herself into his outstretched arms. "Daddy! I missed you."

He hugged her tight. "I missed you, too, princess."

His son followed suit with the hug. He was glad Seth was as demonstrative as Sara. He'd raised them not to stereotype, and it was good to see it worked.

Drawing back, he studied the twins. Every time they came home, they seemed changed. Sara's hair was longer, Seth's shorter. The sun made them even blonder. "You both look great. And older... Geez, I hate that."

"No bad thoughts, Dad," Seth said.

"Need help with your things?"

"We don't have as much as we had last May." For the sophomore year, they'd gotten an apartment together and kept it year round. Seth was taking a class in the early session, and Sara was doing research for one of her professors. So Jack had them for only about ten days. The notion made his heart hurt this time.

They carried in suitcases, and Jack went to get the last stuff out of the trunk. But what was left wasn't clothes. It was a crate. "What the...?"

A tiny bark.

Oh, my God, they hadn't! "Sa-*ra*!"

His daughter scooted back down the sidewalk. "I was going to tell you."

The Harrisons had never had a dog, because when his kids were little and wanted one, Jack had had all he could do to take care of the twins and himself.

With uncustomary gentleness, Sara opened the crate door. Out of the small enclosure crept a puppy so small Jack could hold it in cupped hands. It was a Yorkshire terrier with beautiful copper markings.

"Boy or girl?" he asked.

Sara snorted. "Girl, of course."

"How old is she?"

"Five months."

"You have to take care of her while you're home."

Seth joined them. "I told her it was a bad idea. The beast keeps us up at night."

"She's still little." Sara nuzzled the pet and sent a nasty glance to Seth. "Besides, I'm the one who tends to her at school."

"Not always." Seth and Jack exchanged an indulgent look.

Then Jack took the pup from her and held her close. She smelled like dog but in a good way. "What's your name, sweetheart?"

"Hattie," Sara answered.

"Well, Miss Hattie, let's go into the house."

While the twins unpacked, he took the dog outside. After she did her duty, she tried to crawl up Jack's leg. He picked her up again. "I'll bet the outdoors is big and scary to you."

After he walked her down to his room, he put Hattie on the bed and stretched out next to her. "So, how's Sara treating you? She's a pistol. Maybe you can keep an eye on her for me."

Sara breezed in fifteen minutes later. "You talking to my doggie?"

"Yep. She says you've been behaving yourself."

"I have. No trouble. And I got straight As for the semester."

"Which is wonderful, honey. I already told you that."

Wandering around the room—the girl couldn't sit still—she made small talk. Until she turned around, holding something. "What's this, Dad?"

He focused on what she held. Oh, dear God, he hadn't planned on getting into this with his kids. "None of your business."

Her blue eyes danced. "Dad, do you have a *girlfriend?*" She pulled a strand out of the brush. "With dark brown hair?"

His son came to the door. "Who has dark brown hair?"

"Dad's girlfriend."

What to do? Hell, maybe this would be a good time for the kids to get to know Tess some.

"I've been seeing someone, yes."

"Are you sleeping with her?"

"Sara, that's too personal." This time the admonishment came from Seth.

"Why? I told him the first time I had sex. He was great about it." She'd been seventeen and he'd fumbled his way through the whole thing. But apparently, he'd done okay.

"If you're asking if she's stayed the night here, she has. But she won't when you're home."

"Why? I don't care." This from Sara.

"Me, either," Seth told him.

"No. I wouldn't feel comfortable."

Sara smiled. The one that always meant trouble. "Let's discuss it with her."

"No way." He stood. "You're trying to stir things up, kiddo."

"It'd be cool to meet her," Seth said.

"Okay, I'll ask her. Meanwhile, let's go start dinner."

"You can tell us more about her."

Slipping an arm around each kid, he pulled them close and walked to the kitchen. Right now, he was a totally happy man.

oOo

"God, I like this place." Tess hadn't yet been to Badges, the fire and police hangout, in the month she'd been in Hidden Cove. She'd been too busy with her family and work. And Jack. Now she took in the firefighter and police pictures on the wall, a tribute to 9/11 in one corner and the sounds of some oldies on the jukebox.

Jenn linked arms with Connie. "I know you don't come here much, sis, but I want you to be comfortable." There was a time when Connie resented Jenn for being a firefighter and the three siblings excluding her.

"I'm comfortable now, Jenny. Don't worry about me."

They wended their way through the crowd—hearing snatches of

shoptalk: *the fire was really rolling…yeah, a drug bust…my wife's mad I took a second shift…*

At a table in the corner, they found their party. *Girls night out,* they'd called it. Megan was seated with Sophia, Tony's wife and Lisel Woodward, whom Tess had met at the camp workday.

"Hi, Lisel. Sophia."

Tess didn't consider her femininity much, but these two would make Scarlet Johansson wonder if she was enough for her man. Hmm, Tess realized, she liked those words. *Her man.* Maybe too much. Sometimes, when she admitted what was happening between her and Jack, she got scared. Remembered losing Joey. And worried about getting too close to anyone.

While they were still standing, they were joined by another beauty, Faith Ruscio, a friend of Lisel's. Her waist-length blond hair and delicate skin were lovely. After they took seats, she said, "Thanks for letting me come tonight. I love these outings."

"Of course you do." Sophia laughed. Even that was sultry. "Faith has two sets of twins, Tess."

"Oh, wow, how do you manage?"

"I have help from Rick's family and mine. Besides, they're five years apart."

Reaching for the pitcher, Tess poured some beer into a glass. Jenn did, too. Connie and Faith ordered wine.

Soon, Tess was lulled by the cozy atmosphere and the conversation: how the kids were, school getting out and plans for the summer, their jobs.

Lisel turned to her. "Do you like teaching at the Academy, Tess?"

"You know, I do. I'd rather be on the line, but I can't because of an injury."

Suddenly, Tess realized she'd made the comment without rancor. Without resentment. She'd have to think about when her attitude had changed.

"Do you work outside of the home, Lisel?"

"Not in theater anymore. Have you met my sister-in-law, Eve?"

"No," Tess replied. "But I've heard terrific things about her."

"She's retired, too. We run a food cupboard for people in Hidden Cove who are poor and homeless. Believe it or not, orchestrating things takes up a lot of time."

"If you ever need help, I'm available." In Rockland, the fire department practically staffed a downtown soup kitchen by themselves.

Again, the talked turned personal.

From Faith: "Rick's working so hard to keep his business flourishing."

"Mitch is thinking about retirement."

Sophia grinned. "Tony and I have never been happier." She smiled. "Thanks to Jack. I'll never forget what he did for us."

Tess knew the story of Sophia and Tony. She wondered what it would be like to be loved so much a man would quit his revered profession for you.

"Jack's a great guy." This from Lisel.

Out of the corner of her eye, Tess saw Jenn and Connie exchange glances. The look on Jenn's face was familiar to Tess. Uh-oh. Her cousin pretended innocence. "Yeah, I wish Jack had a girl. His wife's been dead a long time."

Please don't let me blush, Tess prayed.

Sophia turned to her. "What about you, Tess. Is there a man in your life?"

It was the first time Tess ever wanted to discuss her love life. But of course she couldn't. Their situation would remain confidential, except for the family knowing, for at least several more weeks. Tonight, the secrecy didn't sit right with her.

oOo

On a special Saturday morning class, Jack watched as Tess finished lighting the fifth fire, which rose up about four feet. Its pinkish-red flames glimmered in the midday sun. Today would be the first time the recruits came in contact with the real deal. The task appeared to be a simple drill, but often, recruits failed to accomplish it.

Today, Tess was in charge. "Before we test you, tell me the four steps to activating an extinguisher."

Anita raised her hand. "The book said to remember it as PASS. **P**ull the pin. **A**im at the bottom of the fire. **S**queeze the handles. **S**weep the fire from side to side."

"Good, Cruz." She scanned the others. "Why do you aim at the bottom of the fire? Murphy?"

"If you aim at the top, the extinguishing element will go right through the fire."

Jack zeroed in on Danny Mauro. His expression was remote today, as if he wasn't even listening.

"Mauro?" Tess's voice was neutral, but she must have noticed his expression, too. "Why sweep the bottom of the fire?"

He looked up, surprised. "Huh?"

"Not paying attention, recruit?"

"This is easy stuff. I've done it before."

"We'll see." Tess crossed to the five extinguishers. "Come get one, everybody."

When she handed Danny his device, she said, "Better pay attention here." To the whole group, she added, "This drill is going to test several things. How well you studied your assignment. How you handle yourself under stress. And how quickly you react. It will be heavily weighted in your RTE this week." The kids knew about Friday evaluations. They dreaded the assessment because it would make or break them.

"I'm going to time you," Tess went on. "When you're successfully done, step back."

Mauro rolled his eyes.

"Go."

Each raced to a fire. Landon went in close and stopped. He'd forgotten what to do already. Tess yelled, "PASS Landon." He started the drill.

The other four had pulled the pins. One aimed at the top of the fire. One at the bottom but forgot to sweep.

And, as Danny Mauro, compressed the handles, nothing happened. He frowned. He squeezed again. He shook the extinguisher, which he should do to see if it was full. "Son of a bitch." He rounded on Tess. "Did you do this on purpose?"

"I did. We dismantle one extinguisher every time we have the drill. We set you up so your adrenaline gets going. Make it important. Then insure something goes wrong to see how you handle it. Your grade is based on your reaction to equipment malfunction."

"That's not what I meant." He was far enough away from her, but he straightened to his full height and took a few steps forward. Jack went on alert. "Did you give me the broken one on purpose? So I'd fail in front of everybody?"

"You mean because you said this was a piece of cake?"

His face reddened and he moved closer. She raised her chin. "What do you think, Mauro?"

The recruit stared at her, then gave her his back. Jack hoped the kid was calming himself. He was silent for the remainder of the class, but Jack sensed he was fuming.

Half of the recruits had made mistakes and, in the process, learned a valuable lesson. Nothing could be taken for granted in a fire. Jack wished he could say he agreed with the method used. Falling into step by Tess as she started inside, he asked, "Go for a short walk with me, will you? They have some free time now."

Her dark eyes were troubled, and the sun made them almost mahogany. "I can't. I've got—"

"It's important, Tess."

Nodding, she headed out toward the woods with him. "What is it, Jack?"

"I want to talk about what just happened there."

"Where?"

"In the class."

She stopped and faced him. "I thought the training went well. When recruits make mistakes, have their shortcomings shown to them, they learn a lot about facing the Red Devil."

"Mauro, especially."

"Mauro wasn't paying attention."

"He thinks you singled him out."

"I *did* single him out."

He jammed his hands in his pockets.

"I'm right about this, Jack. I couldn't let his attitude in front of everybody go unchecked."

"Do you think what you did was wise?"

She took in a breath and let it out slowly. He appreciated that she was trying to control her temper. "Obviously, you don't."

"I'm worried about Mauro."

"Seriously? You should be worried about Cruz."

"Why?"

"She's having a rough time keeping up. I asked her about it. Turns out she has a baby and is juggling the child, her grandmother *and* the class."

"Her file doesn't indicate those things."

"Cruz omitted that on her form because she thought she wouldn't be accepted to the Academy if we knew her family responsibilities."

"Why didn't you report her?"

"Because I listened to what you said about not being too rough on the recruits. Her story's a sad one, unfortunately typical of a lot of women."

"I would have tried to help her. Why did she turn to you?"

"I'm not sure. She came in late once, and I called her on it. She was weepy. Her daughter was sick, and Anita didn't sleep or have breakfast."

"What did you do?"

"I sent her to get some food, told her to go take a nap on the cot in the room off the EMS office. I also said I was sorry her situation was difficult, but she had to follow the rules here—enough so she'd pass."

"Good for you."

She arched a brow. "I did listen to you."

"You did. Still, I'm worried about Mauro."

"He's got to learn he can't be so arrogant."

Jack hadn't wanted to bring this up again, but he had to now. "Like Joey?"

"You already asked me that. I told you I didn't want to talk about Joey."

"Maybe you have to. I'm wondering if you're confusing Mauro's attitude with Joey's."

"If he reminded me of Joey, I'd be easier on him."

"Not necessarily."

Her face blanked. She checked her watch. "I have to go in."

"All right, thanks for listening. I appreciate it."

She stepped in a little closer, touched his chest. "I value your work here, Jack. Of course, I listened. But you have to value mine, too."

"You're right. I do value it, but I'll show that more."

Glancing around—there was no one in the woods—she kissed his cheek and walked away.

Tess was right to want to be treated with respect, but that didn't stop Jack from worrying about Mauro. And Tess wasn't being honest with him. Or maybe herself. She *was* comparing him to Joey. Jack just didn't know what to do about that.

CHAPTER 12

Jack stood at the helm of the boat he'd rented at the Hidden Cove Marina and steered the four of them out to shore. The kids loved boating on the lake, so he had this rig for several days.

And today seemed like a good time to have a meet-up with Tess. Participating in an activity together would help break the proverbial ice. The introductions over breakfast had gone well. Tess was friendly, inquisitive and not a bit nervous. Jack was. He'd never had the twins meet a woman before.

As they bounced on the water and the wind blew in his face, Jack pondered that fact. He was serious about her. He wanted to be with her, and these two weeks were going to be hard because he wouldn't get to see her as much as before. Of his own doing, there would be no opportunity for intimacy. The conversation had been awkward...

Tess, you can't stay overnight at my house while the kids are here.

Her eyes had narrowed, but there was a glimmer in them. *Why, Dr. Harrison, I didn't know you were such a prude.*

Not a prude. I wouldn't be comfortable having sex with them down the hall.

In the other wing of the house.

I guess I am old-fashioned and it's stupid, because both kids have had sex and talked to me about it. I don't know why I'm this way.

She'd given him a big smile. *You know what, Doc. Old-fashioned works for you.*

He'd crossed to her and encompassed her in a big hug. *Except in bed.*

I'm not old-fashioned there.

Unfortunately, we won't be in bed for two weeks.

Aw, shit...

Jack steered them to a little inlet in the cove that he liked. He slowed down, stopped and glanced behind him. At the back of the boat, Tess and Sara were stretched out in the sun on two benches, wearing only their bathing suits. Seth, who wasn't crazy about the sun, lazed under a canopy in the shade, watching the water.

He called out, "Seth, want to drop the anchor?"

"Yeah. The bathing beauties certainly won't help."

After the anchor was in place, he and Jack dropped onto the seats up front. Jack smiled at the child who was so easy to be with. "Want something?"

"I can get it." He reached into the cooler and came up with a bottle of water. "There's beer here, Dad."

"I'll have one of those."

The two of them sat in silence, listening to the water lap, the occasional Jet Ski rider come by and the hum of its motor. The way the sunlight bounced on the surface of the lake was magical.

Leaning back in the cushions, Seth gave him a little-boy smile. "It's great out here."

"We can come as often as you like. I've got the boat for the days you're home."

"I want to spend time with you, Dad."

"Is something wrong, son?"

Seth shrugged. "In some ways, I wish we'd come home for the summer."

Jack had so many memories of summer: swimming in Hidden Lake at his friends' houses, watching the kids climb the jungle gym, building sandcastles.

"Yeah, me, too." He waited. Since he was the dad, he added, "But you'll be glad you're taking calculus now when you have all higher-level classes in the fall." Seth had pretty much settled on being a math teacher.

His son smiled, reminding him of Elizabeth's smile. Today, it didn't hurt as much as usual. He thought again about how much Tess had come to mean to him.

Seth angled his head to the back of the boat. "She's great, Dad."

"Yeah, she is."

"I'll bet she doesn't take any crap from any of the recruits at the Academy."

His heart tightened in his chest. "Why would you say that?"

"I can just tell. She's not intimidated at all by us."

"That a good thing?"

"Really good."

He glanced to the back of the boat and saw the *girls* sit up and swing their legs to the floor. They stood and made their way to the front. Jack watched them. Tess's face was red, and he could see a little outline of sunburn on her chest. Sara had some marks, too.

"Didn't you two put on sunscreen?" he asked sternly.

"Yes, Dad. Tess insisted. I didn't have a choice." Her tone was teasing.

"You must've missed some spots. I've got aloe in our stuff."

"Later." Tess angled her head at Sara. "I challenged your daughter to a swim. I said I could beat her to that outcropping of rocks over there and back."

Jack winked at Sara. "She, um, was on the swim team."

"Oh yeah?" Tess arched a brow. "Me, too."

"I'll watch so nobody cheats."

"Watch, hell." Seth stood. "If they can do it, so can we. But let's make this a boys-against-girls thing."

Suddenly, Sara eyes turned bleak. Sometimes, her mood could change on a dime.

"Honey, you okay?"

She cleared her throat. "Yeah, it's nice to be able to, you know, have another girl around. We never even knew Mom, let alone do things with her."

Because he'd experienced it, Jack knew how this kind of sadness could ambush you. He hugged her close and kissed her hair. "Aw, baby."

Reaching out, Tess squeezed her hand. "I'm glad you like having me here, Sara."

After the moment passed, Jack whipped his shirt off and faced his son. "Ready, kid?"

Seth clasped his shoulder. "Ready, Dad. For a lot of things."

o0o

Tess gripped the railings and hefted herself up the ladder. She was third in line. Jack had won the race. Sara came in second, and she and Seth took up the rear. When she swung her legs over the top, Jack threw her a towel. "I beat you, Righetti."

"And we tied," she said sassily. "Boys against girls."

"No thanks to me."

When Jack's gaze went to his son, Tess caught her breath. He looked at his kids as if they'd hung the moon or discovered the cure for cancer. It made Tess wonder what she'd missed by not having children. After Joey, she'd never wanted any.

Jack and the twins donned shirts. "Seth isn't into swimming, but he's an excellent baseball player." He threw Tess a big T-shirt which said Columbia University on it.

Poking her head and arms into it, she gave Seth a smile. "Do you play in college?"

"I did my first year. But it took up tons of my time."

"He's got a double major in math and computers, as well as the education courses."

Tess liked the boy. He was so even-keeled. He didn't care that Sara beat him in swimming and seemed comfortable with his own successes. She realized then he was a lot like Jack.

"So, who's hungry?" Sara asked.

Everyone was.

They unpacked the cooler, and Tess was surprised to find fried chicken, potato salad, a green salad and crusty bread. "Did you cook?"

"Daddy did. He got up at dawn to fix this for me and Seth." She gave Jack an impulsive hug. "We could have ordered this out, Dad."

"Nah. You're not home that much."

The chicken was tender and perfectly spiced, the potato salad creamy and the lettuce's dressing tart. She liked the food Jack had made. Her heart skipped a beat at another thought. This kind of family stuff was different from how she felt with the Malvasos. She liked that, too.

"Do you have any kids, Tess?" Sara asked. The girl was so intuitive, she could practically read minds.

"No. I've never been married."

"Any brothers and sisters?"

For a minute, Tess froze. Then she cleared her throat. "A brother. But he died when he was twenty-four."

"Oh, God." Sara's eyes filled with sorrow.

Seth gasped.

Seated next to each other, the twins moved closer so they were touching shoulders and hips. "I don't know what I'd do…" Sara didn't finish the thought.

"Me, either." Seth's voice was raw.

"It was a long time ago." The comment was weak, but she didn't know what else to say.

"Does it still hurt?" Sara asked after a moment.

"Yes. Sometimes it's bittersweet, like now." She gestured to encompass the boat. "I was thinking earlier how much I'm enjoying you two. In some ways, it's how I felt being with Joey."

Sara's whole face brightened. "That's cool."

Tess cleared her throat. "It is."

"But I still think you should stay overnight with Dad."

"Sara!" Jack seemed so shocked it brought a chuckle from Tess.

"What?" Sara lifted her chin at her Dad. "Tess and me already talked about it when we were in the sun. She says she respects your wishes and so should we."

"Well, you should listen to her."

"Maybe I will," Sara said, throwing Tess a conspiratorial grin.

o0o

Two nights later, the four of them went to see a movie. Well, two movies. Jack and Seth wanted to see a romantic comedy, and Tess and Sara chose a bestselling thriller that was recently made into a film. No stereotypes in this family, Jack thought again. And Tess fit right in.

On Wednesday morning, the kids met Tess and Jack for lunch at the Fire Academy. Tess was pleased to see how many people loved Jack's children: her cousins, the Ramirez family, even Chief Callahan.

And on Sunday, Seth asked to go to their old church and invited Tess to come along. At first Tess had hesitated. She hadn't been inside of a church since Joey's funeral. Two firefighters had died in her department in Rockland, she'd told Jack, and she attended calling hours and went to the cemetery afterward. But not church. He didn't pressure her, but he was thrilled when she showed up to go with them after all.

In between, Tess insisted Jack spend some time alone with them. By the end of their first week, he was worn out. Flopping down on his couch after their dinner of hamburgers and mac and cheese, he threw up his hands "You guys have to do something on your own tonight."

"Yeah, tryin' to get rid of us?" Sara asked.

"No, I need rest."

"Tess coming over?" Seth asked. He was getting as nosy as his sister. It had become a game with them over the past several days to tease him about her.

"I didn't invite her. Now go see your friends."

"Well, there *is* a party tonight at the lake."

His fatherly instincts went on alert. "Who's giving it?"

"Just some kids." Sara's evasiveness always worried him.

"Not good enough, honey."

"Dad, we're twenty." Now she whined. "And we go out all the time at school without you to check up on us."

"Humor me. I want an address, at least."

Seth said, "That's not too much to ask."

They left with kisses and hugs, and as soon as they closed the door, Jack called Tess. When she answered, he didn't even identify himself. "Tell me you're free tonight."

"Yeah, my boyfriend won't sleep with me for ten days."

"He's an idiot. Why don't get on over to his house."

A very sexy chuckle. "Kids out?"

"Uh-huh."

"I'll be right there."

"Tess?"

"Yeah?"

"I like being called your boyfriend."

oOo

Nervous because she'd never done anything like this, Tess stood on Jack's front porch and hesitated. She was worried that she was being stupid. And then she got mad at herself for going out of her comfort zone. Damn it. She rang his bell with a pounded fist.

In seconds, he yanked open the door. And gave her a quizzical look. "You had time to do all that with your hair?" He peered at her closer. "And makeup. Holy cow!"

"Nah. We just finished doing each other's hair and putting on war paint."

"Who's we?"

"Megan, Jenn, Connie and me. We were all home together."

"Thank them for me."

"Oh, just wait," she mumbled under her breath and stepped inside. Some soft, sexy saxophone played in the background, and candles had been set out over the table surfaces. She cocked her head. "Hmm. You missed me, huh?"

Instead of answering her, he grabbed her hand and put it to his groin. "A lot. And this is from simply seeing you."

He was hard and heavy in her hand. "We're on the same page, Doc." She stepped back and unzipped the sweatshirt she wore. Some lacy thing, white and delicate, greeted him. He swallowed hard. Then she sidled down the pants.

"Christ Almighty, Tess. Where the hell did you get that?"

She snapped the clasp of the garter belt attached to white stockings. "This little thing? The girls took me shopping earlier to buy something to wear with you the next time we were together."

He went to reach for her then stopped. "You didn't tell them that I wouldn't…because the kids were here…"

"What do you think? It was just us girls."

Startling her with his quickness, he pulled her to him. "Tease." He took her mouth in a savage kiss. She bit his lip. He grabbed her ass. She hiked up and wrapped her legs around him. Blindly he backed her into a wall, and pressed her against it. "Don't wait," she whispered harshly. "I'm ready."

Freeing himself from his clothes, he plunged into her. That was the last thing he remembered.

oOo

An hour later they were in bed and making love again. His caresses were tender and slow. His kisses whisper soft everywhere on her body: the inside of her knee, her waist, the little mole she had under her jaw. Lost in a wash of sensation, she drifted along, enjoying each precious brush of his hands and lips. He entered her with the same gentleness, slipping inside, moving slowly until she crested and fell off the edge of the waterfall of pleasure.

They cuddled afterward. She relished in the feel of his hard muscles and the male scent of his skin after sex. Neither spoke. For minutes. Then Tess asked, "How could making love be so different each time?"

He kissed her hair. "The first was passion."

Easing herself up, she braced her arms on his chest. "Don't say what the second was."

"Why?"

"Saying it aloud will give it more power. It's too soon." Panic started to rise from her stomach to her heart, then worked its way into her voice. "I've only been in town six weeks."

"It doesn't matter how long you've been here." His tone never changed. It was sure and certain. "How long we've been together. Something clicked between us in Rockland and never went away. What's between us has only intensified since you came to town."

"It's too soon," she repeated. "Don't say anything more."

"Just this." He eased her onto her back, then angled himself over her, watching her intently. "The intimacy of what happened here in bed, *and* out there in the living room, is real, Tess. We've crossed a line. You'll have to face that."

"I know. I just think we should take it slower. I'm scared."

His frown was deep. "Okay, I'll agree to take it slow. Nothing's going to change, though."

She laid her head on his chest. "I hope not."

oOo

"We'll be at the smokehouse this morning," Captain Hennessey told the recruits on the Monday of the fourth week. After all the book learning and more to go before the practical maneuvers, they needed some hands-on things to do. Danny was bored to death.

"You'll dress in your gear here at the Academy, and we'll hike to the smokehouse out back. Once there, you'll be sent inside alone. The building will be filled with mist, simulating smoke, so you won't be able to see anything."

"You said firefighters never worked alone." This from one female recruit who'd just begun to speak up.

"We don't. Ever. But you might get separated, or your partner may get hurt. We want to test your ingenuity if you have to act solo."

"If it's dark in there, how will we get out?" Johnson asked. Like Hanley, he'd had trouble with the maze.

"You memorize what you did on the way in, then reverse it. And when there's something blocking your exit like what could be a fallen beam, there are ways out. Just don't panic."

Righetti, in the back, added, "There are Mayday alarms on your coats if you need them. We'll set them for seven minutes. If they go off, you come out regardless of whether or not you finished your task."

Danny mumbled under his breath, "As if."

"What was that, Recruit Mauro?" Righetti again. Damn her, she must be watching him like a hawk.

"Nothing, ma'am." She was going to get on him again today; he just knew it. Well, he'd show her. His dad had brought him to the smokehouse on weekends when there was no training and let him go inside—more than once. He remembered the layout.

Following his fellow recruits to the locker room, Danny pulled out his gear and suited up faster than anyone else. While they were still wrestling with their air packs, he exited the Academy and walked at a clip over to the training area by himself. It was stinking hot in all this clothing; even at a slow pace, he was sweating beneath it. After a few minutes, somebody caught up to him.

"In a hurry, Mauro?"

Shit. "The chief told us to head on over."

"Yeah, she did."

They walked side-by-side. Her long strides kept up easily with his. "I suppose you've been in a smokehouse, too."

"Uh-huh."

"Well, stay on your toes, recruit. There might be some surprises."

He stopped and she went ahead of him. "Captain?"

She turned.

"Why are you always riding my ass?"

"Why are you always being such a know-it-all?"

Because I don't want to be here, Danny thought. But no, he chided himself. *She* was the problem.

"None of the other instructors have issues with me."

"Don't bet on it."

She jogged the rest of the way, leaving him open mouthed. Nobody liked him here?

His conscience came front and center. *Why would they? You haven't been yourself, once.*

"Shut up," he said aloud and kept walking.

The gray, concrete building in the far back of the Academy complex rose up three stories high, with several openings for windows and a set of metal fire escapes on the southern corner. Mist resembling white smoke billowed out of them.

Danny arrived first, but gave Righetti the Bitch wide berth. The rest of the recruits and teachers came along shortly. Chief Hennessey looked from him to Righetti, who said, "Mauro was in a hurry. I kept him company."

Hennessey frowned but didn't speak to him. Instead, she focused on another recruit.

"Murphy, since you always raise your hand when I ask for a volunteer, we'll spare you the effort. You go in first." She held up a card. "Your task is on the third floor. In one of the bedrooms is a box of books. Bring it back down. And keep us apprised of your progress through the radio. Everybody is wearing a mic so we'll all learn about recovery calls from each other's experience."

"Right on it, Chief." The guy was always so excited about everything they did. He had a friendly grin and easy way. And he really wanted to be a firefighter. Danny envied him.

Murphy hustled inside. "I'm going up the steps... Ouch, I hit something so there's an impediment on the second landing. On the third floor now...found the box. Hell, it's heavy."

"So are bodies, Murphy." Hennessey's tone was dry.

"Yeah." Silence. "I'm retracing my steps...am at the staircase... going down. Holy shit..." Static and noise over his radio mic.

Silence. For too long. Righetti and Hennessey bolted inside. Even Danny was concerned. Then, finally, from the mic, "He's right here... You okay, Liam?" Hennessey asked.

"I fell flat on my ass and slid down on it the rest of the way."

Both women laughed. "Are you hurt?" This time it was Righetti.

"Only my pride. The books spilled all over, though."

"That's okay. Get on out of here."

The three of them exited. When they reached the group, Hennessey put a hand on Murphy's shoulder. Obviously, they liked him. "He's all right. Make sure you give him some grief for embarrassing himself."

Good-naturedly, Murphy laughed.

Cruz went in next. Same drill, but she had to retrieve a suitcase on the roof. They could hear her breathing heavily as she climbed the last flight of stairs. Something inside of Danny shifted. He hoped she didn't wash out. She was trying hard.

"I'm on the roof... Got the suitcase. It's heavy but I can manage it. Oh, no, I'm back at the door I came in, but it won't open."

Danny realized there must be another teacher inside to set up the roadblocks.

"What are you going to do?" Hennessey asked calmly.

"I don't know."

"Don't panic, Anita." Even Righetti used a first name. "Think hard what the building looked like from the outside."

"The fire escape!" Silence. "I'm there. It's open. I'm coming down."

"Right choice, Cruz," Hennessey said with a big grin on her face. "We can see you. Good job."

Cruz came out, lugging the suitcase, looking as if she'd won a war. Her smile was huge and made him like her.

Four more recruits took their turns inside, had some troubles but got out fine with their booty.

Righetti turned to him. "I hope seven's your lucky number, Mauro. You're next. In a corner of the third floor is a body in the closet. Bring her back."

Hmm, that sounded exciting at least. He put on his face mask and went inside. It was hotter in here. He hurried up the three flights of steps easily because he kept in good shape. Feeling his way down the hall was a snap, but the inability to see *anything* spooked him. His heart raced.

"You there, Mauro? You're supposed to be narrating your progress." Hennessey sounded ticked off.

"Yeah...almost there. I'm at the room... Here's the closet... The door won't open."

No response.

"I don't have a ram to spring it. Can somebody bring one in?"

"Nope." Righetti's voice. "You're on your own."

"Seriously?"

"Think on your feet, recruit."

What to do? Taking off his glove, he fished in his pocket for the screwdriver he'd carried inside. Felt for the hinges on the door. Jimmied the sharp edge under the top one, but it slipped, gouging his unprotected hand. Wetness covered his palm. "Fuck."

"What was that Mauro?" The bitch again.

Determined to show her he could do this, he wedged the tip in the hinge again, and the metal fastener snapped off. The bottom one did the same. The door fell inward but he managed to move it out.

"Okay, I'm inside."

"Good job, Mauro." A compliment from Righetti?

Squatting, he felt for the body. Hardness. Stuffing. Here it was. He yanked on it. Damn, somebody'd tied it down. "Dummy's rigged. But I got my wire cutters." He'd snipped a couple of ties around her chest when an ear-shattering noise reverberated in the building, almost making him fall back. It took him a minute to realize the sound was his Mayday alarm.

Hennessey said, "Come out, Mauro."

"In a few minutes."

"Now!" Hennessey gave him a direct order. He knew insubordination on the fire ground was not tolerated. "If this was a real fire, the alarm would mean you're out of air."

"I'm not."

"Get out, Mauro." Righetti sounded mad.

"I'm coming... Just one more. There I got it."

Silence from the other end. Fuck them, he needed more time and he took it. They should be happy he showed initiative. He exited the stairwell on the first floor carrying the dummy.

Outside, Chief Hennessey greeted him, hands on hips, a deep scowl on her face. "You disobeyed orders."

"I saved the dummy."

"You were told to come out. You'll get a zero for your performance this week on RTE. You know the rule. If you get less than fifty on your total score, you won't graduate and become a firefighter."

Anger rose inside him, fast and fiery. She had to be kidding. He'd done his job. He started to speak, but Hennessey moved in close. "You're already in trouble, Danny. Don't say anything else."

He held her gaze, bit the inside of his jaw, then circled around her and strode away. Heading toward the Academy, he felt the weight of the accusing stares from the other recruits. Who gave a shit?

Captain Righetti grabbed his arm as he passed her. "I tried to warn you, Mauro."

She'd probably set him up.

He flung off the captain.

"What the hell?" She stumbled backward, but he kept going, not waiting to see if she was okay. He had to get out of here.

His mic still connected, he heard the other recruits shouting. "She's down... Hell, what just happened...? Oh my God..."

Then Captain Hennessey. "Somebody go get Ms. James in the EMS office. Tess, you okay?"

Silence.

Then, "Yeah, I wrenched my shoulder. And got some scratches is all."

Whipping off his mic, Danny threw it to the ground and kept walking. He reached his car, yanked off his helmet, tank and turnout coat, flung them to the pavement. He got inside with his boots, bunker pants and suspenders still on. The engine roared to life as if it was angry, too, and he tore out of the parking lot, but he got only about forty yards down the road before he had to turn into a gas station. Off to the side of the parking lot, he put his head on the steering wheel.

oOo

Jack flew into the EMS office, located at one end of the gym. An assistant in the outer area raised her brows. "Jack? What's wrong?"

"Where's Tess Righetti?"

"Inside with Larissa."

His heart beating fast, Jack rushed to the main office door, yanked it open.

Larissa was listening to Tess's heartbeat but stopped and looked up. "Jack? What's going on?"

His gaze focused on Tess, he asked, "You okay?" His voice was hoarse, with traces of panic.

"I'm shaken and sore," Tess answered. "But basically okay." Her pale face with some scratches on it belied her words. Still, she didn't seem seriously hurt. He'd only heard from his secretary that she was in EMS, and he'd gone to find her. Letting out a deep breath, he turned to Larissa for confirmation.

Her gaze was knowing, as if she sensed what was happening. He was beyond caring what the scenario with him and Tess looked like. "Like she said, she's sore and scratched up some, but she'll be fine. Jack, this isn't—"

"Larissa, I need to see Tess alone."

Eyebrows raised, she looked to Tess. "Captain Righetti?"

"Yeah, it's fine. Thanks for the help."

"Take those pain pills I gave you." She squeezed Jack's shoulder. "Calm down, cowboy. Tess is better off than you are."

After Larissa left, Jack crossed to the small examining table. The blinds were slanted and a few rays of sun peeked through, accenting her lack of color. Without saying anything, he pulled her gently into his arms. Still seated, she clung to him.

"Are you really not hurt?" His hand cradled her head.

"I'm not." Her voice was too soft. "I'm shaken over what happened, though."

When he pulled back, he kept hold of her hands. "Tell me. I don't know the details."

"We were doing some basics in the smokehouse. One at a time, to see how the recruits would react independently." She explained the exercise. "When Mauro's turn came up, he drew the unlucky straw."

"This is about *Mauro?*"

"Yeah. He disobeyed orders when his Mayday alarm went off. He wouldn't exit the building until he got the dummy freed. Olive got on him."

"And you?"

"Well, I wasn't nice to him, Jack. He'd blown it this time. I stopped him as he was leaving and he pushed me away. That's when I fell."

"Shit."

"I'm fine, Jack, but *he's* out of control."

His mind whirred. Tess, Danny, Tess, Danny. He tried to sound calm when he asked, "What did you say to him? Did you taunt him?"

Frowning, Tess straightened and slid back some on the table. "I'm not sure I like where this conversation is going. *I* didn't do anything wrong. And I don't have to defend myself to you."

"I'm worried about Danny's state of mind."

The *recruit* is arrogant, Dr. Harrison. He thinks he knows everything."

"There's more to him. Something worrisome is going on inside him." He held her gaze. "I should have foreseen this was coming."

"*This*, involving me?"

"Yeah. The recruits…Mauro…they…" He stopped, unsure of how to proceed.

Her gaze narrowed, then she cocked her head. The angle showed some black-and-blue marks on her jaw "Spit it out, Jack."

Oh, hell. "They complain about you, Tess."

A long pause. She stared at him. "They? Not just Mauro?"

"Yeah. Three or four more. They say you're too hard on them. You *are*, sweetheart. I told you that before."

She watched him. Her eyes were clear and something else... accusing. "What do you say, Jack, when the recruits complain about an officer?"

"I tell them there are different methods of teaching. Some tough, some laid back. What you and I discussed before."

"What else did you talk about? Ways to get around me? Did you tell them to report this to the brass?"

"Of course not." He ran a hand through his hair. "You're overreacting."

"Am I?"

"I'm telling you the truth to help you."

"If complaints about me were so pervasive among the recruits, which I still doubt, and if there was some serious concerns about Mauro's attitude, you should have informed me."

"I said the class was confidential."

"Yeah, well, you said a lot of things."

"What does that mean?"

Temper lit her face. "Would you move back?"

When he did, she slipped off the table and wrapped her arms around her waist. The self-protective gesture cut him to the quick. "You've allowed the recruits to complain about me, because maybe you wanted to be proven right. All the while, you were telling me how much you cared about me. Can't you see the problem with that?"

She'd manipulated what he'd told her. "First off, I had to let them say what they thought. I have a responsibility to deal with issues they have."

"Yeah, that savior complex sure comes out with them."

"What?"

"You think you have to save everybody, even me. You don't."

Was that true about him?

"Look, come over tonight after I cook at House 7. We'll go step-by-step through how these complaints unfolded in class. You've skewed the entire thing." When she hesitated, he begged. "Tess, please."

"I will, depending on how you answer this. Recruits ask my opinion on things all the time. Did they ask for yours, on me being too tough?"

He felt as if he'd gotten socked in the gut. "Tess, I—"

"They did, didn't they? And you agreed with them."

"It wasn't that simple."

"It is to me. Answer the question."

Fuck it, he was upset too, about the things she'd said to him. And now she backed him into a corner. So he lifted his chin and spoke in anger. "They *did* ask me. I *did* agree. But you're making my behavior in class out to be something sinister, and I resent that."

She shook her head. "What a fool I was to get close to you. To trust you again."

That made him madder. Especially because he sensed there was more to her getting angry like this. "You're throwing roadblocks into our relationship. You never let anybody get too close to you. It's because of Joey and your loss. As a matter of fact, this whole thing about being tough is about Joey. If someone had been tougher with him, you think he might have been okay."

Her face reddened and her lips thinned. "Yeah, Doc, well, look in the mirror. You do with the recruits what you do with Sara."

"What are you talking about?"

"You coddle Sara. Maybe you should analyze yourself before you start judging others. I'll bet there's a boatload of psychological things that go into letting Sara get away with anything she wants to do."

"Sara's fine."

"For the time being." With that, she circled around him and started for the door.

"Are you coming over tonight?"

She whirled on him. "No. Never again."

"You don't mean that."

"Yes, I do. We're done, Doc."

For a minute her face got so sad, he was taken aback by it. "I never should have let this happen."

"Tess…"

But she opened the door and strode out. Jack let her go. Hell, he thought, nursing his anger. She'd misinterpreted what he'd done. Shit! He kicked the wastebasket in the EMS office across the room and kept swearing.

o0o

Shaky, sad and still pissed as hell, Tess pulled into the Malvasos' driveway and turned off the engine. Thankfully, the house was dark. She tried to recall what the family's plans were tonight. Mitch was working, and Sabina was out with Will Rossettie. Sabby and Megan had something to do together for Girl Scouts. At least Tess wouldn't have to face anybody. Dazed by the ugly fight with Jack, she wanted to get inside, crawl under the covers and pull them over her head. On the drive home, she admitted to herself that she acted badly and had made decisions in the heat of anger. What she'd said made her cringe. She hadn't meant to say she wouldn't see him again. Didn't mean it now. Her anger got the best of her. Damn it to hell. Exiting the car, she headed to the front door.

Two feet away from the porch, she stopped in her tracks. On the steps sat Danny Mauro. Still dressed in his blue uniform, which accented wide shoulders, he looked big and strong. Very big. Very strong.

Her mind raced. At six o'clock, it was still daylight. He probably wouldn't try to hurt her out in the open, with neighboring houses not far away. But she'd been shocked when he pushed her earlier, and he couldn't be doing well, so her pulse began to race. She darted a glance behind her. Could she get to her car without him stopping her?

"Please, don't leave. I won't hurt you. I didn't mean to today." He sounded desperate. And desperate people did things.

What to do? She didn't feel safe. But when she got a good look at his face, she saw the kind of sadness that was familiar. Now she realized she'd seen the same expression in Joey's face, too, whenever he'd screwed up. But she never recognized it for what it was, either time.

"All right, I won't leave. But I'm taking my phone from my pocket"—she slipped it out—"and pressing 9-1. If you get out of line, I'll hit the last button, and the police will come."

"I won't get out of line. I promise." He sounded like a little boy. "I'm sick of getting out of line." He scooted over on the steps. "Wanna sit?" Again, the hoarseness, the gravity of his tone.

But she had to beware. "I'll stand, for now anyway."

He glanced to the side. The evening sun hit his face and she realized his cheek was wet. The kid had been crying. Again, Tess was thrown back into time, when Joey had been arrested for reckless driving. At the jail, he'd sobbed.

So she tried to soften her tone. "What's going on, Danny?"

"You never called me that before."

"I haven't?"

He shook his head. Took a deep breath. "First off, I'm sorry I pushed you today. I didn't know what I was doing. I was ready to explode and had to get out of there."

"I can accept that. But what about the rest of the time? You've been surly and rude this whole four weeks."

A half smile. "I could say the same about you."

The comment made her stop. She knew she'd been tough, but had she been...mean to him?

"I probably shouldn't have said that. You're the instructor. You have to be hard on us."

"If you know that, how can you explain your behavior?"

His whole face tensed as if he was trying to get something out but couldn't. Finally, he said in such a low voice she had to struggle to hear, "Because I don't want to be at the Academy." His voice even lower. "I don't want to be a firefighter."

She never expected that. "Then, why are you in the program? You're smart. You could do anything with your life."

His body folded over itself, and he slid his arms around his legs. He looked ready to break. "I know. I, um, got into Notre Dame the week I was accepted in the fire department."

"That's great."

"I didn't tell my parents."

"Why?"

"Because it's expected that I'll be a firefighter. I didn't want to let anybody down, but now, getting kicked out of the Academy is going to be worse than if I never went. My dad's retired, but my brothers still work in Camden Cove."

Jack's accusations, no matter how mad she'd gotten over them, made her think hard about what she would do in the next few minutes. What if this was Joey? What would she want an adult to do here? Tess felt the importance of this moment. What she did, what she *chose* to do, was going to be crucial to this boy's life. "Danny, the jury's still out on what will happen to you because of today. You haven't been asked to leave."

"I will be."

"Not necessarily." She nodded to the step. "Move over now. We'll sit and talk about this."

"Seriously?"

"Yeah." Her smile was genuine as she dropped down on the hard cement. "Seriously."

CHAPTER 13

"How's the flight attendant, McCabe?" This from Lisa Beth Duncan. Both were paramedics on Quint and Midi 7 night shift. This group had asked Jack to cook another meal soon after the first, which he usually didn't do. But they wanted to talk about an issue they'd had with a person who subbed in the house often. Firefighters using him as a sounding board for daily issues was what he wanted to happen because of his visits, so he'd agreed.

McCabe, the handsome black man, grinned at his HCFD partner. "You won't believe the stories she has about the passengers. Last night, a woman got on the plane with a stack of magazines a foot high."

"To read?"

"Nope. When the plane hit a bumpy patch, they heard a tearing sound from seat 9B. Lacey checked it out and saw the woman had ripped apart an entire magazine." His warm brown eyes sparkled. "Every time they hit a bump, she tore more magazines."

The firefighters laughed. At the stove, stirring cheese into the fettuccine Alfredo he'd made, Jack focused on the banter instead of the debacle he'd had an hour ago with Tess. He wouldn't think about that until later, when he could see her. If she didn't come to him, he planned to march right over to the Malvaso house and confront her.

"Hey, Doc, how would you analyze the woman's actions?"

"Everybody has a coping mechanism, but that's a new one to me."

McCabe chuckled. "It was mess to clean up."

"Better than if she barfed," one of the group said.

"Dinner's on," he said, playing the dad role. "No talk about barfing."
While they lined up, Jack stood back and tried to enjoy their
enthusiasm for his meal. But his mind didn't cooperate—he still could
see Tess, hurt and shocked, sitting on that exam table, at the door,
leaving him for good, she'd said. Man, he'd blown it by focusing on
Danny and not her. He also suspected hers was a knee-jerk reaction,
and she hadn't meant what she said about them calling it quits.

"What you thinking, Doc?" Grady O'Connor asked. He seemed to
be doing well in his new role as an officer.

Jack watched Grady; the guy was such a happily married man.
Jack wished he could ask him for advice about Tess. But of course
being the fire department shrink precluded that kind of camaraderie.
"Daydreaming."

After they were seated and diving into the rich, creamy macaroni
and crusty Italian bread, they made small talk. Discussion of problems
would wait until after the food.

Halfway through the meal, the PA crackled over the speaker. "Quint
and Midi 7, Rescue 7, fire on Baker Street. Go into service."

The group stilled. "What the hell?" Lisa Beth said. "A house doesn't
get calls when Jack cooks for them."

O'Connor was already up. "No matter. Let's go."

They raced to the bay. Jack stared at the half-eaten meals. Just what
his rotten day needed. Still—there never *had* been even one call during
his visits, as Lisa Beth said. He knew his luck had to run out, but he
didn't like the feel of things tonight. So he went to the bay, and after
the rigs catapulted out, he followed them in his own car to the scene.
When he reached it, he felt foolish. For thinking there was a problem.
For thinking they needed him here. He recalled Tess's accusation…

*Yeah, that savior complex sure came out with your kids… You think you have
to save everybody, even me. You don't.*

But because he was still unnerved, he stayed. He watched the three-
alarm fire spit and flare, belch dark gray smoke and gobble up the
wood. Behind him, Engine 4—Jane's crew—and Ladder 15—swerved
in just behind the Midi.

A sea of firefighters hopped off the rigs, the cacophony of the
trucks and shouts from men deafening. Then the fire chief pulled
up. Jack's premonition didn't seem so odd to him now. Noah came to

serious fires. "Hey, Chief. This a big one?"

"Yeah, the building's connected to a series of row houses. Which means if we don't contain the fire in one, it'll spread to the others. I called in even more trucks than this." He angled his head to Incident Command. "I'm going to go check in with Malvaso." Jack hadn't realized Mitch was the BC in charge.

Sticking his hands in his pockets, Jack watched the action, his concern growing. Sometimes a fire had a nasty, mean feel. This one was one of those. His pulse sped up.

Because they were paramedics, as well as firefighters, McCabe and Duncan waited in front of the building for victims to come out, or to see if they'd be called in.

Another guy from the Quint got behind Grady O'Connor on the hose, and they started inside.

House 15 guys hauled ladders to the front, back and sides.

Jack recognized all this as usual stuff as he headed to Incident Command. He'd not quite reached it when he heard, *Pop, pop, pop.*

Stymied, he glanced at the house. Had something exploded in there? *Pop-pop-pop-pop-pop-pop-pop.*

McCabe jumped on Lisa Beth. They both went down.

Mitch pitched forward to his knees.

Noah Callahan lurched to stand behind him.

Pop-pop-pop-pop.

The fire chief jerked backward and fell flat on his back. *Oh, my God,* Jack thought as he dove behind the truck.

Somebody was shooting at firefighters.

oOo

Sirens sounded in the distance. Jack crouched behind the truck. Mitch and Noah lay flat out on the ground, so the vehicle protected them, too. Jack prayed neither tried to crawl away and reveal himself. The shooting had stopped only seconds ago. He listened for it to start up again. Nothing. The sirens got louder. After a few grace minutes, he made his way on his hands and knees over to Mitch.

His best friend's eyes were wide and his breathing shallow. "Ch-check Noah," Mitch croaked out. "He got hit when he pushed me down."

"How badly are *you* hurt?"

"A shoulder wound. Tend to him." He clutched at Jack's arm.

"Please, Doc. He shielded me."

Sirens screeched now. One by one, cop cars slammed to a halt inside the fire ground. Behind them the big white ambulances arrived. Amidst the noise and activity, Jack reached Noah.

The chief was out cold. A gaping wound near his heart bled profusely. Whipping off his shirt, Jack balled it up and pressed it onto Noah's chest.

Mitch called out, "Is he alive?"

Noah's breathing was shallow. "Yeah."

"How bad is it?"

"He's unconscious, so I don't know." Jack felt Noah's neck. The chief's pulse was thready.

Kneeling between his two friends, Jack watched the police surround the area and fan out. But there was no more shooting. Jack stayed down and kept the cloth on Noah's chest, waiting for the medics to come.

o0o

"All clear, all clear!" Jack heard the message, but he didn't know how much later it was. Maybe just minutes. Noah lay still as death, and Mitch moaned. The person who'd called out added, "The son of a bitch is dead."

Ambulances hurtled into the fire ground. Several medics piled out. One cupped his hands and ordered, "Make your position known if you or someone near you is hurt."

Jack stumbled to his feet. "Over here. Two victims. It's serious."

Others shouted, then more. And more.

Two medics hustled to Incident Command. They bent over Noah, and Jack turned back to Mitch. He was sweaty and pale. Jack reached for his hand.

"Who else is hurt?" Mitch rasped out, gripping him.

"I don't know."

"Go see."

Another attendant came up to Mitch, so Jack stood back and surveyed the scene. Groups had formed around the bodies of the wounded—or worse. His gut told him they weren't getting out of this without fatalities. He hurried to one group. A paramedic worked on Jackson McCabe, who lay on his back, unmoving. "How is he?"

The medic looked up, his eyes bleak. "Not good, Doc. He's one of our own."

Placing his hand on the guy's shoulder, Jack squeezed. It was about all he could do in the way of comfort.

Lisa Beth, seated on the ground, watching, stared at her partner blankly. Jack crossed the few feet and crouched in front of her. She looked up at him, shook her head. Tears coursed silently down her cheeks, and he pulled her into his arms. "I'm so sorry, Lisa Beth."

"He…he pushed me down and covered me with his body."

Jack held on to her until some members of Group 7 found her. Then he stood and crossed to three other people on the ground. One lay spread-eagled, his helmet off, his legs at an impossible angle. "Mary, Mother of God!"

Beside Jack, a medic whispered, "I can't believe it."

Someone else said, "I thought Senate went to the Academy."

"Cramer's only been a battalion chief for a month," a woman bending over another body whispered.

They were dead, Jack realized. They were all dead.

o0o

Tess and Danny had talked for over two hours, and it wasn't until she got in the house did she note that no one had come home yet. The first floor was dark inside, so she switched on a foyer light and headed to the kitchen. She checked the clock. It was nearing nine. Where was everybody? Frowning, she poured herself some red wine and sipped it. The spicy Malbec went down smooth. She went upstairs to Zach's room, kicked off her shoes and lay on the bed, thinking about the young recruit and how she'd contributed to his angst.

Down deep, Danny Mauro was a normal kid, a talented one. His behavior in class had been rooted in the fact that he wanted to go to college, but he'd turned down a full scholarship to fulfill his father's wishes. The story rolled around in her mind.

Eventually, thoughts of Danny were replaced by thoughts of Jack and what had happened to their relationship in that EMS office. They'd said awful things to each other, words that couldn't be taken back. The notion made her eyes mist. Damage had been done. He'd asked her to come over, though, and she'd said no. Should she go now? Deciding to finish her wine first, she switched on the TV to catch the news.

Breaking News flashed in big white letters across the bottom of the screen. A sober-faced anchor from a local channel stared out at the camera. His eyes were grim as he said, "If you're just joining us, there's been a shooting in downtown Hidden Cove."

Megan! Oh no! But wait, she was with Sabby. Still, Tess had gotten to know others in the police department who could have been hurt.

"We're going live now to Baker Street, where our team is on the scene." A female reporter appeared on screen. "Julie, what's going on?" The woman's face was pale and her lips thinned. "We've had no official word about the incident. And we can't get near the area because it's cordoned off as a crime scene. But we saw ambulances race by." She swallowed hard. "All we know for sure is from the 911 call we monitored. Some firefighters are down. We don't know the extent of the injuries or if there are any fatalities."

The glass Tess was holding dropped onto the bed, the wine soaking the spread. She bounded up and yanked her phone out of her pocket. Oh, God, she'd tied it up with the 911 thing she'd punched in because of Danny.

Hurriedly, she clicked into her voice mail. Zach had called more than once. She listened to the first message. "Honey, it's Zach. There's been a shooting. So far, we know that Mitch and Noah were at the fire. Ladder 15, Engine 4 and the Quint and Midi 7, Rescue Squad 7 night shift were called."

Jack had said, *"I'm going to cook for Quint and Midi 7 night shift. Come over to my place later."*

Her heart galloping in her chest, Tess punched in Zach's number.

He answered with, "Tess?"

"Oh, God, Zach. Any more news?"

"No. We still don't know who was shot"—his voice cracked—"or worse."

Tess gripped the edge of the night table and bit her lip. She wouldn't burden Zach by falling apart. She mumbled soothing words, then said, "Jack was cooking for House 7 tonight."

"They never get calls when he cooks, so there's no reason to think he went to the scene."

And he was hoping to meet her. Oh, God, maybe he didn't follow them to the call. "Where are you? I want to be with you."

"Jenn, Meggie and I are as close as we can get to the scene. An ambo is leaving now. Damn, it just stopped. Wait a sec."

She heard the running of a motor and, over it, someone call out, "Zach, one of the victims is Mitch. We've got him. You guys can get in if you want."

The phone went dead. And Tess was left alone to wonder what had happened to her beloved cousin and the rest of her firefighter brotherhood.

o0o

Forcing himself to blank his mind and ignore the wrenching in his heart, Jack sat once again with the Malvaso family, Eve Callahan and Ian Woodward at Memorial Hospital. They were in one of the rooms designated for the families of the victims of the shooting. Others waited in spaces next door, down the hall or in the hospital lobby.

"Fuck it," Zach said. "I can't believe three of ours died. It reminds me of Sinco."

Years ago, a warehouse had caught on fire, and ten people had died. The loss reverberated through the department for years and had literally changed Zach's life.

"Rightfully so, Zach," Jack answered. "This tragedy is as horrific."

Jack scanned the group. Connie and Jenn were holding hands. From their trip in with the ambulance, the Malvasos knew Mitch was stable. Grady, who hadn't been hurt, was grief stricken and Connie's husband talked softly to him. Sabina had also come in with Will and sat stoically, as did the former police chief, who was Noah's best friend. Jack noticed they held hands.

Megan had gone to the ladies' room, to cry probably, as Tess had that day Sabina was in danger. Briefly, he thought of Tess, then pushed her out of his mind. No time for regretting his own fuckups.

Just then, though, she walked through the door. Her face was ashen. She headed right to Zach. Both he and Casey stood, and Zach grabbed her. Jack was within hearing distance of the conversation, but he was out of her range of vision. "Mitch is wounded but stable, honey."

"Thank God. It took me an hour to get here. I made the mistake of calling a cab, then there was an accident..." She trailed off.

"There's more, honey." Zach swallowed hard. "Three of our people are dead."

Her face drained of any color it had left. "Jack?"

"What? Oh, no. He's fine." Still listening in, Jack heard his friend tell Tess the morbid news—who had died.

She pinched her eyes with her thumb and forefinger. "Were others hurt?"

"Noah Callahan. It's pretty bad."

Knowing he had to see her, Jack joined them. "You okay? You're still in your work clothes."

She turned and, right there in front of everybody, she threw herself into his arms. It should have meant more than it did, but he was numb by now. Still, he clasped her to him.

"I thought… I knew you went to House 7." She gripped his neck tighter. "I'm glad you're all right."

When she drew back, Zach touched her arm. "He was at the fire scene, too."

"You were in the shooting?"

"Yeah, I was with Mitch and Noah at Incident Command."

She grasped his hand. "Thank God you weren't hit, too."

"He helped Noah," Zach told her. "Mitch only has a shoulder wound, but Noah got hit in the chest. Jack staunched the flow of blood with his shirt until help could get there."

"This is so unreal." He watched her scan the area. "Poor Eve and Ian."

Jack fisted his hands so hard, they hurt. "I know. They've had so much to deal with in their lives." He glanced over at them. "I think I'll go talk to them."

They sat like mannequins, Eve on a chair, Ian in front of her, holding her hand. "Can I get either of you anything? Coffee? Water?"

Eve, unable to talk, shook her head. Ian said, "No thanks."

Taking a seat next to Eve, not saying anything, Jack waited with them until the doctor came out. Eve bolted up.

Even the doctor was pale. "Noah's still alive. But he's unconscious, and that worries us."

"What does that mean?" Eve asked.

"It'll be touch-and-go, Mrs. Callahan, when we operate. The bullet went right through him, but it nicked an artery. We have to fix it ASAP."

Ian gripped her hand. "Right now?"

The doctor nodded. "He's being prepped as we speak. I have to go, but I'll send out updates." He squeezed Eve's arm and nodded to Ian, then walked away.

Eve burst into tears. Ian tugged her onto his lap. Jack saw Ian's eyes fill, too. Jack didn't offer platitudes. They were firefighters and knew death could come at any time.

To give them their privacy, Jack walked over to the other side of the room. He'd never felt more helpless in his life.

oOo

The news of Noah's condition shocked everyone. As Tess watched the scene unfold between Ian and his sister, she was almost leveled by their sadness.

Zach, who'd gone to check on Sabina, came back to her. "The doctor says we can go in and see Mitch."

"You first," she told him. "I want to talk to Jack."

When the family left, Tess crossed to the window where he stood facing out, his shoulders stiff, his head down. As if in sympathy, the sky had filled with ominous gray clouds. "Jack?"

He turned.

"I'm so sorry about what's happened."

"Me, too. I have to go meet with the families of the three people who died." He swallowed hard. "One was Tom Senate."

His face got so bleak she wanted to hold him. But something stopped her. He had a remoteness about him. Suddenly, she realized it was his coping mechanism. She wouldn't try to breach his defenses.

"I hope I can be strong for them. He has a wife, son and daughter."

"Why wouldn't you be? You're skilled in these situations."

The grief in his eyes deepened. "I—if I hadn't—it's my… Never mind. I have to go."

"We'll talk later."

"Maybe."

Staring after him, she tried to decipher what he was saying. It was about Tom Senate. Ah, now she remembered. He was the line firefighter who had signed up for Academy teaching, but Tess had taken his place. Was he mad at her for that? No, this wasn't about her. Oh hell! Could it be guilt?

"Tess, I came out to get you." Her cousin frowned. "You okay?"

"Zach," she said grabbing his hand. "I think Jack feels responsible for Tom Senate's death."

"What? Why?"

"He quit the Academy because of Jack's class. If he hadn't…"

"That's ridiculous, but you're right. That's exactly how Harrison would feel." He glanced around. "Where is he?"

"He went to console the families of the deceased."

"Shit. He'll suffer through this alone."

Shaking her head, Tess stood straighter. "Not if I have anything to say about it."

"Let's go see Mitch. He'll have some suggestions about dealing with Jack."

Zach slid his arm around her. He felt solid and strong, and she needed that now. Together, they walked down the corridor to see Mitch, but Tess's mind was still on the hurting doctor.

o0o

The next morning, Jack stood by the window, staring out again, this time in his office. Contrary to yesterday, the sun beat down harshly on the buildings nearby and on the pavement of the road that ran by the Academy. Cars whizzed by. The outdoors was too busy and bright, too cheery for what the immediate future held. He'd hardly slept because he was dreading the day to come. From previous experience, he knew he'd be bombarded with people who wanted to talk about the three deaths, the seven injuries and the fact that even though Noah's surgery had gone well, he was still unconscious. The chief could die, Jack knew, and that notion clenched his heart like a jagged vise, so much so, he pressed his chest with his hand to stop the pain.

Then there would be the recruits to deal with. Their training couldn't continue as normal today. He didn't know what Olive was planning, but it probably included him. He whispered, *Please, God, give me the strength. And forgive me.*

No, no. He wouldn't think about himself now.

A knock sounded on the door. "Come in." He turned expecting to find Olive. For a brief moment, when he saw Tess, his whole body lightened. He wanted to hug her close to him and never let go. Instead, he said evenly, "Tess?"

"Hi. I came to fill you in on our plans for the recruits today."

He was glad she was all business. Firefighters had to be disciplined and get beyond their emotions, like she was doing right now. "Tell me."

Coming closer, she stopped far enough away that he couldn't smell her lotion or see the little pulse in her neck. "First, we're going to take them outside on a long jog. They can work off some of their anxiety and sadness that way."

"Good idea."

"After the run, we're serving coffee and donuts, and Olive will talk to them about risks firefighters face every day. It'll be hard, but safety, or lack thereof, has to be brought out into the light after yesterday."

"You should let them ask any questions they have afterward."

Her hands fisted at her sides. "We're planning to."

"Do you want me there for all this?"

She gave him a sad smile. "We thought you'd be too busy with the rest of the department. We can handle the kids on our own."

"I'll come to the beginning of the meeting. Let me know when you get back from the jog."

"Will do."

"And thanks for planning all that. I *will* be swamped today."

"I know, which is why we're going to have *this* talk." Turning, she went to the door and locked it.

Looked like her firefighter reserve had a crack. This time, she came in very close. He backed up, like a coward. "I know you now, Jack. I know what you're feeling."

"Yeah, well, Tess, it's dangerous to think you know everything." His bitter, bitter tone shocked him.

"What are you referring to, exactly?"

"That wasn't meant as a criticism of you."

"No, it was of yourself."

Hopelessness filling him, he looked away.

"I figured it out last night when you didn't return any of my calls. You think you're responsible for Tom Senate's death."

He stared at her silently. Hearing it said aloud cut him to the bone.

"You're not," she told him. "But nobody's going to convince you otherwise right now. I just want you to know we figured this out."

"We?"

"I told the family."

"Fuck it, Tess. They don't need my problems now."

"Mitch is home."

He shook his head. "He's gotta be worried sick about Noah."

"We all are."

"Then, go tend to them. And to the recruits who I also fucked up." He hadn't meant to say that aloud, but the notion plagued him, was in the forefront of his mind.

She folded her arms over her chest, which meant she wasn't leaving.

"What are you saying?"

"I failed with them, too, and look where it got Mauro. I was so sure the Recruit Concerns class was a good idea. But it wasn't. Has anyone seen him?"

"Not today." The expression on her face was odd—softer, he guessed.

"What aren't you telling me?"

"I talked to him yesterday. Things aren't as bad as you think. But we can discuss him later." She lifted her arms to hug him.

"Don't, Tess."

"Take some comfort from me," she whispered softly.

"I don't want comfort."

"Jack…"

"Please, Tess, don't make this about me, or me and you." His voice rose a notch. "There's a lot of hurting people out there, scared people. We have to take care of them."

"Fine." She stepped back. "I'll let you put your guilt aside, for now, but you'll talk about it eventually."

"We'll see." He looked down at her and was astounded at the love in her face. He almost reached out to her, but he held back. He had to be stoic. "Now go take care of the recruits, and yourself, too."

"Same goes for you, Jack."

o0o

The jog had turned into a run. It was too hot for all out running, but the instructors allowed the recruits to set the pace. Back at the Academy, they headed into the classroom, most dripping with sweat. Fatigue etched itself out on each of their faces, and Tess was sure nobody got much sleep last night.

Olive, who hadn't even conducted roll call, addressed them. "No need to change into your uniforms. Get your donuts and coffee. We're taking it easy for the rest of today."

Questioning looks abounded. Of course. The instructors had been rigid about routines. Too rigid? Tess, too, was questioning her role in everything, like Jack. Only she wasn't beating up on herself for mistakes she might have made.

While the kids gathered around the coffee urn, murmuring among themselves, Danny Mauro approached her and Olive. Tess hadn't told anybody about what'd happened last night between her and the kid.

"Mauro." Olive's voice gravelly. There was no bite in her words.

"Chief. Captain." He focused on Olive. "I know what I did yesterday has to be dealt with. I apologize for my actions. But maybe you should just concentrate on helping the other recruits today."

"Yesterday seems minor now, Danny." Olive choked back emotion. "We'll talk later this week."

Danny glanced at Tess. "I won't be here later this week. I came today because I think I might be able to help the others with what's happened. No arrogance meant in that. Both my dad and my brothers have gone through deaths of guys on the line, and by osmosis, I have, too."

"That'll help, Danny." Olive stared over his shoulder. "There's Dr. Harrison. If you'll excuse me…"

Tess didn't look at Jack. She'd said her piece this morning. And she meant what she'd said. She'd give him space now, but what was between them was far from over. Instead, she gave Mauro what passed for a smile. "You doing okay, Danny?"

"After all this, I feel foolish for whining yesterday. For pouting all these weeks."

"You're entitled to your feelings. But I understand them, too. I feel bad for whining about my ankle."

"Thanks for saying that."

Cocking her head, she noted that despite his sorrow, his brown eyes were clear and his wide shoulders relaxed. She realized she'd never seen him this way. The burden he'd been carrying around for over a month had been a heavy weight on his shoulders and not the *chip* they'd all assumed he had. "Why won't you be here at the end of the week?"

"I plan to tell my parents that firefighting isn't for me." He waved his hand to encompass the classroom. "They'll probably think I'm a coward, that I'm just afraid now, but I'll handle it."

"Good for you. And thanks for coming in today."

"Can I say one more thing?"

"Sure."

"You helped me last night when I'd done nothing but try to alienate you. I'm not sure why, but I've learned from that. About forgiveness, for others and myself."

"What a nice thing to say." Tess squeezed his arm. And thought, *I wish we could convince the doc about that.*

After Danny went to sit down, Olive called the recruits to gather. Chairs were dragged into a semicircle around the instructors, the sound unnaturally loud. Only Quinn Frazier and Tess and Olive were in attendance. Tony was off with his crew, of course, because Jackson McCabe had been one of theirs. Jenkins knew the battalion chief who'd been killed. And Larissa was with the medics.

Olive squared her shoulders and scanned them all. "We'd like you to get your feelings about what happened last night out in the open. I'm hurting, too, a lot, as are the rest of your teachers, so let's be kind to each other."

Subtly, Jack leaned forward. "We know you're scared, maybe questioning whether you even want to be a firefighter. But try to reserve judgment for a week or so. Big decisions shouldn't be made in desperate times."

"You've covered safety on the fire ground in class," Olive said. "And you'll be talking about it again, today. But it's obvious that you are never really safe on the line."

"Nobody's safe." This from Mauro.

Olive stirred, expecting trouble.

"Airplanes are sabotaged and crash. Kids are shot in big cities when they're on the playground. The world is full of risks."

Murphy nodded. "I agree. But firefighters walk into danger intentionally, so we're *more* at risk."

Cruz spoke up, too. "In the big scope of things, today isn't any different from yesterday. We've known all along that firefighting is a dangerous job. Sure, we aren't expecting to be shot at when we go to a fire, and I *don't* feel safe out there, but I never did."

"That's an interesting point, Anita." Jack's voice was calm. "Does anyone want to share his or her feelings, other than fear, now?"

Mauro waved at Jack. "I would." He glanced around. "First, I wanna apologize to all of you for how I behaved these last few weeks. You'll know why I've been such a jerk soon. But, right now, I feel sorry for the families of the people who died or were injured. And for Chief Callahan."

"Danny," Tess said. "You told me your father and brothers have dealt with deaths in the line of duty. Want to tell us how they coped?"

"Mostly by being with other firefighters. You'd think they'd heal quicker by spending time with their wife and kids, but it wasn't that way for them. They turned to each other. Dad said it was the only thing that helped. I know my brothers admitted more of their emotions to their colleagues than he ever would have to us."

Olive brightened a bit. "I have an idea. Why don't you all come over to my house? About four. After we're done here, classes are canceled, and you should catch some sleep. But we'll get together off campus and just be with each other."

Every single one of them agreed to come.

Jack stood. "I'm headed out to be with the Callahans at the hospital." He surveyed the class. "I'm proud of your maturity here. Thanks for rising to the occasion."

Because she couldn't leave, Tess said aloud, "Dr. Harrison?"

He shot her a surprised look. "Yes, Captain."

"Remember what Mauro said. You should be with your colleagues, too."

"Point taken."

He walked out, and Tess turned back to the recruits. They needed her now, as did Jack, but only these kids knew it.

CHAPTER 14

Jack held Eve's hand and placed his other one on Ian's shoulder. Lisel clutched her husband's arm when the doctor told them Noah might never recover. These people were strong, had dealt with tragedy, but this...

Instead of bursting into tears, Eve dropped onto a chair. Silent tears coursed down her cheeks. It was more heartbreaking than a fit would have been. Ian, who loved Noah like a brother, struggled to stay calm for his twin. But he swallowed hard and bit the inside of his jaw. The pall that settled over the room was thick enough to cut with a knife.

Jack turned to the doctor. "Is the diagnosis because he hasn't woken up?"

"That, and his vitals are erratic." The doctor leaned in closer. "We already had to revive him once."

"It hasn't even been twenty-four hours." Eve's voice was raw.

"I'm sorry, Mrs. Callahan. But I think you should be prepared. I don't believe he's going to make it through the day."

Now Eve started to cry in earnest. Drawing her up, Jack held her to his chest. She felt slight as she clung to his shirt and sobbed into it. This was going to get worse before it got better, so best she get rid of some of the emotion stuck inside her. The doctor waited until she calmed.

Eve drew back and scrubbed her cheeks. "I want to see him."

"I'll show you back."

"Want me to come, Evie?" Ian asked.

"Not yet, if that's okay."

"Of course it is."

On shaky legs, she crossed to the entrance to the ER and went in to see Noah alone.

Ian stared blankly after her. Lisel gripped his hand. She wasn't crying, and Jack knew she was holding back for her husband. He'd try a stab at comfort. "I'm so sorry, Ian."

"I can't believe it." His voice was hoarse and hollow. "I wouldn't even be here if it wasn't for him."

Dropping down on the chair Eve had vacated, he came level with Ian. The bleak look in his friend's gray eyes was familiar. "You talked about that in our PTSD group." Jack remembered the horror of Ian's confessions.

"I was suicidal and he was instrumental in my recovery." Ian shook his head. "He kicked my butt six ways to Sunday to get me to the Academy."

"He's helped a lot of people." Jack thought back to Noah's accomplishments: Hale's Haven which, without his support, would never have flourished. Promoting women. Handling the bad seeds like Ed Snyder, who'd been a blight on the department even before the guy turned into an arsonist.

When Jack started to recall the hours he and Noah had spent together professionally and personally, he had to battle back his own grief.

"Jack?" He looked at Ian. "Your phone's ringing."

Fishing the cell out of his pocket, Jack checked the caller ID. "Hello, Nancy." Noah's secretary.

"I'm sorry to bother you at the hospital, but people have been coming to me all morning. Everybody's upset. Terrified, really. And they want to know how Noah is, when *you'll* be back..."

"I'm not sure. I'm at the hospital with the chief's family."

"Jack?" Ian again.

"Hold on a second, Nancy."

"You can go to the office. I imagine you're in demand right now."

"I should check in." He told Nancy he'd be there soon. To Ian, he promised, "I'll be back." Just as Jack stood, Mitch and Megan came through the waiting room door.

"What the hell are you doing here?" he asked Mitch. The man's shoulder was in a sling and he was pale. He'd been gravely injured, too.

"It's bad, isn't it? With Noah."

Time for the truth. "Yes, Mitch, it is."

Mitch stepped aside to reveal Noah's adult daughter, Valerie, his granddaughter, Abby, and…oh my God, seven-year-old Iana.

Jack almost lost it at the sight of Noah's family. They'd say goodbye to him today.

o0o

L imp and exhausted, Tess blew out a heavy breath when the recruit session ended and the kids filed out the door. They'd poured their hearts out, and the morning had been draining. Word had come down that Noah might not make it through the day—and the cloud of doom over all of them intensified.

"See you later," Olive told her hoarsely.

Bedraggled and drained, they both still wore their sweaty shirts and shorts. Tess could see Olive was barely holding it together as she walked out the classroom door. These people who'd known Noah for years were suffering. Since she was an outsider, who hadn't known Noah well, she vowed to try to make things easier on the rest of them.

While Tess was still seated, staring out at the sunny day, Danny came back inside. "Captain Righetti? You okay?"

"As much as I can be."

"Is it all right if I come to the gathering at Chief Hennessey's today?"

"We'd all like that."

"I'm so sorry about the chief."

Tess could only nod. Danny squeezed her arm and left.

Minutes later, she went in search of Olive. She found her looking through the window of her office. Her back impossibly stiff, the battalion chief had wrapped her arms around her waist. Tess thought of Jack and his similar stance this morning.

"Olive?"

The woman shook her head. "Please, give me some time."

Tess was torn about pushing this. So she crossed the room and placed her hand on Olive's shoulder. "It's okay. You might be better off if you let go."

Olive shook her head. "I can't. Later. Not yet."

Still torn, she walked away, letting the strong, brave woman, who'd fought like hell to get where she was, deal with this tragedy in her own way.

oOo

The halls of the Academy were deadly silent, broken only by phones ringing. Jack had spent most of the day with people who were already mourning Noah's death. Now he was headed to Noah's office area to console more staff who loved the chief.

When he reached the area, Noah's secretary looked up. Her eyes were swollen, her nose red and runny. "Thanks for coming, Doc."

"How are you holding up?"

She shook her head.

"Could you get everybody together in the conference room? I want to give them a chance to vent."

"It'll be horrible. But welcomed." Her voice cracked on the last word. She'd worked for Noah for his whole stint as chief.

Once the staff had gathered, Jack went into psychologist mode and comforted them as best he could, but the pain in his gut almost leveled him. When the meeting ended, he headed out the door to return to the hospital.

oOo

Tess was walking to her car when she noticed Jack come out of the Academy. She waited until he caught up to her. What she saw on his face made her want to weep. "You're a wreck, aren't you?"

His gaze sought hers, and he gestured to the building behind them. "So many people in so much pain."

"In addition to your own. He's been your friend for decades."

"Fuck." His eyes welled, and he looked to the heavens. "I've got to be strong, I…" He didn't finish.

"You *do* have to be strong, Jack. But not right this minute. Come on, get into my car with me."

The fact that he didn't object told Tess he was barely holding it together. She clicked open the vehicle, and he got in the passenger side. She closed the door, circled the car and slid behind the wheel.

His fists were white-knuckled. His head back, his eyes were shut. He was a man on the edge.

She put her hands on his shoulders and tugged him around. He went into her arms in an awkward embrace over the gearshift.

When she clasped his neck to keep him close, Jack came apart.

oOo

Danny went home to rest and change his clothes. In his room, he found his mother seated on the bed, a pile of shirts in her lap.

"Mom, I told you not to do my laundry. You're not a maid."

She didn't pick up on the humor, so he crossed to her. And saw she was holding a paper. Her hands trembled a bit.

"What's that?"

"Your acceptance to Notre Dame." She looked up at him. "Honey, why didn't you tell us you applied to a college?"

Before his talk with Captain Righetti, he would have lied. Instead, he knelt down in front of her and grasped hands that had guided him through childhood and adolescence. "I haven't been honest with you."

"I know something's wrong. So does Dad. You haven't been yourself these past weeks." Holding up the paper, she asked, "It's about this, isn't it?"

Danny nodded. "I wanted to go to college."

"Why didn't you? The letter says you got a scholarship. A full scholarship. So it couldn't have been the money."

Captain Righetti's words echoed in his head. *You have to be honest with them, Danny. And if they don't support you, you'll have to be strong.*

"I was afraid of disappointing Dad and the guys."

"By not wanting to be a firefighter?"

He nodded.

"Oh, honey. Even if that's true, they'll get over it. They want you to be happy. Dad's noticed your mood, too. He worried that you weren't doing well at the Fire Academy."

Danny felt his eyes sting... It had been an emotional day anyway, and now this. He wished he'd talked to her before and spared everybody the grief he'd caused them.

You know, you can make up for your mistakes, Captain Righetti also said yesterday.

He thought of Chief Callahan dying in the hospital right now. But Danny still had time to fix things. "Then I made a mistake. But I can change this, Mom."

Standing, she pulled him up. "Yes, you can, buddy. Now give me hug and we'll talk about how."

oOo

Dressed in her best tie-dyed skirt and a white top, Anita Cruz rang the bell of Chief Hennessey's house; one of the recruits pulled open the door. Danny Mauro. He looked different.

She said, "Hey." The foyer was empty behind him, but she could hear talk off to the side.

Danny stared at the child she was holding. "Who's this?" He didn't sound sarcastic.

"My daughter, Charlotte."

"You got a kid?"

Anita nodded, waiting for an attack.

"Come on in. Holy cow, we didn't know."

"I kept it a secret."

When she stepped inside, a few of the other recruits came out to the foyer.

Anita held Charlotte up straight. She was done hiding things, being afraid. "The baby's mine."

"Well, hell." Murphy rummaged his way through the others to get to her and reached out his arms. "Let me hold her. Hi, baby. What's your name?" He frowned at Anita. "And what were you doin' keeping this little miracle a secret?"

Relieved, Anita smiled at his easy acceptance. "I was… I don't know. I guess we all have secrets." Her gaze narrowed on them. "I brought her today because I'm revealing mine. And I wanna know all yours."

Murphy wiggled his brows. "Not sure you do, but let's go tell everybody."

"Can I get you a drink?" Danny asked.

"Yeah, sure, ice tea."

After each recruit had a chance to coo over the baby, Captain Righetti joined them. Anita asked her, "Any word on Chief Callahan?"

"None. Dr. Harrison said he'd call us if there was."

Anita saw the shadows in the woman's eyes. The unnatural way she held herself. Impulsively, she gave the captain a hug.

And was surprised when the captain hugged back. Hard.

oOo

Jack watched his friends wait for the devastating news. Thank God, he'd let down with Tess. He wouldn't have been able to handle the next few hours any other way. He was missing the recruits get-together at Olive's, but he couldn't leave these people. Olive had stopped by, spent some time with Eve, then gone home to get ready for the gathering.

Firefighters packed the downstairs lobby, waiting for the verdict on their beloved boss. Up here, the family talked quietly with each other and the Malvasos, who'd gathered along with Will Rossettie. Right now, Mitch held Eve's hand. While Lisel stood by, Ian cuddled his niece Iana on his lap. She sensed the somber surroundings.

Will got up and headed toward Jack. He nodded to Eve. "She's so strong," he said.

"I know she is. Eve and her brother have been through a lot." He studied Will's face. "What about you?"

Rossettie's eyes moistened. "I can't believe I'm gonna lose my buddy." He barely got the last word out.

Jack clapped him on the shoulder. Physical contact helped at a time like this. "I understand, Will. I understand."

The others approached him…

Jenn Malvaso. "Hell, Jack, this is awful."

Mitch. "How you holding up?"

To which Jack replied, "Forget me. Go lie down on the couch."

Zach. "Man, I love the guy." Previously, they'd been at odds. In his old life, Zach had an affair with Noah's wife.

When Iana started to squirm on her uncle's lap, Jack crossed to them. Crouching in front of the little girl, he noticed her eyes were the same color as her dad's and her dark blond hair curled a bit, like his. "How you doing, sweetheart?"

Her lips trembled. "I want my daddy."

"I know, honey."

She clutched a faded blue bear, old and well loved. "He gave this to me. To hold when he wasn't here."

Jack choked back emotion. The bear would be used, a lot, from now on. "Come with me a minute. Maybe we can draw over by the window."

Uncurling herself from Ian, she slid her hand in Jack's. Lisel gave him a grateful smile. The little girl didn't need to know yet she was about to lose her father. He managed to get her settled at a table with paper and crayons.

"I'm gonna make a picture for Daddy, for when he wakes up," she said innocently. Jack bit his lip so hard he tasted blood.

They were drawing pictures of fire trucks when suddenly the waiting room went silent. He glanced up to see Noah's doctor had come out to speak to the family.

o0o

The recruits were in chairs and on the floor of Olive's living room, sharing secrets, when Tess's phone rang. She looked to Olive. Olive's eyes widened. Tess checked the caller ID and saw it was Jack. They were about to get the bad news.

Her heart heavy—Tess knew what it was like to get this call—she clicked into the phone, gripping it so tight her hand hurt.

"Tess, it's Jack."

"Hi." She couldn't say more.

She didn't have to. "Tess, oh God, Tess, it's a miracle. Noah woke up."

o0o

When Jack finally got in to see the chief, his face was almost as white as the sheets tucked around him. The lines at the corner of his eyes had deepened. Yet he'd insisted on seeing every last one of the people waiting outside. Beside him, Eve clutched his hand. Her complexion was normal, her eyes brighter, now that Noah was out of the woods. But Jack knew the aftermath of this kind of trauma would be long standing.

Noah smiled at Jack. "Hey, buddy, I wondered when you'd come in."

"I waited till the others got their chance to visit." After the adrenaline high of finding out Noah was okay, Jack's body was limp and his temples pounded. He couldn't remember the last time he'd eaten.

"You all gave up on me." Jack couldn't read Noah's tone.

"Hell, the doctors told us to expect the worst. I guess we had a miracle in the department."

"Thank God." Eve kissed their clasped hands.

"I hear you staunched the blood right after I was shot and kept me alive."

"Nothing anyone else wouldn't have done."

His friend's brows furrowed. "We lost three. The doctors said the injured would recover."

"It's a tragedy."

Lying back, the chief sighed heavily. "Eve said they ID'd the shooter and he had no connection with the fire department."

"Which is good, Noah. If he'd been one of us, this whole thing would be more of a nightmare."

"Yeah, it would."

"Since he shot himself, too, the police don't know his motive."

His friend closed his eyes briefly. "I can barely think about all this."

"Then, don't. Just get some rest. You have a whole staff to tend to the others."

Eve got up and saw Jack to the door. "I can't thank you enough, Jack, for being there for him at the scene. And here, for us. We couldn't have survived without you."

"That's not true. You're all very strong. But I'm glad I could help." He kissed Eve's cheek. "I'll stop by tomorrow."

After he spoke to those still lingering in the waiting room downstairs, Jack headed to his car. All he wanted was to find a cave to hide in, to forget about what had happened with Tom Senate and the others, but he had to check in with the recruits. He owed them and the teachers that. Then he'd go home and collapse.

He found them all outside in Olive's backyard. The warm air felt good after the air-conditioning of the hospital, but Jack still felt cold inside. Pasting on a smile, he walked through the gate.

"Yay! Captain Harrison is here." Murphy crossed to him. "Chief Hennessey said we could dispense with protocol when we got the good news." He slapped Jack on the back. "Isn't it's great about Chief Callahan?"

The rest of the recruits greeted him, too. Jack endured the celebration as best he could. But as each minute passed, the three deaths, and his part in Tom's, ate away at him. When the kids finally left and he was alone with Olive and Tess, the three of them dropped into Adirondack chairs.

Olive nodded to the gate. "They grew up a lot today."

Jack said, "Tragedy does that for people."

Brows narrowed, Olive's face darkened.

"What's wrong, Olive?" Tess asked.

"I'm thinking about McCabe, Lawson and Senate." She bit her lip. "I haven't been letting this in, but I wish I had talked Tom into staying at the Academy. He'd be alive now."

"Olive, you can't feel guilty about that." Jack came to the edge of his seat. "It wasn't your fault."

"I don't feel guilty. I feel bad. There's a big difference."

"He jumped to that conclusion because *he* feels guilty about Tom Senate."

"Tess!" he snapped. "You're out of line."

Anger flared in her dark eyes and she sat forward, too. "Fuck it, Jack." She looked at Olive. "He thinks if he never started the Recruit Concerns class, Senate would have taught the class."

"If you never started the Recruit Concerns class, those kids who just left wouldn't have made the strides they did today." Olive's voice was sharp now. "You've been feeling this since last night?"

Jack scowled but didn't speak.

"Yes, he has."

"Well, Doc," Olive said again, "That's just stupid."

"I told him that."

His eyeballs pinging back and forth between them, Jack felt as if he'd been ganged up on by the Amazons.

oOo

Six days later, after the last of the three firefighter funerals, Jack accidentally met up with Tess in the Academy gym, where he'd come to run off some of the negative feelings he still harbored inside him. When she reached where he stood, he fell in step beside her.

"Tess."

"Jack."

The greetings were cold and hollow—or maybe it was a reflection of what he felt inside himself. "The funerals were moving."

"The pageantry of a firefighter or police funeral always is."

Thinking about the slow mourn of the bagpipes, the trucks draped with black bunting, hundreds of men and women in dress blues made his mood worsen. "Yeah." He waited. "I, um, haven't seen you around much."

"I've been busy with the recruits." She didn't look at him, hadn't spared him more than a glance. "You canceled the last two Recruit Concerns classes, so we've had to take up the slack."

"I thought it was best."

"So, what's new? You always think you know what's best."

Unable to read her, he shut up but kept jogging with her. Finally, he couldn't stand it. "How have you been?"

"I'm coping, Jack, which is more than I can say for you."

That's it. He halted and snagged her arm so she had to stop, too. "What's with the cryptic remarks?"

Her brown eyes flared like hot coals. "Are you kidding?"

"You're mad at me?" The notion outraged him. It felt good to replace the nothingness with some kind of emotion.

"Of course I'm mad at you. Look at you. Your eyes are bloodshot, your face is lined with fatigue, your whole stance stiff and unyielding. Instead of moving on, you're wallowing in self-pity."

"Moving on with you? In case you've forgotten, you were the one who broke off the relationship with me."

"Yeah, I was pissed. I would've gotten over it. I *have* gotten over it. We could have fixed things between us. But instead, you shut out me, the recruits, everybody."

"I'm doing my job, Tess."

"Sure you are."

She started running again, and again, he caught up with her. "Look, I'll admit I haven't been myself. But I'm entitled to my grief."

Staring straight ahead, she quipped, "Then, you got it. Let me know when you're done feeling sorry for yourself."

"What the hell does that mean?"

She stopped of her own volition this time. He was struck by her anger and, at the same time, sabotaged by how he wanted to hold that beautiful body close again and take comfort in her. "I'll spell it out for you. I don't want a relationship with you until you reconcile this whole thing."

"Thanks for the sympathy."

"You don't need sympathy. You need a swift kick in the ass."

"Consider it given."

"Yeah, well, let me know when you're better."

He glared at her.

"But don't wait too long." She started to run again. Then looked over her shoulder at him. "I got a date with Cory Cameron tonight."

Well, hell, he thought as he walked off the floor. He'd never expected *this*!

o0o

Pissed off royally at Tess, Jack took two days furlough from his job and drove down to visit his kids at State College. The campus was truly beautiful: sun glistened off the buildings, trees had filled out and turned a lush green, and flowers bloomed everywhere. Since only a small number of classes were held for the first-session summer school, and many of the staff had taken a month off, the grounds were also absent of their usual hustle and bustle. As he opened the door to the student union, he was glad he'd thought of coming here. He needed a good dose of Sara and Seth to cheer him up. As he found a seat—there were only scattered tables with occupants—he thought of Tess's words: *Let me know when you've decided to stop feeling sorry for yourself.* How dare she?

After he waited a few minutes, his daughter bounced into the place with someone. Shit, her denim dress was too short. And he didn't want to have lunch with her friends. She raced over, and as always, when he stood, she threw herself at him. "Daddy!"

"Sweetheart." He held her tight, relishing the solid, alive feel of her.

When she drew back, she tugged on the other guy's arm. "Dad, this is the professor I'm working for this summer, Michael King."

The man put out his hand. "Good to meet you, Jack."

Jack shook. "You, too."

He smiled affectionately at Sara. "You've got quite a daughter here."

"Yeah?"

"She's influencing my research. She's come up with some ideas for a thread I should follow that I hadn't thought of. She's a risk taker, I think, but in a good way."

"Not always, Michael."

"I guess you've got to take the good with the bad." He touched Sara's arm. "See you, tomorrow."

They sat. Jack said, "He seems nice."

"He is." Her face sparked with mischief. "Don't worry. I'm not attracted to him."

"I'm not worried about that."

"No, but you would have been later when you got home."

Just then, Seth appeared at the table, wearing khaki cargo shorts and a white T-shirt, again seeming young and healthy. He gave his Dad an awkward hug, as Jack was seated. Seth got everybody coffee, then dropped down next to his sister.

Sara touched Jack's arm. Her big blue eyes were filled with sympathy. "How are you, Dad? All that stuff with the shooting. I wish you'd let us come home."

"I was busy every second."

"I'll bet." She studied him. "Want to talk about it?"

"No, I don't. Truthfully, I'd like to escape the fire department for a bit."

"Then, tell us about Tess." Sara wiggled her brows. "Did she take care of you during all this?"

She would have, he thought. *If I'd let her.*

"Yeah, she did."

"What's wrong?"

"Nothing, except that I feel bad about everything that happened."

"Not bad." Seth's gaze narrowed on him. "Hell, Dad, you look guilty."

He'd forgotten how astute Seth was. When he was feeling particularly lonely and overwhelmed or when something was wrong at work, Seth had always sensed it.

"The internet said the guy was a torch. He'd set fires all over New York City. Then he started shooting people. You aren't blaming yourself for that, are you, Dad?"

"Of course he's not. Why would he?" Sara, on the other hand, never saw through him.

"Look at him, sis. We know that expression in his eyes. Every time we did something wrong or you missed one of my games or her dance recitals, you got that expression that said, *I blew it with you guys.*"

"I did?" Jack was open mouthed.

"Yeah." Seth's expression was impatient. "You gotta get over things. Be easier on yourself."

"You could take lessons from me," Sara quipped, only half joking. "I get over everything too fast."

Astounded, Jack leaned back and watched his children. He had no idea they knew he'd been guilt ridden all his life at the times he let them down, because, as a single parent, he couldn't do everything. Shit, essentially they were saying the same thing as Tess.

o0o

"So, why hasn't Jack been around for a week? You sneaking over to his place?"

Tess and Mitch had come out to the back patio after dinner. Her cousin had asked the question out of the blue. It had been almost two weeks since the shooting. Mitch still wasn't back at work, and he was nosing into everybody's business.

"We, um, we're taking some time apart."

"Honey, I know I gave him a hard time at first, but he's my best friend outside of the family. I'd be happy to see you with him."

"We've got problems, Mitch." She wouldn't betray Jack's secrets. If he wanted Mitch to know about his suffering over Tom Senate's death, he would tell him. "We have to work them out."

"By staying away from each other?"

"Yeah, well, he did take a couple of days off."

"Where'd he go?"

"I have no idea."

Turning in his seat, he tipped her chin. "Tess, what's all this about?"

Just then, Megan came out to join them. With the warm breeze ruffling her hair, she looked cool and collected in shorts and a tank top, unlike at the hospital, where everybody had been a mess. Healing had begun. Megan sat on the arm of Mitch's big wooden chair and put a hand on his good shoulder, rubbed it. The small gesture of affection made Tess hurt inside. She missed that kind of closeness with Jack.

Megan asked, "Did you tell her?"

"No, we were talking about how she and Jack are blowing their relationship."

"Mitch! She's not your daughter." Megan looked to Tess. "Is that true?"

"Maybe it is. I got mad, he got mad, I got mad again...hell, it sounds stupid to say it aloud." She shook off the thought. "What were you supposed to tell me?"

Mitch's gaze narrowed, as if he was deciding whether or not to let the discussion go. "Noah Callahan's retiring."

"Because he almost died?"

"In a way. Eve left the HCFD a while ago, and he's been contemplating retirement, too. I guess when you have a near-death experience, you come out of it looking at things different."

"Good for him."

Jack could use lessons from his friend Noah Callahan about moving on.

"That's not all of it," Megan told her.

Mitch added, "He wants me to replace him."

"Wow! Are you going to?"

"I'd have to be chosen by the mayor."

"No, I mean, would you want it?"

"I'm not sure. Meggie and I have to discuss it more."

Tess smiled. "That's good, Mitch, that you have a choice."

"You say that nostalgically. You have choices, too, Tess, with Jack."

"I gave my ultimatum. My choice is made. The ball's in his court."

oOo

"Good to see you, Jack."

"You, too."

Don Caruso was one of the most respected psychologists in New York City. Tall, looking a bit like a younger Robert DeNiro, he had a pleasant smile and shrewd brown eyes.

"Is this appointment a consultation on a patient?"

"No, Don, the session's for me."

His friend's brows raised. "Since you're one of the sanest men I know, I'm surprised."

Absently, Jack rubbed the arm of the dark leather couch where he sat across from the psychologist. The office windows let in natural light, bright and sunny, but Jack couldn't get past the darkness inside him. "Something's happened. I can't get over it."

"Then, you're right to seek help. Why don't you tell me about it?"

Since Jack had never been to a counselor before, it was odd being on the other side of the couch. Still, he forged ahead.

He started with the background with Tess.

Went on to talk about the Recruit Concerns class.

He stopped after he told Don about Senate and two others' deaths.

"I read about the shooting, Jack. I'm so sorry." He thought for a minute. "Didn't the police discover he was a pyromaniac who decided to take his task one step further?"

"The consensus is that he probably thought if he killed firefighters, more buildings would burn. It's crazy thinking."

"Sociopaths twist reality that way."

Jack stared at the man blankly.

"This is where you tell me how you fit into the situation."

"I know it is." Laying his head back against the cushions, he took in a deep breath and said what was in his heart. "I want a future with Tess."

"That's a good start."

"But she won't see me until I *get my act together*. My guess is she thinks I won't move on if she's there to…tolerate my behavior. Enable me. Or maybe she just doesn't want to."

"The cold-hearted bitch."

He came to the edge of his seat. "You know, that's what I…" His voice trailed off when he saw the expression on Don's face. "Ah, you were being sarcastic."

"I was."

"You think she's using tough love, that she's trying to help me by not seeing me."

"Maybe."

"Fuck it. How do you *get over* something like the death of men in your department? One that maybe you could have prevented."

"Whose could you have prevented?"

He explained about Tom Senate.

Don leaned back on the chair. "Let me ask you. What would you tell a patient who came to you with this problem?"

Though he knew what Don was doing, he went along with it. "First, I'd tell him he'd feel better with time, when emotions weren't so raw. But I'd also dig into his background to find out where this sense of responsibility came from."

"Both sound great to me."

"Hey, I'm doing all the analysis here. You're supposed help me see this clearly."

"I am, Jack. I am."

o0o

On a Saturday night, three weeks after the shooting, the Callahans invited a group of friends to their house. Mitch said Noah was going to tell them about his retirement. She wondered briefly if the chief had consulted with Jack.

She hadn't seen Jack much. He worked every day at the Academy, but mostly he just nodded to her in passing. In down times and at night as she lay in bed alone, she questioned herself for giving him the ultimatum. Had she been wrong to do that? Should she have stood by her man? God, she sounded like a karaoke song.

The gathering was in full swing by six o'clock. A catered barbeque waited on the deck of their house in the heart of Hidden Cove—which had specially built ramps for Ian—and Eve was keeping a tight rein on Noah. He hadn't been allowed to do anything but sit in a chaise and talk to his guests.

"Where are you, Tess?" Zach had come up to her, where she stood on the grass sipping a glass of wine.

"Just thinking. How you doing?"

"Better now that Noah's out of the woods. Hell, that was the worst."

"It was."

His gaze never left Tess's face. "Jack took it super hard."

"Yeah?"

Always astute, damn it, Zach studied her. "Why don't you know that?"

"Long story, which I don't want to discuss tonight."

"Okay. There he is now."

Searching the crowd, Tess found him on the deck. He'd just come out of the house. God, he looked good. He wore gray shorts and a T-shirt to match the stripe in the pants. She studied him from head to toe and felt a longing so great she gasped.

"You sure you don't want to talk about it? You're drooling like a schoolgirl."

Immediately, her hand went to her mouth.

"Gotcha."

She shot her cousin an annoyed look.

Pulling her around to face him, Zach gentled his grasp. "Honey, one thing we've all learned after the shooting is that life is short. Terrible things have happened. It's not okay to waste time. And before you say it, I know I've wasted years of my life along by acting bad. But I've learned lessons from it all. And these last weeks have been a good reminder. I think we forgot about Sinco." The fatal fire in which Zach almost died.

For some reason, Tess's eyes teared. Droplets ran down her cheek. "I—"

From the side, she heard, "You makin' my girl cry, Malvaso?"

Zach scowled at Jack. "No, Harrison. You've done that all by yourself."

Tess, still stuck on *my girl*, couldn't keep up with the conversation.

"I'm gonna leave you two alone. Patch it up, will ya?"

Zach walked away. Jack stared down at Tess. His expression was warm, but something else. Determined? "You're coming with me" was all he said.

Taking her hand, he led her down a slate pathway on the side of the house, to a door which, when opened, revealed a laundry room. He pulled her through that to…where else? "Another bathroom."

"Yep." He eased her inside.

She went willingly.

oOo

Jack meant to talk to her first. But when he saw her wearing a skinny-strapped top that bared her shoulders and made her look fragile, and especially when he noted the tears in her eyes, he'd been overcome with emotion for this woman he'd hurt. Pressing her gently into the closed and locked door, he lowered his mouth to hers. She went up on tiptoes to meet him, to take and take and take.

Buttons popped. The rasp of a zipper. All the while, they kissed. His hands went inside her blouse, molded her full breasts. She touched him everywhere as she wiggled out of the shorts and panties he'd undone.

He freed himself from his clothes. She grasped him, massaged his hard length.

Hiking her up, he stopped kissing her and looked in her eyes. They were full of acceptance. For him. "I love you, Tess," he said as he slid—still gently—inside her.

The spasms began then for both of them. He came in a rush of pleasure, of sensation so great it eclipsed his vision. She joined him, calling out his name.

Then they collapsed into each other; he was breathing hard, and so was she. When he could, he stepped back. She looked up at him.

Righting his clothes, and helping her with hers, he dropped down on the tile and drew her next to him. Her hair was a mess from his hands, she had a slight brush burn on her cheek and her gaze was soft and satisfied.

"I have things to say."

"Me, too."

"No, I want to go first."

"No, me."

He rolled his eyes. "All right."

"I was wrong to give you an ultimatum. I should have just stood by you."

He shook his head.

"Don't, Jack. We belong together. You said you loved me. Let's work this out."

"I am." His words were simple.

Those lovely eyes widened. "What does that mean?"

"I've been seeing a psychologist in New York. He's good. I've had three two-hour sessions."

"You have?"

"Physician heal thyself and all that."

"I'm so glad for you."

"It's for us, too. You were right. My guilt over Tom was excessive. I'm working on finding out why—the kids said I've always been like this. Interestingly, my exaggerated sense of responsibility seems to have a lot to do with Elizabeth dying and me trying to be everything to everybody. It's *my savior complex*, I think you said."

"I can see where that could happen to anyone, especially a good man like you. I'm glad you're getting help."

"And pleased?"

"And pleased."

"Whew! At least the excruciating pain of baring my soul ain't for nothin', sweetheart."

"Now you know how your clients feel."

He laughed, then turned serious again. "It's killed me to see you in the hall or at a meeting and not have contact." He brushed hair out of her eyes. "How about you? Tell me where your head's at these days."

Fair was fair. She came up on her knees, took his hand and cupped his cheeks. "I love you, Jack Harrison. Faults and all, though there aren't that many of them."

He met his forehead with hers. He wanted to savor the tender moment.

Loud pounding on the door interrupted that. "Hey, Tess, are you in there? We've been looking for you."

"She's with me," Jack said, irritated. "But she's not coming out anytime soon. Go away, Mitch."

Laughter, both inside and outside the door.

Tess glanced around the large space. "This bathroom's fancier than any we've ever fought or made up in."

"Yeah, I think we should test it out again."

She drew him close enough to smell her lotion, the scent that was just her. "You're on, Doc."

EPILOGUE

Beginning of September

In the foyer of an auditorium in downtown Hidden Cove, Tess stood next to Jack, waiting for the procession to begin. Graduation day for the newest recruit class from the Anderson Fire Academy had dawned bright and beautiful. She smiled to herself. She and Jack had had their own private *graduation* of sorts earlier. When his hand grazed hers, she leaned over and said, "Watch it, Doc. We taught these recruits to be very observant."

"Yes, ma'am." His smile was deep and genuine. It had been getting broader and more sincere since he'd seen Don Caruso for therapy, which had ended last week. Tess's heart did a little happy dance at the notion of how much better he was.

Liam Murphy, the de facto head of the class, faced the group. "Okay, everybody shut up. It's time to start."

The newly minted firefighters looked spiffy in their dress uniforms. Dark blue jackets and pants, light blue shirts, black ties and spit-shined shoes. Each outfit of course, was topped off with a wide-brimmed navy hat. Jack and Tess wore identical clothing, except their shirts were white and maybe their shoes not quite as glossy.

Twelve of them lined up. Two classmates had dropped out of the Academy right after the shooting because of their inability to get over their fears, no matter how much Jack had tried to help them. With Mauro gone, that left an even dozen.

The recruits walked down the aisles with their shoulders straight and their heads held high. As they should. They'd accomplished a lot in the remaining weeks after the shooting. Seats on the stage waited for them, and off to the left were more seats filled by the instructors and the county brass.

After everybody was settled, Anita Cruz rose. Tess had gotten to know her well and admired her for what she'd accomplished. "I'll now lead you all in the Pledge of Allegiance. You might not know this, but my parents were immigrants, so these words have special meaning to me."

Afterward, Liam Murphy, who'd been asked to address the class—Jack had helped him with his speech—approached to the podium. He looked tall and handsome in his dress uniform. "Classmates, instructors, fire department personnel and mayors. Welcome to our graduation. We'd like to thank you for the support you've given us over the last fourteen weeks, for all you've taught us by your words and your actions. No one could have foreseen the tragedy that would befall the department, but we had good role models and people who took care of us when they were hurting. We'd like to thank Dr. Harrison in particular for his Recruit Concerns class, both before and after the event. Even though we didn't *talk* for the first ten days, it was a tremendous help."

A rumble of laughter on the right side of the stage.

Tess squeezed Jack's arm and he winked at her.

First off, the kids gave Olive Hennessey a standing ovation and read her a poem someone had written about leadership. Then they thanked each instructor individually—Larissa James for filling in at the last minute, Quinn Frazier for letting them stop for water when he took them out for Confidence Walks, Haywood Jenkins for being "stern and supportive." Tess thought that was interesting.

"Last but not least, we'd like to thank Captain Righetti for helping us to understand which of us were meant to be in the department and what our particular skills are. As a side note, the *girls* want to give their appreciation for her *Boys Chat.*

"The captain talked at length about how to treat female firefighters." He cleared his throat. "Us guys are still stinging from that."

More easy laughter.

Last, Murphy showed some candid photos: he and Johnson

wrestling with a hose full of foam. Anita training as an EMT, with Jack as her patient during practicals. Landon making faces in the mirror of a fire truck. And more.

After the levity, the mayors of the surrounding areas congratulated the class, and the one from Hidden Cove introduced another speaker. "Next up is the acting fire department chief, Mitch Malvaso, to present the certificates."

Mitch, with a huge grin and an easy demeanor, approached the podium. His quest for the white hat had begun. "I thank each and every one of you for your dedication and hard work. You're about to become members of one of the greatest sister- and brotherhoods in the world."

He spoke glowingly of Noah and his part in the success of the class. Of the battalion chief and the instructors, from whom he couldn't have asked for anything more. And for all firefighters who put their lives on the line for others every day they came to work.

Then he said, "Class members please stand... Raise your right hand... Repeat after me. I Firefighter—say your name—pledge and declare that I will support the constitution of the United States and of New York State... I will faithfully discharge the duties of a firefighter at—here say the department you'll join—to the best of my ability."

Huge applause erupted from an audience packed with proud friends and family, and they clapped again when he handed out the individual certificates.

As the ceremony ended, Tess was awash with something she'd never felt before: contentment. Looking at the recruits, the teachers and the family that had come to celebrate, Tess shook her head. Who would have thought?

o0o

Jack kept his hand at Tess's back while they waited for the recruits to come backstage. "That was the perfect ceremony, wasn't it?"

"Almost as perfect as this morning," she told him.

"Almost."

The recruits filtered back in shifts. They spoke to each teacher, and when they reached Tess and Jack, Anita Cruz just looked up at them, her eyes teary and slipped her arms around Tess's waist for a meaningful hug.

Murphy stepped forward. "I probably shouldn't do this but—" He picked Tess up and swirled her in a circle. "Thanks, Captain Righetti."

"All right, Murphy. That's enough."

Holding on to Tess's hand, Murphy looked down. "What's this?"

"What do you mean, probie?" Jack asked sternly.

"The captain has a gold ring on her finger that she never wore before."

"Oh, that." Tess shot a glance at Jack. "Well, yes, it's because I just got this band this morning."

"You got married this morning?" Anita could barely contain herself.

"Uh-huh."

"Who's the guy?"

Murphy jumped in. "I know who it is. Let's see your left hand, Dr. Harrison."

Jack held his hand up, facing out, and grinned. Several of the recruits gasped. Tess laughed out loud. "You're thinking he's going to tell me what all of you said about me in the RC class, aren't you?"

"Well," Johnson mumbled. "You were nicer after the shooting."

"I learned from it, too."

"Besides," Jack put in, "she needed to know you were unhappy with her methods. And before you say anything about the privacy I promised you, I realize now I should have found a way to let the instructors know how happy or unhappy you were. I've got to think of a way to build in something like that for the next recruit class."

The congratulations were hearty. Jack chuckled when the group broke up and walked away and someone muttered, "I didn't think they even *liked* each other."

He and Tess were about to head out for the graduation reception at a local restaurant when someone else came backstage "Hey, you two, I was waiting in the front for you, but you didn't come out." Jack recognized the voice even before they turned around.

"Congratulations," Danny Mauro said. He looked different, dressed in a swank gray suit, tall, broad-shouldered. His confidence was obvious.

"And to you, too, son."

Danny sighed. "I'm looking forward to the fall now." He went directly to Tess and grasped both her hands. "Thanks again for everything."

They spoke more to Danny, then he left them alone. The two of them walked back through the auditorium and stopped on the stage, looking at the now-empty seats. "It was some class, wasn't it?" Tess remarked.

"Yeah, and Danny came to the graduation."

"I'm glad he's taking classes at Notre Dame instead of waiting a year to go. I'm surprised they let him in without matriculating."

"Hmm."

"You had something to do with that, didn't you?"

"I know people. I made some calls. But he got his scholarship back for next spring all by himself." Jack added, "He told me you were the one who made him realize he could fix the mistakes he made, and he did."

She sidled up to Jack. "You too, Doc. You fixed us."

"Remember that, when we have our first fight as a married couple."

Tess went up on tiptoes and gave him a peck on the cheek. "I decided we aren't going to fight. We're just going to head for the nearest bathroom." She glanced off to the side. "Speaking of which..."

"Nope, not today. I plan to carry my *wife* over the threshold of our house properly, lock the doors, turn off the phones and have her all to myself. There will be no disturbances today."

She looped her arms around his neck and grinned. "Works for me, Doc."

For notification of Kathryn's new work and information about her books, be sure to sign up for her newsletter at http://on.fb. me/1bLS0bN.

o0o

Dear Readers,

I'm hoping you enjoyed THE FIRE INSIDE, and that you could experience the events that happened to the characters along with their emotional responses. I think that's the strength of the book. Every time I proofread the scenes where Noah is dying, I got teary eyed. And, of course, I felt relief after he recovers. When I reread the shooting incident, I experienced fear—every time.

Writing Jack's story was long in coming. He appears in every book, but you never find out much about him, except that he's widowed. I developed his backstory for this novel, and as always, things changed. I had no idea Sara would be a risk taker, or Jack had a savior complex. And I'm sure everybody wanted some sweet woman to make him happy after all he did for the Malvasos and others. That didn't happen, either. Suddenly, he was involved with a not-so-easy-going woman whom he doesn't like much at first. I didn't expect that to occur, but, as I said before, my characters always react in ways I didn't anticipate.

Tess was one tough cookie. As a teacher myself, I could appreciate her need to be stern and disciplined, but Jack's argument made sense, too. And, as a teacher, I'm not sure how I would have felt if the administration set up a group for my students to vent their feelings about me—and I would never know what they said. Tess was also complicated. Her life experiences, particularly in losing her parents and brother, informed most of her actions. But she grew and changed over the course of the novel. I let that develop naturally, and I hope I succeeded in portraying her as a well-rounded character.

This was a hard book to write in that it addressed some difficult issues about the fire department. I intended it to be the last in the Hidden Cove Series, but we'll have to see. Every six months, I seem to get an urge to write about my smoke eaters. I could start a new series, I guess.

As always, thanks for reading my work, and please spread the news if you liked the book.

Best,
Kathy Shay

Visit or Contact Kathryn at www.kathrynshay.com
www.facebook.com/kathrynshay
www.twitter.com/KShayAuthor
http://pinterest.com/kathrynshay/

If you liked this book, you might want to post a review of it.

Don't miss the other books in the Hidden Cove Firefighter Series.

After The Fire

After being trapped in a fire, the Malvaso brothers and sister decide to make changes in their lives. Follow Mitch Malvaso as he struggles to get closer to his kids and out of a doomed marriage. Jenn, his sister, wants to have a baby and asks Grady O'Connor, her best friend, to be the father.

On the Line

Fire Chief Noah Callahan and Albany Fire Investigator Eve Woodward butt heads while she investigates the cause of accidents at Hidden Cove fire scenes. Who knew they'd fall in love? And watch Zach Malvaso become the kind of man he wants to be with feisty firefighter Casey Brennan.

Nothing More to Lose

Injured 9/11 firefighter, Ian Woodward (Eve's twin), and a disgraced cop, Rick Ruscio, struggle to salvage their lives with the help of the women who love them.

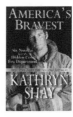

America's Bravest—Six Novellas

The men and women on another Rescue Squad in the Hidden Cove Fire Department have complicated personal relationships due to the nature of their jobs. Each of the six novellas details the love and work of one firefighter, but the stories are tied together with an arson case and a blogger out to discredit them.

It Had to Be You

Beckett Sloan is an Iraq and Afghanistan veteran who comes home with PTSD. He joins the fire department and finds the love of his life in army nurse Lela Allen, but his demons keep them apart.

 **Chasing the Fire—Three Novellas**
In another set of novellas, CHASING THE FIRE, the past catches up with three brave firefighters and they must wrestle with it to find love and contentment.

To browse Kathryn's impressive list of titles go to http://www.kathrynshay.com/books/.

Continue reading for an excerpt of BEGIN AGAIN. The first book in Kathryn Shay's new series *The Ludzecky Sisters.*

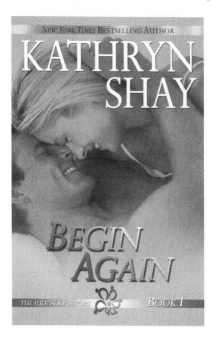

Now, for a look at Kathryn Shay's new series: **The Ludzecky Sisters**. Many fans will remember them from PROMISES TO KEEP, Secret Service Agent Luke Ludzecky's story, and CLOSE TO YOU, the second book in The O'Neil series, featuring C. J., the oldest sister. The girls also have cameos in the other four O'Neil books. Now, the six sisters have their own stories. Alike in looks, but completely different in personalities, their lives will tug on your heart strings.

BEGIN AGAIN
The Ludzecky Sisters
Book 1

The Ludzecky Family was well acquainted with the trials and tragedies in life, but none was as horrific as this one. The matriarch, Donuta Ludzecky, affectionately known as Matka, sat in the front pew of a Catholic Church next to her best friend, Rosie Pettrone. The woman had suffered the worst loss any mother could have visited on her—losing a child, or in this case losing two. Twin boys. Thirty-five years old. They'd been married to Paulina and Antonia, Donuta's two daughters. Like the good Polish woman that she was, Donuta sat stalwart, holding back any display of her own emotions. Of course, she suffered with and for her friend. But she also couldn't help thinking of the effect this obscene event would have on her eight Ludzecky children.

Her gaze traveled first to her twin girls, sitting on each side of Rosie. Antonia had dissolved into tears the moment they walked into church and hadn't stopped crying. Lukasz had to take care of her two year old son Salvador, who wept softly into his uncle's chest. Paulina, stronger both physically and emotionally than her twin, had slid her arms around her boys, and remained stone-faced. The crying would come later for her girl, Donuta knew. And their lives would never be the same without their husbands. Donuta learned that fact from the death of her own husband when she was in her forties.

Her gaze landed on her boy, Lukasz. He and his wife Kelsey had come down from Binghamton. Their near-perfect lives had been long in coming, and, now, their happiness would be shadowed by their sisters' trauma. The same was true for Caterina. She was content as a mother of two, working in linguistics for the Secret Service, madly in love with her husband Aidan O'Neil. She'd want to protect the girls, which was impossible. She'd already made plans to stay in Queens with them for three weeks.

Ana, the third oldest, had helped take care of the others, especially when more babies came along and Donuta was in the hospital giving birth or twice with exhaustion. Though Ana was happily married with one child, she'd smother her twin sisters trying to right things for them.

Magdalena, a year younger than Ana, would take over the logistics. A successful venture capitalist, she'd try to organize, strategize and "fix" whatever she could for her sisters. She didn't yet know there was no fixing tragedy, that the girls needed to grieve, but Magdalena had a stubborn streak.

And then there was Sofia, who'd had tragedy of her own in her life. At sixteen, she'd developed leukemia. The treatment forced her to give up her beloved dancing aspirations. This child would go into herself unless someone stopped her. Fragile, almost waif-like, Donuta hoped she could withstand the sorrow that had come their way.

And last was Elizabeita. Who knew what her youngest would do? Bright enough to be a Rhodes Scholar and earn two degrees at Oxford, pretty enough to be a model and bold enough to take all kinds of safety risks, the girl had been impossible to control all her life. Donuta worried about her. How would her baby handle the overwhelming grief?

When the priest asked them to stand, Donuta chided herself. She was thinking about her family's welfare, and here was poor Rosie, who'd suffered such loss. However, the facts remained: Donuta would be a good friend in every way, but her role as Matka would make her priorities her children, as always.

CHAPTER 1

Three Years later

"Stop fidgeting. I'm almost done." The statement came from Magdalena, Paulina's older sister, who right now was fussing her hair into a French braid.

Paulina stared in the mirror. "Sorry, I just don't see the point of this. Clipping it back would be easier."

"You're meeting with the architect for this new project. You should look presentable."

"Why? I won't get more jobs from him because of my hair."

Magdalena, who always looked as if she'd stepped out of the pages of Vogue, sighed. "I hate that you hide your beauty."

"I don't hide it. It's just not important to me." Paulina touched her face, wide and freckled. "So don't you dare ask for me to put on makeup."

"There, I'm done." She picked up a hand mirror and Paulina turned around.

Thick and tightly woven, hanging past her mid-back, the braid *was* pretty. But the sight made her sad. She could still see her husband, his big hand fisted in her hair. He'd whispered, *Grow it long again. That's sexy as hell.*

"You don't like the style?" Magdalena asked at her expression.

"I love it."

"But?"

"My hair was short when Donnie died. He wanted me to let it grow but I couldn't see the point."

Her sister's smile disappeared. "Yours grew the fastest."

In some kind of unconscious solidarity, the seven of the Ludzecky girls had grown their hair long since the Pettrone brothers' deaths, to match Antonia's, which she'd had always reached down her back. No one planned it, but now they all had the same thick, sun streaked blond hair of the same length. Donnie *would* have loved it.

Magdalena kissed Paulina's head to signify she understood. "Think happy thoughts today and put on the dress I brought you."

"Really, Mags, I have some dressy clothes of my own." Well, not quite dressy, but presentable enough for a business meeting.

"Humor me."

As Paulina slipped into the sheath, she could appreciate the soft copper colored silk flowing over her skin. It made her think of a man's hands touching her.

"What's wrong? You flushed like you accidentally saw some porn."

Paulina sat to slide on her shoes. "I was just thinking."

"About?" A hesitation, then, "Spill it, girl." Sometimes all of the sisters, not just the twins, had a sixth sense about each other.

Paulina looked into Magdalena's eyes. They, too, were the same hazel, though Mags' were almond shaped. "I miss having sex. There I said it out loud."

"Ah." Magdalena took Paulina's hands in hers. "It's been three years. Donnie wouldn't want you to live like a nun."

No, he wouldn't. Once, when they were drawing up wills and designating the guardianship of their kids, they'd talked about what they'd hope for each other if one of them died. Donnie, big, macho and protective as hell, had said, *Don't mope over me, baby. Go on with your life.*

"No, Donny wouldn't want that. But Nia does."

Her twin had not moved past her grief—and loyalty—to Peter, Donnie's twin, since their accident three years ago. Paulina had to tiptoe around her in order to go forward, even making changes in the business. Paulina certainly couldn't confess her desire to be with another man.

Magdalena kept hold of her hands. Two years older than Paulina, this sister was the most worldly of any of them, having gone to Harvard

Business School and then building a wildly successful career in venture capitalism. "Honey, we all know Nia is in a different place from you. And we respect her timeline in getting over the grief. But you can't let her hold you back."

"That's not the only thing." Even when she shrugged, the silk caressed her. "I never go anywhere to meet men. I work with them all day, but can't get involved with my employees. There's nobody to date."

"Then take up hobbies. Join a gym."

Standing, Paulina looked in the mirror. At five-eight, her figure was full, but muscular and toned. "I don't need a gym. I do physical labor every day."

"Let me think on this."

Drawing back, Paulina checked her watch. "I have to be in town in half an hour."

"My driver's waiting for us. I can take you to Armstrong Associates."

Paulina's whole body softened. "My rich, beautiful sister. Have I thanked you enough for coddling us the last three years?"

"Hush. No need. I love you, Paulie. Always."

"And I love you."

Paulina was still thinking about Magdalena when she arrived at 16 Park Avenue. After she got out of the car, she stood and stared up at the chrome and glass building. Befitting an architect, it had interesting peaks and angles that the April sun sparkled off of. She wondered what this new architect would be like. Most of the professionals she worked with on a job had preferred to deal with Donnie, and were respectful to her, but Paulina had been in charge since her husband died and together with Nia, ran their contracting business. She still wasn't used to making deals.

Shaking off her thoughts, determined to succeed, she entered the building and shivered. The dress was sleeveless and light and she hadn't thought to bring a sweater, though Mags had insisted she carry a purse. She took the elevator to the twenty-third floor, which opened to the firm she would work with on this new building—a music hall in Queens. Her company, Pettrone and Ludzecky Builders, had gotten the construction bid from the city, and Armstrong Associates were chosen to design it. She and the architect were meeting over the preliminary plans already drawn up by one of their own structural engineers, the firm and the city.

Though Paulina preferred older, classic structures, the contemporary suite of offices was stunning. Teak double doors opened to a large anteroom with a receptionist. The woman sat behind a sleek desk, with curved legs and an angled top. "Hello. I'm Lana Bright. You must be Ms. Pettrone. Our ten o'clock with you."

"Yes to both."

Lana rose and said, "Follow me." They went down another short corridor, to a second set of double doors, which mirrored the outside ones. Lana knocked, and a deep voice within called out, "Come in, Lana."

A man stood looking out at a panorama of windows that faced New York's skyline. He turned at the whisper of the door and approached them. "Ms. Pettrone. Nice to meet you. I'm Adam Armstrong."

"Nice to meet you, too, Mr. Armstrong."

He was…arresting. His features were chiseled, his blond hair cut short enough to be neat, but long enough to let the sun highlight it. His eyes were grass green.

Holy shit, she thought. If she was scoping out her business associates, Paulina really needed to find a man.

oOo

The woman's fingers were callused, Adam noticed when he shook her hand, and she didn't wear a speck of makeup. But she looked quite different in person than she had on her firm's website. More feminine, he guessed, though he never went for rounded cheeks and freckles. Adam appreciated the ability of women to use makeup cleverly to enhance their looks. "Come in. May I call you Paulina?"

"Most people call me Paulie."

God, no, not a boy's name. Though she was plain, he preferred the more sophisticated form of address. "Call me Adam, too. Can Lana get you something?"

She shook her head and a few tendrils of hair escaped her functional braid. Soft, blonder, they kissed her face.

"Then let's sit."

They took chairs at an oval teak table facing the city. Her eyes widened like a child's as she perused the skyline. Right away, he knew this woman wouldn't dissemble, which would be a welcome change from some business partners he'd dealt with. "What a pretty office, Adam, and a gorgeous view."

"It's inspirational."

"I'll bet." Smiling, she still gazed out the window. "I love all the styles, sizes, heights of the buildings in the city."

"I do, too." Though nobody had ever voiced his love of New York like that. Glancing down, he'd unfolded the rolled up blue prints. "Ready?"

The corners of her mouth turned up.

"What?"

"You sound like a little kid opening a present."

He chuckled. "I guess that's how I feel about my work. Even though you've gone over the preliminary drawings with your structural engineer out at the site, you haven't seen the actual building."

"Go for it."

The façade was the first sheet on top. Paulina Pettrone recoiled when she saw it. What the hell? He waited as she leaned back in and examined every inch of it, then raised her gaze to his. Tinged with green now, her eyes were filled with appreciation. "I didn't expect this."

"Is something wrong?" Not only did the notion tick him off, but he felt a bit like somebody had told him his baby was ugly.

"I'm surprised at the traditional arches and windows. Carvings into the stone. The classic lines." She gestured to encompass the office. "I was anticipating something more modern like this."

"The city wants a classic look for the exterior. That style fits in with the neighboring buildings. But the inside has more modern elements." He stared down at his plans. "Besides, it will house some of the greatest music in the world so it should be a combination of both."

This time, her brows furrowed. "I'm glad you believe in matching the exterior with its surroundings."

He'd been compared to Frank Lloyd Wright, whose mantra was just that. He wouldn't brag to her, though.

She took a bead on him. "I checked you out online. Now I remember the comparison to Wright. Very nice."

"Thank you." Her gaze went back to the plans, as if she couldn't stop looking at them. That tickled him. After he let her study his designs, he asked, "Do you think you can handle the outside?"

"Of course." She seemed amused at his question, making him feel silly. "We've done older facades like this before. I've worked on all of them." Now her eyes twinkled. "Literally. I helped set stone in place and built the arches."

"You've been in the contracting business for ten years."

"Uh-huh. I started right out of high school, but ended up getting a degree in building construction at a local college and took several more structural engineering courses."

Since he was aware of what had happened to her, he felt he needed to confront it. "I know your husband and his twin brother started the business fifteen years ago. Is it all right if I say how sorry I am for the accident?"

The light went out of those eyes. It didn't dim, it was doused completely. And was startling. He'd never seen that kind of transformation before. "Yes, you can say that. It's worse when new people ignore that he's gone."

Adam squeezed her arm. Now that part of her skin was silky. Interesting! "Then I'm glad I said something."

"Don't you want to know if I can handle the job since I've only been in charge three years?"

"Word on the street says you and Don were equal partners."

Her laugh was soft. Sincere. "I like that. He would, too."

"Good. Let me show you the inside of the building. There are some complicated sections."

Her chin raised and his attention dropped to the cuffed neckline of the dress. "I'll be able to handle them."

"You wouldn't be here if I didn't think you could, Paulina."

"I know. Now show me your baby."

o0o

Adam sat in the back seat of his limo fingering the cell phone Paulina Pettrone had left behind in his office. She'd checked the time on it, and must have thought she'd slipped it back in her purse. Lana spotted it under the chair.

She seemed uncomfortable with the leather purse she carried and maybe even in the dress she wore. He hadn't expected the woman he saw online to have clothes like that. He'd pegged her as what they used to call a tomboy, but she was certainly feminine when she showed up today.

But what the hell did he really know about women?

Do you realize you call your buildings she? You're married to them, not to me. All you think about is work.

To be honest, at the time, Bethany had been right. He'd just joined his father's firm after graduating from Cornell and in typical dad fashion, Andrew Armstrong had told him he'd have to earn his way. Adam had not only risen to his father's expectations, but enjoyed the sense of accomplishment. He'd worked hard to please his dad, but himself, too. Unfortunately, Bethany couldn't wait for success to come their way and had an affair with his best friend. He didn't know what hurt more—losing his wife, or his longtime buddy, which in itself said something about his marriage.

"The site's right up here, Adam."

Adam could see the trailer labeled *Pettrone and Ludzecky Builders* and the frame of a building behind them. The scent of fresh cut wood filled his head after he opened the door. "Thanks, Joe. I'll only be a minute."

Joe had been with him for years so it wasn't odd that his driver turned around in the seat wiggled his brows. "Must be some woman to go this far out of your way."

"What?"

"Bringing the phone to her instead of having me run it out. You must like her."

"No, actually, I just met her. And she's not my type." He thought of Elyssa, the woman he currently dated, with the sleek short hair and long lean body.

Joe faced forward again. "Uh-huh."

Since it was seven at night, the site was deserted. No vehicles were parked on the grass, but there was a light on in the trailer. After he exited his car, he walked over to it and knocked. No answer. He knocked again. Then he heard, "Who is it?"

"Adam Armstrong. You left your cell phone in my office and I had a meeting out this way, so I'm returning it."

Nothing. Then he heard the lock snick. Paulina opened the door. The first thing he noticed was she held a baseball bat. The second was she wore men's clothes, reinforcing his tomboy expectation. And last, she was dirty...really dirty. Her face was smudged. The T-shirt that was once white, was...dingy. Jeans sported patches of mud. Clunky work boots scuffed and caked. "Hi." She nodded to the phone. "You didn't have to do that."

"No problem."

"I'm not used to carrying a purse. I usually stick the cell in my pocket. But then again, I didn't have one of those, either."

Her confession stumped him. No coyness from her. And she certainly wasn't trying to impress him. "Um, okay."

She shook her head. Her hair was pulled back and tied at her neck with a big clip. "It's Mags' fault. She made me take the damn thing."

"Mags?"

"Magdalena, my sister. She dressed me for our meeting." Her hand went to her mouth. "Oops, I don't think I was supposed to tell you that."

"Why?"

"She thought I should look more sophisticated." The sound that came out of her mouth was almost a snort. "As if."

"You looked perfectly lovely." He gave his version of a snort, then scanned her up and down. "Quite a difference from now. What the hell did you do today?"

"They were putting in the bathroom piping and somebody had to go into the crawlspace beneath. I went because I'm the littlest. Not that I'm little. But smaller than the guys."

"Interesting." He couldn't help but smile. Who would have known once he got her talking, she would ramble on. And reveal a lot about herself.

"Sorry for running my mouth. I got nervous when you came to the door."

He nodded to the bat, which she still gripped in a gritty hand. "That's not much protection. I could wrest it away from you in seconds."

"Ha! No way."

"Want to bet?"

"Sure. You can buy me a beer sometime if I win, and if I lose, I'll treat you to one of those stupid, fancy martinis that comes in all flavors."

It was his turn to chuckle.

She eased her way outside. Night hadn't fallen but they were in shadows. He thought briefly how this so wasn't him, but her playfulness was contagious. Whipping off his jacket and hanging it on the doorknob to the trailer, he took a crouching stance. "Go ahead, try to hit me."

Raising that bat, she winked. "Don't worry, I got good reflexes. I won't hurt you."

She aimed for his shoulder, but he parried out of the way. She pivoted fast and went for his hip. Again, he evaded. When she tried to get around him, he caught the end of the bat and snatched it from her. "I told you…"

His feet went out from under him—and he went sprawling face first in the dirt.

She laughed. "I wouldn't call that a win."

Sitting up, he dangled his hands between his legs. "I got the bat but you got me. For the record, I wasn't prepared for a street fight."

"Always be prepared for a street fight. My brother taught me that." She held out her hand.

Taking it, he rolled to his feet. But he didn't let go. "When?" he asked.

"When what?"

"When can I take you for the beer?"

"Oh, forget it. Let's call it a tie."

Suddenly, he didn't want to forget it. "I--"

"Mr. Armstrong?" the voice came out from under a nearby tree—full of humor.

"Hell, did you see that, Joe?"

"Every bit. I'd say you're losin' your touch."

Adam smiled. "Joe Corleone, this is Paulina Pettrone. She's building the music hall."

"So you said." Joe turned an affectionate look on Paulina. "Hello, Mrs. Pettrone."

"Mr. Corleone." *Her* expression turned mischievous again. "Should I, like, be afraid of you?"

A deep laugh rumbled out of Joe. "Maybe. I got connections, lady."

Was Joe flirting with Paulina? She must like Italian men given who she married.

Paulina bestowed an equally flirty smile on Joe. "Well, I have a few things to finish and then I'm leaving."

Glancing around, Adam frowned. "Where's your car?"

"My truck's back home. Magdalena drove me into the city this morning, I caught a train back out here. I'll call a cab tonight."

"Won't your family come?"

"Yeah, they would. But then my sister will…never mind. I'll be fine."

Joe said, "We aren't goin' anywhere without you. You shouldn't be out here all alone."

Her face saddened. "Yeah, you're right. I have to be careful for my boys. You never know when disaster will strike."

Stillness, full of grief invaded the night.

"So you'll come with us."

"I'm a mess. I'll dirty up the car."

"No problems, I'll get a blanket out of the trunk."

They waited while she locked up, then headed to the car. Joe opened the back door for Adam, but Paulina grabbed the blanket and then the handle of the front door. "I'll ride up here with your chauffeur."

Once inside, Adam said, "He's a great deal more than that."

She climbed inside and the door shut. Adam followed suit. Why the hell did it bother him that she obviously didn't want to get in the back seat with him?

o0o

Be sure to look for these six Ludzecky novellas coming soon: BEGIN AGAIN, PRIMARY COLORS, RISKY BUSINESS, THE WAY WE WERE, HANDLE WITH CARE and LOVE STORY.

ABOUT THE AUTHOR

A New York Times bestselling author, Kathryn Shay has been a lifelong writer and teacher. She has written 54 books—17 self-published original romance titles, 36 print books with the Berkley Publishing Group and Harlequin Enterprises and 1 mainstream women's fiction with Bold Strokes Books. She has won five RT Book Reviews awards, four Golden Quills, four Holt Medallions, the Bookseller's Best Award, Foreword Magazine's Book of the Year and several "Starred Reviews." Her novels have been serialized in COSMOPOLITAN magazine and featured in USA TODAY, THE WALL STREET JOURNAL and PEOPLE magazine. There are over five million copies of her books in print, along with hundreds of thousands downloaded online. She lives in upstate New York with her husband and children.

28235936R00142

Made in the USA
Middletown, DE
21 December 2018